ALMOST PRIEST

MCCULLOUGH MOUNTAIN 1

LYDIA MICHAELS

Lydia Michaels

Romance
ALMOST PRIEST {McCullough Mountain 1}
Copyright © 2019 Lydia Michaels
First E-book Publication: July 2013
Originally Published as SACRED WATERS
Cover design (c) 2022 by Lydia Michaels

www.LydiaMichaelsBook.com

DEDICATION

For the Dougherty girls.
Thank you for a beautiful day at the lake and inspiring me to write again.

McCullough Mountain
Publication Order

Almost Priest 1
Beautiful Distraction 2
Irish Rogue 3
British Professor 4
Broken Man 5
Controlled Chaos 6
Hard Fix 7
Intentional Risk 8

Find more McCulloughs in Jasper Falls!

Wake My Heart 1
The Best Man 2
Love Me Nots 3
Pining For You 4
My Funny Valentine 5
Side Squeeze 6
And many more...

CHAPTER 1

$\mathcal{S}$he was making a mistake, Samantha thought for the hundredth time that evening. She distracted herself with her phone as they headed over the interstate toward the darkening west. Braydon tapped out a beat on the steering wheel as the chiming sounds of Coldplay filled the car. Unlike Sam, he appeared to be suffering from zero misgivings about this trip.

The signal finally picked up on her wireless network and she quickly logged into her mobile email. Grades had to be posted by now.

"You get through?" Braydon asked at her sigh of relief.

"Yeah, let's just hope it loads."

"The closer we get to Center County the harder it'll be to get a signal. I don't know why you're worried anyway. You know you got an A."

Sam tapped her foot on the carpeted interior of his Passat with fidgety impatience. The chances of her getting less than an A were unlikely, but she wouldn't be able to relax until she knew for sure.

"I probably wouldn't be so concerned if it was a normal semester for me, but student teaching and senior seminar ate up all eighteen of my credits this semester. That one grade carries more weight than a typical three credit course."

He shook his head in resignation. "Samantha, you showed up every day, your cooperating teacher loved you, the principal of the school requested you to forward your résumé directly to her when you graduate, and you've carried a four point oh GPA since you were a freshman. You shouldn't be stressing over this."

She pursed her lips as the swirled rotary image cycled on her phone. There seemed to be a cyber traffic jam at thirty percent loaded. "Come on." Her phone suddenly let out three obnoxious beeps and informed her that the wireless connection failed. "Damn it!"

"When we get to the house you can use my parents' computer."

"I don't want to impose. Can we stop at a McDonalds or some other fast food place with wifi before we get there?"

Sam didn't share Bray's amusement when he chuckled. "Samantha, we don't have fast food joints out here. Just let it go. Once grades are out there's nothing you can do about them anyway. Put your phone away and embrace the fact that you have three weeks of vacation before you have to even think about college again."

He was right. She sighed and slipped her cell back into

her bag, but for some reason she still couldn't relax. Rather than stress about her grades or the fact that she was only six credits away from graduating, she stressed about their journey.

It was the start of summer, yet to Sam it was the end of an era. Her flip-flops and shorts were only irrelevant accessories. Her mind was solely focused on the light at the end of the tunnel. As the air from the sleek black vent on the dash tickled her exposed knees, Sam imagined what the end of the summer would feel like. Such relief. By mid-August she'd be, if everything went according to plan, settling into her new classroom and zipping through textbooks and novels for her lesson plans.

She shouldn't have agreed to go home with Braydon. She wasn't sure why he even asked in the first place. The minute they pulled onto the highway, however, the belated acknowledgement that they were in a relationship set in. For some reason it never occurred to her to see their acquaintance that way. Sure they had a mild, mutual attraction and shared a few meals and kisses together, but as far as being a couple, well, Sam wasn't quite there yet. She only hoped his family didn't read too much into the significance of her visit.

The truth she never would've agreed to join Braydon if her parents weren't in Florida for the month. The idea of returning home to her mom and dad's empty house seemed a depressing way to spend her summer break. It was the image of her watching played-out movies on basic cable, never once taking off her slippers, and destroying one pint of Ben and Jerry's a night, that struck her as pathetic and had her quickly agreeing to spend her break with the McCulloughs. Now she was thinking she would've been better off returning home and waiting it out on her own.

Braydon laid his hand on her thigh and gave an affectionate squeeze. His hands were large and masculine, but pampered and surprisingly smooth. "It'll be fine. You'll see. You'll love the mountains."

Samantha offered a halfhearted nod and settled further into her seat. She'd never been this far away from the suburbs of Pennsylvania other than her time in the city and was unsure what to expect. She'd probably get a crash course in nature and the great outdoors over the next three weeks, but she wasn't worried. She prided herself on her ability to adapt to almost any setting.

This would be an adventure of sorts, a chance to learn, and experience new things. She just hoped the McCulloughs didn't mind her being there. Houseguests were tedious no matter how loved, after a certain length of time.

Braydon had a large family. Hopefully she could fall into the shadows and not cause too many waves in their normal routine. "Who's going to be there? At the house I mean."

"Well, you got my mom and dad, Sheilagh, who's graduating in a few days, Kelly, who'll probably live with my parents until he's forty. If Colin isn't there already he'll be there eventually. Kate and the kids will be around, but she lives close so she'll travel back and forth. You'll get to meet Morai and Nonna. Luke lives in the guest house so he'll be in and out for meals and other stuff and I think Finn just broke up with Erin so I think he's back in the house too." Samantha stared at him dumbly for a second. "What?"

"When you said you had a big family I didn't realize it was that big. I'll never remember all that. How many brothers and sisters do you have total and are you the only one that left the nest?"

"There are seven of us total. Katherine, that's Kate, is the oldest. She has her own place with her husband, Ant, and they are expecting their fourth kid soon. Colin's been away for years. He's the oldest brother. He left for college right after he graduated.

"Finn works with my Uncle Paulie and my dad as a logger, but Luke, his twin, went away to Notre Dame for four years on a football scholarship. He never planned on returning home, but after he hurt his knee he kind of just showed up. I think eventually, once he gets over his hurt pride and bruised ego, he'll take off again.

"Kelly, I guess, is our black sheep. He never showed any interest in leaving, but I wouldn't be surprised if one day he suddenly declared he was going to drift across country for the pure novelty of it. And Sheilagh, well, hopefully she's mellowed out, but from what my mom tells me I don't think that's the case. She's graduating this year."

"What do you mean mellowed out?"

He laughed.

"Ever hear the saying 'if you want trouble find yourself a redhead'? That's Sheilagh. It's her life's ambition to prove that redheads truly have more fun. Don't let her intimidate you though. She acts hard, but she's really a marshmallow on the inside."

"Oh. Is she planning on going to college in the fall?"

"Who knows? Do yourself a favor and don't bring it up in front of my dad. Sheilagh's crazy smart. She was accepted at Princeton, Catholic U., and Penn State Main. She won a grant for the school of her choosing that'll cover a huge part of her tuition, which in a family of seven kids is nothing to sneeze at."

"So which one do you think she'll choose?"

"That's the thing. I don't think she'll choose any of them. She's still figuring out what she wants to do and she doesn't want to leave home until she's sure. See, at home, Sheilagh's a force to be reckoned with, but take her out of her fish bowl and she's just a scared little girl from a redneck town."

"So you think she's nervous?"

Braydon twisted his lips and tilted his head in consideration. "Yes, but she'll never admit it. Girl's got more guts than brains and for a girl who's IQ's been off the charts since elementary school that's saying a lot."

"And what about Kelly? Does she work?"

"First of all, Kelly's a guy and he makes sure anything with female parts is completely aware of it. He may be lacking in ambition, but he has an overabundance of confidence."

"You say that as if you don't get along with him."

"Kelly's fine, but sometimes it gets old, you know? Like, grow up already. He's twenty-two, works at my aunt

6

and uncle's bar, sleeps in a different bed almost every night, and never takes anything seriously."

Sam was cataloging everything Braydon said in her mind. If she was going to be spending three weeks with the McCulloughs she wanted to be prepared. There was nothing worse than living with people whose names she constantly confused.

"And who are the twins?"

"Luke and Finn. They're identical, but Luke's a little more built from playing sports all his life. He's your typical athlete, star quarterback in high school, and in a small community that equates to being the town hero. He was homecoming king, dated the prom queen until he left for college, plays hard and takes losing harder. He used to be the go to guy when you needed to laugh, but since he hurt his knee he's been in kind of a mood. He would've been recruited to the pros. You'll see. When he plays sports from time to time, there's this fire in his eyes, like a passion. That's still there, but he'll never go big now. His field injury can't take the relentless pressure. He went from being predicted as the upcoming draft sensation to a risk factor no one would gamble on."

"That's a shame. Does he have any other skills?"

"Not really. Football was his life. Once that got taken away from him he kind of pulled into himself. When he graduated and came home he moved right into the barn and began fixing it up as an apartment. He never went back to his old room. I think all the trophies and newspaper clippings were an ugly reminder for him. Once my mom realized he wouldn't be living there anymore she boxed up all his awards and turned his room into a nursery for my nieces and nephew."

"Kate's kids?"

"Yup. Frankie, Skylar, and Hannah. You'll meet them tomorrow. Katherine probably is spending the night because she knows I'm coming home."

"So you're close to your older sister."

"Yeah. Kate's almost ten years older than me so she's always favored me. Where Colin and the twins were close enough to her age to fight with her like true siblings, I fell into that perfect era of her life where she wanted a real baby to nurture. My sister was born to be a mother. She'll probably have a baseball team of children someday."

Braydon wore an affectionate smile as he spoke of his older sister. He obviously loved her very much. As if he could read her thoughts he admitted, "She spoils me rotten."

"And what about the other twin?"

"Finn? Finn's quiet. He likes to read and mostly keeps to himself. He was sort of in the transition of moving in with Erin, but I guess that didn't work out. I don't think anyone's really disappointed. She didn't really mesh with the family. We're pretty close, so things like that matter."

Sam was almost starting to relax until she considered about what would happen if the McCulloughs didn't mesh with her. Sensing her tension Braydon squeezed her leg and reassured, "Don't worry. They'll love you."

He adjusted the volume of the radio and Sam assumed he was done with her inquisition for now. She settled back into her seat and stared out the windshield as they drove into the black night. Worried what his family would think of her, she replayed each of his siblings' characteristics in her head, committing them to memory, and hoped she'd make a good impression.

Her ears popped and although she couldn't see past her reflection and the glow of interior lights in the car window, her equilibrium told her they were deep in the mountains. She covertly watched Braydon as he navigated off the highway and onto a dark patch of road.

His wavy blond hair fell onto his forehead in unruly curls Sam imagined most women would find it tempting to run their fingers through. His pale blue eyes traveled over the road, and in the dimness of the car his five o'clock shadow showed darkest at the thin cleft of his chin. He was one of those peculiarly handsome metropolitan men that could model department store sweaters and get away with wearing pink. He was masculine enough that one could actually call him pretty. It was frustrating kissing someone you knew was prettier than yourself.

Sam was never referred to as anything beyond cute. She supposed she had that American girl-next-door thing going for her. Plain, straight brown hair, boring brown eyes, skin that only burned and freckled in the sun, and dusty colored eyelashes. By the time she was sixteen, she already accepted that no amount of makeup would hide the freckles that covered the crests of her cheeks and the bridge of her nose. She was plain, pure and simple. She wondered if Braydon's family would question what he was doing with such a girl.

She didn't even own makeup. She wore Chap Stick, but she didn't think that counted. Going to school in the more metro section of Philadelphia brought out a lot of impulses to appear more sophisticated, but it was too much, on top of school and worrying about her parents, to keep up with the Joneses as well.

She'd resigned herself to being a cotton-blend kind of girl. While the rest of the world fought to squeeze their hips into skinny jeans, Sam decided her worn in boot cut ones were just fine. They were only clothes. What mattered was what was on the inside.

But if that was true, why was she suddenly wishing she brought a more impressive wardrobe with her to meet the McCulloughs? She was being ridiculous. Having never suffered from superficial insecurities before, it didn't make sense, at age twenty-four to give such silly doubts space in her mind. She supposed it was hearing Braydon refer to her earlier as his girlfriend that triggered this unusual train of thought.

Was she his girlfriend? He hadn't asked her out. They hadn't slept together. When she met him four months ago he asked her if she was going to an event being sponsored by Villanova at the student union building. She was and of course told him so.

It was through the interference of mutual friend that she found herself sitting next to Braydon for the day of the event. A week later they were having lunch together at a local brewery, but, again, friends had orchestrated their meeting. It wasn't until they'd been set up several times that Braydon finally asked for her number. And once he had her number it took a week for him to use it.

At that point there was no lengthy phone call that left her exhausted the next morning or with butterflies in the pit of her stomach. No. When he'd used her phone number it was simply to text her and ask what time she was heading to the cafeteria for dinner on a random night. Their lackluster acquaintance progressed as such over the following weeks.

She wasn't dense and she wasn't sending mixed signals, so of course she was surprised that Braydon wanted her to come home with him. Apparently he felt a stronger connection, or at least was assuming one, more than anything *she* felt between the two of them so far. Not to say the possibility of a strong connection didn't exist Sam just hadn't sensed it yet. Perhaps these upcoming weeks would deepen their connection. She should probably be nervous at the possibility of becoming more with Braydon, but all she could muster was a curious sense of indifference. She liked him, but their chemistry was... manageable. She wasn't concerned with losing herself in the moment or having a sudden attack of butterflies in her stomach. Maybe there was something wrong with her.

She enjoyed Braydon's company, but the bottom line was that she was a realist. They simply hadn't spent enough time together to truly know one another and, as far as casual sex, well, Samantha had never been that type of girl.

She'd be willing to see how things progressed, but she

wasn't some hard-up romantic prepared to settle for the shell of a relationship lacking any depth. If Braydon expected her to actually be his girlfriend then he'd have to open up a bit more, let her see what exactly was ticking in that head of his. Because, to be perfectly honest, half the time Sam had no idea what he was thinking. It wasn't until he walked her back to her apartment late one night at school and kissed her that she realized they were courting more than a friendship.

After that night Braydon frequently slipped in a kiss here and an affectionate pat there, but it was all very meaningless in the grand scheme of things. It was nothing she thought to worry about. Until now.

She was graduating at the end of summer and Braydon still had a year to go. Whatever they were entertaining for the time being, Sam didn't see it lasting. She was surprised he even made the offer for her to come with him for their break.

She felt mildly like a snob for being so taken off guard by the invitation. Braydon seemed to genuinely care that she'd be going home to an empty house if she went to her own home. She hadn't given much thought as to how he would spend the three weeks. She supposed coming from a large family like he did, the idea of being alone was intolerable to him. She was used to the solitude.

Since she was fourteen, it had been just her and her parents. They were close, but never overbearing. After her father suffered a massive heart attack two years ago, he gave up his job at the mill and her mother turned in her resignation at the local elementary school and the two of them finally followed their lifelong dream of opening a bed and breakfast.

The change of pace suited them. It kept them occupied with frequent bouts of business yet also allowed them to schedule time for themselves. This was the first time Sam could ever recall seeing her parents take time for an extended vacation together. It was good for them and Sam was glad for it. If she would've gone home her mother would have fretted over not being there with her daughter and her worrying would've spoiled their trip. It was better for everyone that she was spending this time in the mountains with Braydon. Her mother was pleased to hear Sam would use this time with friends. Sam didn't see the necessity in telling her mother Braydon was little more than a stranger.

She must have dozed off because the next thing she knew the lulling, paved back roads and undulating hills gave way to a gravelly drive worn by time and weathered with deep ruts.

"We're here." Sam heard the exhaustion in Braydon's voice.

"What time is it?"

"Eleven-thirty. My mom will be waiting for us, but everyone else is probably asleep by now."

Sam reached into her jeans pocket and pulled out her Chap Stick. After rubbing some on her lips she ran her fingers through her hair. Her belly flip-flopped with anxiety and she laced her fingers together over her lap so not to give away her nervousness.

Everything was black. If she squinted she could

vaguely make out a canopy of evergreens trimming the drive. Stars winked in and out of the dark feathery green covering. She looked ahead, but there was only blackness. They followed a bend in the path and she gasped. They were at a higher altitude, but good grief she never saw so many stars before in her life. It was as though she could catch one if she only stood on her tiptoes. And there were so many, surely the gods wouldn't mind if she slipped one into her pocket.

Her fanciful thoughts were distracted when a large house came into view. The structure was impressive even when its size was partially cloaked by shadows. Only a few windows glowed here and there and there was a porch light burning, illuminating a wide set of wooden steps.

Evenly spaced pillars portioned out a long wrap-around porch encased in a spindled railing. She suddenly remembered a dollhouse she and her sister used to play with as children, but quickly pushed the thought away. This was not a time to think about her childhood. She needed to stay focused and in charge of her emotions.

Braydon parked behind a Jeep Cherokee that appeared to be in surprisingly good shape considering the model was over twenty years old. He plucked the keys from the ignition and let out a groaning stretch. "Why don't we head in and say hi then I'll come back and grab our bags?"

Sam nodded and unbuckled her seatbelt. They'd been in the car for hours and her legs were screaming for her to stand up and stretch. Braydon opened his door and Sam followed suit. She climbed out and extended her arms far over her head and followed Braydon toward the house.

There was almost a deafening hum of wildlife filling the air. The combination of crickets chirping and locusts trilling in such a symphony-like roar told her how expansive the dark woods behind them were.

She wished it were daylight so she could see more of her surroundings. Subconsciously, her mind had already decided the McCullough home was beautiful. The moment she realized it was a traditional log cabin she admitted it was love at first sight. When had she become such a slut for architecture? She supposed it was the novelty of a real life log cabin that tapped into some nostalgic memory of Lincoln Logs and *Little House on the Prairie* and in turn released a secreted, unrequited longing for country living. Suddenly excited to be there, she wanted to thank Braydon for bringing her.

The heavy wood door at the top of the steps opened and a woman with fiery copper hair stood smiling with her hands clasped tightly at her heart. "You're here!"

Braydon smiled.

"Hi, Mum. Sorry we're so late. We couldn't leave until almost eight o'clock."

She waved away his excuses and pulled him into an affectionate embrace. She was no small woman, yet the sigh she emitted when hugging her son told Sam she was soft and loving despite her aggressive handling of others. When she had her fill she stepped back and held Braydon at arm's length, her wide fingers holding him in place.

"You're in need of a haircut, you are," she rebuked, her

sternness bellied by her cheery expression and the glassy sheen of merriment dancing in her eyes.

"Do you not like my hair, Mum?"

The sudden change in Braydon's speech caused Sam to do a double take. The cadence of his words picked up a clipped lilt and sounded almost Gaelic. Mrs. McCullough laughed and smacked an affectionate kiss on her son's cheek.

"Don't you go getting too cheeky now. Kelly will get jealous. You know how he likes to pretend he's the rogue of the clan."

"How is Kelly?"

Mrs. McCullough smirked and rolled her eyes as if she were laughing over a well-known secret. "There's enough time to talk about your brother and his reprobate ways later. For now why don't you introduce me to this lovely lassie?"

They turned and faced Sam as Braydon said, "Mum, this is Samantha Dougherty."

"Dougherty." Mrs. McCullough pronounced her name the proper Irish way sounding like *Doe-hearty,* lacking the hard G most American's used when speaking the name. "Well, that's a good strong Irish name. I believe you'll fit in nicely around here."

Before Sam had a chance to answer, she was smothered in the woman's arms and being hugged near the point of suffocation. When Sam was released she quickly grasped the railing behind her to prevent her body from stumbling down the steps.

"Thank you so much for having me, Mrs. McCullough."

"Oh pish, you call me Maureen, love. Let's head on inside; it's hot out tonight."

"Why's it so warm here? I was expecting it to be at least twenty degrees cooler than the city." Braydon commented as they followed Mrs. McCullough, no, Maureen, into the house.

"We haven't had a bit of rain in over two weeks. The woods are growing dryer than a nun's tits. We won't be having any bonfires this side of the forest any time soon, that's for sure."

Braydon's mother's language jerked Sam's attention away from her inspection of the house. She couldn't remember ever hearing her own mother say tits. Her mother could barely say breasts and that included discussing a cut of chicken for dinner.

Sam kept up with the two, keeping an ear open for comments pertaining to her, as she eyed her surroundings with covert curiosity. A grin flourished across her face when she realized the log home was authentic inside and out. The perfectly stacked logs matched the wooden tongue and groove planks covering the floor and ceiling.

Following the others into a kitchen, she was impressed by the wooden cabinetry. Sam could tell immediately, even with no architectural background, that the woodwork was all custom made. The designer, whoever he was, clearly took a lot of care in carving out every detail down to the mortise and tenon joints that interlocked the sturdy framework.

She took a seat next to Braydon at the large farm table filling the enormous kitchen while Maureen informed her son of the family's current events, speaking with agreeable frankness.

"Kate's here, but she couldn't wait up. Her sciatica's been bothering her something fierce this time around. Not that I minded her making her excuses early. I'll warn you now, Bray. Your sister's been leaving air biscuits in every room. You know, with Frankie it was her ankles, with Skylar it was the heartburn, with Hannah it was her sciatica, with this one it seems it's her arse. She's all those ails and now farts too! She's makin' my house smell like a pile of cabbage shite, that's what she's doing."

"Mum!"

"Well, she is. But don't tell her I told you so. She's weepier than a willow tree this pregnancy. There's no wonder why Anthony decided to wait until tomorrow to get here."

Sam had no idea what to make of Braydon's mother. Maureen continued to speak with hybrid comments filled with loving and crass observations about the McCulloughs while she bustled about the kitchen heating leftovers.

Sam noticed a microwave tucked between two raised cabinets, but Maureen continued to pull out pots and pans as she heated up food. Sam was willing to make the assumption that a women like Maureen never used a microwave. In just the brief few minutes she'd been in her presence, she could already tell Maureen McCullough was a woman who took great pride in working hard for her family and would scoff at shortcuts.

When the food was heated she placed a hefty bowl of stew in front of Braydon and Sam. There was also a bowl of roasted potatoes seasoned in rosemary and a basket of homemade biscuits wrapped in a dishcloth with red ticking that looked hand sewn.

The food was different than anything she ever tried in the city or anything she ever saw her own mother make, but it was still quite good. As Maureen prattled on about Frank, Braydon's father, Sam watched Braydon shut his eyes in pleasure as his mother's cooking settled into his belly.

Sam smiled. Most comfort food was embellished because it came from a mother's love. Braydon obviously tasted more than just stew with each bite. He tasted recipes shaped by traditions and was likely remembering memories of being in this familiar place. She was happy to witness this settling side of him. She liked watching Braydon at home.

Once she finished her supper, Sam pushed her bowl away. Without pausing for even a syllable, Maureen chattered on as she stood and carried the dishes to the sink and began washing them. The kitchen was clearly her domain. She navigated through the motions of tidying up without ever taking her eyes off Sam or her son.

It occurred to Sam that her anxiety about being here had disappeared the moment she met Maureen McCullough. She analyzed the women and wondered what magical gift she held that made her able to put guests at such ease. Maureen was a natural when it came to hospitable courtesy, even if she didn't necessarily follow propriety.

As they all laughed at an anecdote Maureen shared about a woman at the butcher, Sam decided that for as much as she loved the McCulloughs' log cabin, she loved their mother more.

Contrary to her first impression, Samantha saw the beautiful woman that was Maureen McCullough. She imagined her hair was once a fiery red to match her spicy personality although now it was more fawn colored with natural highlights in the deepest shade of orange. Laugh lines softened her dark green eyes. Her clipped un-manicured fingernails spoke volumes about how no nonsense she was when it came to taking on the labors of mothering seven children.

At first her brisk mannerisms made Maureen come off as abrasive, Sam would now describe her as soft. Not due to her round bosom or generous curves, but because of the way Maureen would titter and giggle in between stories with absolute femininity, her eyes twinkling like a little girl's. It didn't matter how many times she said bollocks or cock in a sentence. It was all just noise coming from a sweet, loving woman with a dirty mouth.

They talked until well after one in the morning. After such a heavy meal and four hours of travel, Sam was ready to call it a night. They still had to carry in their bags from the car. The idea of carrying anything at this hour made sleeping in her travel clothes tempting.

Maureen said, "Well, I'm off to bed. I'll see you two in the morning for breakfast." And with that she was gone.

Braydon's mother bustled out of the kitchen and climbed the steps. When Sam turned back to Braydon, he was smiling.

"What?" she asked.

"What do you think?"

Seeing no need to lie, Sam smiled and admitted, "I love her."

He beamed and Sam was certain he was about to kiss her, but the front door opened and someone yelled, "Jesus, Mary, and Joseph has the prodigal son returned?"

Braydon pulled back and groaned as he stood from his seat when a young man with rakishly spiked hair and sharp crystal blue eyes came into the kitchen.

"Kelly," he greeted as he embraced his younger brother in a backslapping hug.

Ah, so this is the loner.

"It's good to have you home, my brother."

"Good to be home."

They broke apart and Kelly turned to Sam. He leered at her with faintly sinister amusement while she tried not to bristle under his scrutiny.

Whoa. That expression should be photographed and put in the dictionary under the word smolder.

"Well, hello, pretty lady. I see you've come with the wrong brother, but I'd be glad to remedy that for ya and make sure you come again."

Braydon shoved his brother out of the way. "Kelly, this is my *girlfriend,* Samantha."

"Braydon, don't interrupt me when I'm speaking with the lassies. How long are you here for, beautiful?"

Sam wasn't sure if Kelly realized he was pissing his brother off, but she didn't really want to get in the middle.

"Three weeks."

He made an expression that Sam could only describe as disappointment.

"That, love, is a shame. Three weeks with this lot and you'll be crazy as a loon by the time you head home. I can't be exposing myself to anymore crazies." He leaned in a theatrically whispered, "You see, they all know I'm the McCullough with the biggest cock and, the crazies, well, they don't like to share."

This time when Braydon shoved his brother Kelly actually stumbled and landed in a kitchen chair. "Shut up, moron. She's not one of your trollops."

Kelly laughed. "Oh, now Bray, it isn't kind to call your friends' mothers trollops."

"I don't even want to know what friends you're referring to, but I hope they kick your ass when they find out you're diddling their mums. You're disgusting. Samantha, I'm going to get our bags. Kelly, try not to repulse or corrupt her within the next three minutes."

"Oh, come on now, Bray. I'm not you. Give me a little credit. I cannot corrupt a beautiful woman in three minutes. With stamina like mine I'll ask for at least an hour."

Braydon rolled his eyes heavenward in clear frustration. Truthfully though, Sam was having a hard time not laughing. As Braydon walked toward the door he turned and said, "You know what, Kelly?"

"What, big brother?"

"Take that big cock you're so proud of and go fuck yourself."

With that he stomped out of the house.

Kelly turned back toward Sam and was smiling at her as if they shared a secret. She finally gave into her smile and said, "You're mean."

He laughed. "Not mean, smart. You'll see. Everyone around here kisses Bray's arse. I make sure he doesn't get ahead of himself and grow too cocky."

"Ha! And you're not cocky?"

He gave her a wicked half smile and said, "Samantha, love, I thought I already made it clear, out of all the McCullough men, I'm the cockiest."

Braydon walked in and dropped the bags onto the wood floor. "You ready to head up to bed, Samantha?"

"Where am I sleeping?"

"In my room with me."

It took her a minute to find her words. Kelly was distracted with making some kind of sandwich, but Sam was certain he wasn't missing a single word. "Braydon, I cannot share your room. This is your parents' house."

"So?"

"So it's rude and not proper."

"They won't care."

"Well, I'm sorry, but I care. I'll sleep on the couch, but I can't sleep in your bed with you."

"Samantha, that's ridiculous. I'm twenty-three. They

know I'm not a virgin. They probably assume we spend the night together all the time at school."

She gasped. "Well, we don't!" Realizing she wasn't telling Braydon anything he didn't already know she turned to Kelly and affirmed, "We don't."

He smiled as he prepared to take a bite of his sandwich. "Don't get your knickers in a bunch over what I think. I don't judge. I am a gentleman though, so I will say, if you don't want to share Bray's bed you can use mine."

She pursed her lips and rolled her eyes. "Let me guess, you'd be willing to keep me warm too."

"Samantha—"

"Ah, love, my bed's never cold."

Before things got heated Sam held up her hands and interrupted them both. "Look, I'm not sharing anyone's bed. Kelly, since you have room in yours I'm sure your brother would appreciate half of it. I was up late writing papers all week, I've just traveled all night, and it's well past two in the morning. I'm going to bed. Braydon, we can work out better arrangements in the morning, but for now I'd appreciate it if you showed me to your room."

Kelly must have found her speech very amusing. He smiled grandly and said, "Dear God, Braydon, if you don't marry her, I will. You must be amazing in bed, aren't you, love?"

She groaned. "Braydon, show me where your room is."

She scooped up her larger suitcase as she left the kitchen and followed Braydon up the stairs. The wood creaked as they climbed the steps. The second floor was as dark and silent as a tomb.

"I can't believe you're sticking me with Kelly," Braydon whispered.

"Well believe it. I can't believe you expected me to share your bed under your parents' roof."

He let the comment go, but Sam could tell he was irritated.

She didn't think she was being irrational. His family didn't know her. She was here for the duration of the next month. How difficult would it be to sit across from them at the breakfast table if they were all thinking about what a whore she was? No, she could not share his bed. Tomorrow she'd see if there were better arrangements for him, but for her first night this would have to do.

Braydon opened a door and flipped on a light. The room was painted slate gray with matching bedding. The furniture was modern with sharp geometric angles. The only thing inside the room that remotely complimented the style of the house was the gray and white fur blanket at the foot of the bed and a skull with six points of antlers hanging from the wall. There was a large gray metal cabinet with a lock taking up a good portion of the room.

"What's that?"

"Gun safe." Braydon was obviously being short with her.

"You hunt?"

"Everyone hunts around here."

"Did you kill that?" she asked pointing to the antlers hanging on the wall.

"That was my first big kill. Got it with an arrow when I was thirteen."

Samantha had a hard time assimilating the Braydon she knew from Villanova with the Braydon who cursed in an Irish tongue and shot animals with a bow and arrow. She suddenly longed for the comfort she experienced earlier in Maureen's presence, because up here in Braydon's bedroom she felt very alone and confused.

Braydon placed her bags at the foot of the bed and opened a drawer to pull out some clothing Sam assumed he'd sleep in. Without looking at her he briefly opened up a door on the right side of the bed.

"Here's your bathroom. It has a shower and everything you need. The closet's over there if you want to hang anything up. Kelly's room's two doors down the hall if you need anything. I guess I'll see you at breakfast."

He began to walk out into the hall and Sam felt the weight of guilt.

"Braydon, wait."

He paused and looked at her.

This was his room. She was being selfish. He invited her here so she wouldn't spend her break alone and now she was forcing him out of his room and into a room with a brother who clearly irritated him. But his presumption that they'd go from a few shared kisses and dates to sharing a bed took her off guard and she didn't want him to assume too much.

"I..." Yet she still didn't want to give his family the wrong impression. Maybe Maureen would understand, but she had yet to meet the other nine hundred McCulloughs. Who knew what they'd think of their brother shacking up with her? She'd have to wait and see. "Maybe tomorrow you could sleep here and I'll see about sharing one of your sister's rooms."

"Don't sweat it. I'm just tired. It's fine. Really."

He appeared fine, but Sam suspected he was trying to keep the peace.

She walked over to him and gently kissed his cheek. "Thank you."

He ran his hand over her ponytail and playfully tugged the end.

"You're welcome, Samantha. Goodnight. I'll see you in the morning."

CHAPTER 2

*S*am awoke to the echo of rolling thunder. The unusual sound had her immediately opening her eyes, reminding her she was in an unfamiliar place. She was in Braydon's bed at the McCulloughs'.

The roar of thunder sounded again, only this time it sounded more like a stampede coming from the hall. Elephantine footsteps echoed up and down the narrow wood flooring of the hall followed by an excited shriek and bubbling laughter. Sam sat up and pushed away the soft fur blanket twisted around her waist.

She climbed out of bed and stretched. What time was it? She walked to the window and pulled aside the drapes. The isolated splendor that greeted her took her breath away. Sitting in front of the reddening dawn were enormous mountains with nothing but flush pine trees sitting upon their shoulders.

The green rolling hills were bathed in roseate tints as the golden sun slowly climbed over the fleecy clouds to claim its place in the eastern sky. Breathtaking. This was nothing like the scrubby forelands of the New Jersey Coast. This was nature at its purest, so tremendous and humbling.

For the first time in a long time, Sam thought of God. Only he could create such perfection.

The stampede sounded from the hall again. Sam moved quietly to the bedroom door and peeked out to find the culprit. Because she was wearing only a pale blue cotton tank top and white cotton briefs, she made sure not to open the door more than a crack.

A cloud of black hair rushed by fast enough to send a small puff of wind over Sam's uncovered calves. Just as Sam processed that it was a little girl in a cupcake night-gown, a small boy yelled and charged down the hall in full battle cry. The girl shrieked and the boy gave a villainous laugh. Uncontrollable, nervous giggles escaped the child's lips as the boy neared, backing her into a corner.

Suddenly they both burst out laughing as the boy shouted, "You're it!"

"Skylar! Frankie!"

The children stilled and looked down the stairs toward the adult female voice Sam couldn't see the owner of. "Don't make me come up there and knock the beef off ya! People are sleeping. Come down here and eat your breakfast."

The little girl looked up at the older boy nervously,

now seeing him as her protector rather than her playful predator. "Told you it was early."

"You started it. Ah well, come on. Let's go get Hannah."

The children tromped down the steps, still unaware of how loudly their steps fell. Sam shut the door and smiled. This house was nothing like her home.

The smell of bacon permeated the halls and lingered in her room. Once the days started around here, the McCulloughs likely didn't stop until well past dusk. If she wanted to join the others, she'd better get dressed and be prepared for anything.

She lifted her suitcase to the bed and unzipped the cover. Flipping through her items she pulled out a pair of khaki shorts and a fitted white tee. Unfolding the clothes, she laid them out on her bed, placing a fresh pair of cotton panties and a bra on top.

She frowned at the wrinkles, but decided they'd have to do for now. After retrieving her toiletry bag and a towel from her suitcase she moved toward the bathroom. She turned the knob and wondered if Braydon brought in her other bag that held her sneakers. She wanted to explore today and sneakers would probably be—

There, standing naked in her bathroom, was a man – a beautiful man.

All thoughts fell out of Samantha's head like a spilt jar of marbles scattering out of reach. Standing stock-still, mouth agape, personal items clutched to her chest, she stared—openly gawked in dumb shock—at the vision before her.

She must've been taken him by surprise as well,

because he stood still as a statue, his damp hair clotted in sharp spikes in every direction, his shoulders still coated with a sprinkling of droplets from his recent shower, and nothing but a towel dangling from his left hand suspended just between his well-defined hips.

Holy mother of God, Sam had never seen such a breathtaking show of nakedness.

His olive skin smoothly caressed the muscles climbing his torso like a Jacob's Ladder. His tapered hips led to toned thighs, strong calf muscles sprinkled in dark hair, and two big tanned feet.

"Pardon me. I forgot to lock the door," he said in a deep voice that was wholly masculine.

Her gaze jumped to his and she had to actually think hard in order to make sense of his words.

He was beautiful. Tall, with short hair blacker than a raven's wing. His defined jaw was clean-shaven. His lips looked soft and slightly pinker than his olive pigment. His nose was straight, enunciating the symmetrical perfection of his face. Stunning blue-green eyes stared back at her.

He couldn't have been more than thirty, but his eyebrows added something appealing to his visage, made him appear more distinguished, older than she assumed he truly was. Two perfectly black slashes she suddenly had the urge to smooth the soft pad of her thumb over pulled together as he frowned at her.

Her eyes returned to his deep sapphire ones. He was staring at her expectantly.

"I..." A thousand words ran through her head. Stunning. *Ass. Bite. Lick. Sweat. Entwined. Thrust.* None of them remotely appropriate for the situation.

Her faltering tongue seemed to take up the weight and space of a battleship in her mouth. If she tried to form words only clumsy talk would fall past her lips making the situation worse.

Embarrassed, Samantha hastily turned and slammed the bathroom door, closeting herself away in Braydon's room and shutting out the beautiful man.

BRAYDON SMELLED sausage and bacon and sighed contentedly. His mother was cooking. Without opening his eyes he reveled in the familiarity of being home. Focusing on the distant sounds of his family bustling about below, warmth spread through his chest.

His smile faltered as the weight of strong arms holding him registered with his brain. *That's not right.* He suddenly opened his eyes and jack-knifed off the bed.

"Get off me, you fucking pervert!"

"What? We were snuggling," Kelly complained.

Braydon groaned. "There's no way I'm spending another night in here with you."

"I think that sassy piece of fluff you brought back from college may have something to say about that."

"Her name is Samantha and she'll get over it. Once she meets Dad and the others and realizes they don't care about stuff like that she'll be fine."

Kelly laughed and rolled over.

Braydon frowned. "What's so funny?"

"You. I never thought I'd see the day when the golden son couldn't bed the girl he wanted."

"Fuck you."

"Nah, I'll just watch you try and fuck Samantha. Has she even let you sample the goods yet, brother? No, don't answer. I can tell she hasn't. I suggest you go ask Mum to get you a bag of ice, because I'm guessing your bollocks will be bluer than a smurf's before you head back to school."

Braydon threw a pillow at his younger brother and stomped out into the hall. After using the bathroom he went to his room to retrieve some clothes.

His fist knocked, but there was no answer so he entered. Samantha's clothes were set out on the bed and the soft, trickling rush coming from the adjoining bathroom. She was in the shower. He wanted to bridge the gap from the platonic purgatory Sam seemed to be holding them in and move their relationship to the next level.

He considered popping in on her to see what she'd do, but figured that wouldn't be very gentlemanly of him and Sam would likely freak. Rather, he quickly dressed and headed downstairs to join the rest of his relatives.

As he came down the stairs he heard his younger sister Sheilagh talking. "Well, what does she look like?"

He paused by the door to the kitchen to see how his mother would answer her question.

"She's pretty enough. Plain like. Quiet. I cannot say I see her being right for your brother though."

"So you don't like her."

"Now, I did not say that. I like her just fine. She's

34

polite, Irish, sweet, easy to talk to. I just never imagined Braydon settling with someone like her. She surprised me. That's all."

Braydon shoulders sagged like sails turned out from the wind and betrayed by the weather. He deserved a decent woman and suffered no misconceptions about his appearance. He was tall, fit, heading toward a successful career. Resentment tickled his spine as his confidence wavered.

"There's nothing wrong with plain," he heard his older sister, Kate, declare.

If ever there were a champion of Braydon's, Katherine was it.

"I imagine it would take a simpler kind of girl to leave the city and not be turned off by Center County. It isn't like we're anything fancy out here."

He wondered at their use of words like "simple" and "plain". Samantha lacked the lace and frills of most females of his generation, but she was by no means lacking. She was pretty. Of course her type of pretty was inconsistent with what he normally deemed beautiful. Typically he leaned toward leggy blondes. Samantha had a nice set of legs, but he never saw her in any kind of high heels.

Still, she always looked nice. Samantha was smart and easy to spend time with. She was graduating and becoming an English teacher in the fall. She was wife material. Braydon always imagined he'd meet his wife in college and get married soon after graduation.

With only a year left to graduate he figured he better

start shopping in the wife department. Samantha Dougherty was model wife material. What wasn't to like?

"I've no doubt Samantha will enjoy the land," his mother added. "I could see it in her eyes how taken she was with our home. I imagine when she sees the territory in the light of day it'll take her heart for a spin."

"Does Braydon love her?" Kate wondered. "Do you think she'll break his heart?"

"Ah, my boy must first give his heart in order to risk having it broken. When Braydon finds the woman he'll marry you'll all know it. She'll own every bit of his soul and he'll be hopelessly ruined for all other women. I saw it with your father. I saw it with your Uncle Paulie, and I saw it with Anthony when he asked to marry you, Katie.

"Braydon thinks he's ready to settle down, but he isn't. He isn't ready to let go of reason enough to let someone else in, to truly fall in love. And anything less than true love is a sham, one I certainly would not want to see a child of mine settle for. This woman's a good girl and she seems to understand exactly what she and my son share. Braydon's making assumptions, but I believe Samantha doesn't have a misleading bone in her body. She will clear the air soon enough. At least before he makes a complete arse out of himself."

"Well, no man's ever going to own my soul," Sheilagh announced.

Kate overrode Sheilagh's statement, "Then why did she come here with him?"

His mother sighed. "Braydon invited her. They may not be soul mates, but they're friends. If your brother wants to bring a friend back from school with him he's more than welcome to. Let them work things out on their own. He doesn't need you cautioning him now, ya hear, Katie? I know you don't want to see your brother get hurt, but sometimes a touch of wounded pride can go a long way. It's high time Braydon learned the world is bigger than our little corner of the mountain. If he doesn't want a woman from Center County then he's going to have to put in a bit more effort. Not every woman's waiting around for a handsome golden haired boy from a small town to smile prettily at her."

The back door opened and Braydon heard his brother Luke, "Morning, Mum."

"Luke, we've a house guest with us. Go put on a shirt." Braydon took the distraction to slip past the kitchen and out the front door.

As Sam softly stepped into the foyer she took a moment to gather her courage. It sounded as if over twenty voices collided from within the large open kitchen. She wished Braydon had waited upstairs for her or at least woke her up when he journeyed down with the rest of the family.

Taking a solidifying breath she drew back her shoulders and took a step into the kitchen then froze.

Over all of the voices she could only make out a few distinct words. Someone yelled to pass the poundies, whatever they were, and a shirtless man yelled across the table, "I heard Kelly was wasting time with Ashlynn Fisher last night."

"I was not and you know it. I cannot help it if she likes to spend her free evenings staring at me. I hardly even looked back."

"Ah, well, little brother, I'm not sure if anyone told you, but you can enjoy a woman with your eyes closed," said another man Sam hadn't seen before. Braydon was nowhere to be found in the kitchen.

"Enough of that talk at the table," Maureen scolded as she hefted a large plate of flapjacks onto the center of the table. "Ashlynn Fisher's no mutt. If you cannot keep your eyes open for her you don't deserve her. I better not hear tales of you misleading that sweet girl, Kelly."

"Wouldn't ride her if she had pedals, Mum."

"And why not? She's quite pretty. Don't you think she's pretty, Luke?"

"Pretty enough," the shirtless man agreed without giving the question much thought. As he lifted his fork to his mouth Sam noticed he had a large Celtic cross tattooed on the side of his muscled rib cage.

A toddler with strawberry blonde pigtails began to cry and the boy and girl Sam had seen earlier were listening raptly to something their Uncle Kelly was whispering in their ears.

A young woman with fiery red hair Sam guessed was Sheilagh announced, "Kelly doesn't want to diddle Ashlynn because she scares the shite out of him."

She smiled proudly when Kelly looked up then she shoved a large bite of potatoes in her mouth with smug pleasure.

"You shut it, whelp."

"It's true."

"Now why would you be afraid of a good girl like Ashlynn Fisher, Kelly?" Maureen asked, finally taking a seat at the head of the table.

"I know why," Sheilagh proclaimed.

Kelly seemed very interested in his plate.

Maureen turned to Luke. "Do you know why?"

Luke looked equally as interested in his plate.

She turned to another son, "Finnegan?" When he didn't answer she complained, "Well, someone better tell me what's so wrong with Ashlynn Fisher."

"I'll tell you," Sheilagh smiled, clearly baiting her brother.

She was quite a beautiful girl. Amazing that someone could have such red hair and not a single freckle marring her face.

"Let it go, lassie," an older man with black hair peppered with silver around his face grumbled.

"Yeah, whelp, drop it," Kelly warned. It was the first time Sam actually detected a note of seriousness in Braydon's younger brother.

"Why should I?"

"Because if you go spreading around Ashlynn's personal business I'll explain exactly why the same dilemma does not apply to you."

"It better apply to you," the older man whom Sam now assumed was Mr. McCullough growled.

Sheilagh glared at Kelly with hardened lips.

Maureen threw up her hands in frustration and complained; "I just don't understand why it has to be a secret from me if everyone at this table already knows."

Another red headed woman feeding the no longer crying toddler tossed down a baby spoon in exasperation and cried, "For the love of Mike, Mother. The girl is a virgin!"

Maureen made a small "o" with her mouth then picked up her fork and mumbled, "At twenty-two? Well...There's nothing wrong with waiting in this day and age I suppose. A little temperance never hurt anyone."

"Happy now?" Kelly asked Sheilagh.

The talk moved on to other subjects. It was absolute mayhem. How anyone followed a single word of it was beyond Sam's comprehension. She was already getting a neck ache like one would at a tennis match from simply trying to follow the thread of the Ashlynn Fisher conversation as comments volleyed back and forth.

There seemed to always be four or more topics being discussed at once. The family spoke loudly, cursed freely, and parried verbal jousts with clever and witty quips. It was very overwhelming.

Sam wondered if she could slip outside without being noticed. Perhaps she should go look for Braydon. Rather than play the coward, she stiffened her shoulders and stepped into the melee.

"Good morning."

Like a record scratching, all mouths stopped moving and the sound of silverware and dishes clattering was silenced. Approximately twenty eyes turned toward her.

With wide eyes she slowly raised her hand and finger-waved. "Hi. I'm Sam."

Everyone said his or her own version of hello at once. Sam didn't catch a single name that was thrown at her. Maureen stood and bustled over to the cabinets. Kelly slid down and offered her a seat at the long bench they all shared. The redheaded woman Sam assumed was Katherine lifted the toddler off her lap and told the three children to go play.

Sam sat next to Kelly and watched as he loaded enough food to feed a village on the plate Maureen placed in front of her. Realizing Braydon's brother wasn't going to cease until the food spilled over the edge, she stilled his hand and whispered to him that was enough. Everyone at the table smiled at her and she fought the impulse to check that nothing was in her hair or on her face.

She cleared her throat. "Has anyone seen Braydon?"

"He took a ride out to check a fence for me. Should be back soon," the older man said. He had to have been Mr. McCullough. He looked just like Braydon's brothers. They all shared the same blue eyes and strong jaw. Although the twins had a lighter brown hair compared to Mr. McCulloughs and Kelly's black, it was clear they were all related. It was interesting that Braydon was the only member of the family with golden hair and fairer features.

"I'm sorry I interrupted all of you. I'll just eat and get out of your way."

"Don't be silly, dear. You're our guest for the next two weeks and we won't have you hiding away from us. Best you get comfortable with us as quickly as possible. That way when someone upsets you, you'll have no problem setting them straight. We've got a tough lot here and best you show them you're no shying violet from the start."

Sheilagh stood and carried her plate to the sink. "You're gonna scare her, Mum."

"No, Samantha's tough. I've faith in her. She can handle herself. Can't you, dear?"

Clueless of what a proper reply would be, Sam smiled and took a sip of her juice. If she hadn't immediately liked the McCulloughs so much she'd probably label them all crazy. She focused on eating her breakfast while each family member took their turn introducing themselves.

Katherine was indeed the other redhead. Older than the rest, but still beautiful and vibrant. Sam was quickly realizing all McCulloughs were. She had red hair to her shoulders and bangs that covered her forehead yet always seemed to part in the center. She was the type of woman that pulled off natural as if it were an art. Wearing no makeup that Sam could detect, her ears didn't appear pierced, and the only jewelry she wore was a gold Claddagh wedding band. She also was very pregnant.

The twins seemed the most reserved of the bunch, but perhaps that was because it was still early and they weren't quite awake yet. Finn left the kitchen soon after Sam sat down so she hadn't gotten an opportunity to analyze him yet. Braydon was right. They were identical. What he failed to mention was that they were both off the charts gorgeous.

Luke appeared respectful yet careless. There was something guarded about his posture and the set of his eyes. All through breakfast he wore a short brimmed hat that reminded Sam of a paperboy from the turn of the century. It made his ethnicity all the more apparent and he kept the hat pulled low over his eyes. This brother was the one Braydon said lost his chance at being a professional athlete. He definitely had the body of an athlete. Yet there was something mysterious about him she couldn't quite figure out. Other than a short hello, he said nothing to Sam and very little to anyone else.

Mr. McCullough, who insisted Sam call him Frank, was polite and quiet. Sam supposed being married to a woman like Maureen, didn't leave much to be said at the end of the day.

He wore a red flannel, blue jeans, and faded yellow work boots. Realizing she had imagined what Frank McCullough looked like, he fit the acceptable logger image her mind subconsciously preordained.

And then there was Sheilagh. No wonder she had a reputation of being somewhat of a wild child. Even sitting next to her was intimidating. She was so beautiful it almost defied what Sam thought acceptable for normal people who weren't airbrushed supermodels. Sam fought the urge to keep staring at her in search of at least one flaw. In her glances she found none.

Sheilagh had bright green eyes, the same color of Maureen and Katherine's. Her lips looked naturally made up, as if she was eating berries and the juice permanently stained them. The youngest McCullough was like a thistle flower, beautiful and tempting, but impossible to hold without being cut.

The sound of a car pulling up the gravelly drive followed by a car door slamming filtered into the kitchen. A dog barked and Katherine went to the door.

"It's about time!" She smiled as she pushed open the screen door at the back of the kitchen, her belly filling most of the entrance.

Braydon stepped in and Sam silently sighed with mild relief at his return.

"Beautiful Kate. How are you?"

He hugged his sister with unguarded affection and she whispered something in his ear that made him flush and smile. When the siblings separated Braydon placed a hand on his sister's belly.

"Another boy, eh?"

Katherine smiled and cradled her protruding belly. "I'm fighting to get you a namesake, but Ant says Braydon Marcelli just sounds ethnically wrong."

"Well, that's what you get for marrying an Italian."

A dog scratched at the screen and Katherine leaned past Braydon to let it inside the house. It was a mangy looking beast with gray brown wiry hair. Sam tried not to react outwardly when she noticed it only had three legs.

"Here you are, Rufus," Maureen called as she dropped scraps into a metal bowl on the floor. The dog hobbled over and gratefully nibbled at the trimmings.

Braydon kissed his mother on her rosy cheek than moved over to Sam and did the same before sitting next to her on the bench.

Leaning close he whispered to Sam, "How are you this morning?"

"Good. Where'd you go? I would've gone with you."

"I had to go check something at the end of the property for my dad. If you want to go out later to see the land I'll take you."

He began to eat as the rest of the family returned to the table with mugs of coffee. Frank was perusing the local paper. Kelly drifted back upstairs, and Luke disappeared shortly after Braydon returned. The children played across the foyer in what Sam assumed was the den. Katherine questioned Braydon about his recently completed semester at school and he quizzed her on his nieces and nephew's recent achievements.

"Are we having a game today?" Braydon asked to no one in particular.

"Aye. We're meeting at two. Colleen and Rosemarie have already each called this morning to see if you got in okay."

Braydon smiled and turned to Sam. "They're my aunts. You'll meet them today and the rest of my cousins. We always start the summer with an opening game of baseball."

A ball game. That'd be fun to watch. Sam tried not to get overwhelmed at the idea of more family. These were busy people, lots of offspring. Sam thought it charming the way the family pronounced Colleen as C'leen and Rosemarie as Ross-mer-ree.

The conversation lazed in and out of topics from which wooded areas Frank's company was recently clearing to the family's overall opinion on Finn's recent breakup. Through it all Maureen steadily set the kitchen back to rights and finally joined the others at the table to relax. The small toddler, Hannah, returned to Katherine's lap and napped in her mother's arms using her soon-to-arrive little brother as a pillow.

When the screen door opened again Sam almost choked on the coffee slipping down her throat. It was the man from the bathroom with the sapphire eyes flecked with jade. He greeted Braydon first and then turned directly to her.

"Hello, I'm Colin."

She took his hand. "Sam."

"Samantha's Braydon's friend from college. She'll be staying with us for the next three weeks," Maureen informed.

"Wonderful," Colin remarked as he gave her hand a slight squeeze.

She didn't understand her disappointment at the loss of contact. Obviously she was the immature one, for where Colin kindly decided to forget her humiliating blunder this morning and be a gentleman to his brother's friend, she could not help imagining him naked. When he shook her hand it was formal and without emotion beyond appropriate politeness. The way it should be. Yet for some reason this irritated her.

He moved to the counter and poured himself a cup of coffee then took a seat next to Katherine. Running an affectionate hand down Hannah's sleeping head, he smiled.

What was it Sam noticed in his expression? Not quite

longing, but perhaps some sort of resigned acceptance. There was definitely love in the gesture, but something more. This man, for some reason, stood apart from the rest.

"How was Mass?" Frank asked as he dumped the remainder of his coffee down the drain and stashed his newspaper in a wooden crate of old papers.

"It was fine. I spoke to Father Newsham about moving the later Sunday Mass back an hour since they dropped the Saturday Mass. I don't think he was fond of the idea until I pointed out that a later crowd could possibly bring younger parishioners."

"Lord knows Kelly hasn't been to Mass since they moved it to nine a.m."

Colin chuckled. "Well, Kelly's a proud heathen. I was thinking more about the kids Sheilagh's age."

"I'll remind you I am now a legal adult," Sheilagh told Colin pointedly. "And I never miss Sunday service. However, I'd appreciate being able to sleep in a little longer."

As they spoke Sam couldn't resist watching the oldest McCullough brother. He had a soft yet strong voice. His teeth were perfectly white and straight and now that his hair was combed he displayed a level of refinement the rest of the family lacked. He was devastatingly handsome in a classic way, a cross between a sexy Clark Kent or Gable. He seemed a distinguished gentleman, sure and confident.

"Is you're family Catholic?" Maureen asked Samantha drawing her back into the conversation.

"Um, I have all my sacraments, but we haven't practiced in quite a few years."

Maureen and the others accepted her honesty without judgment. She turned back to watch Colin some more when Maureen proudly announced, "Colin is finishing his Transitional Diaconate this summer. In August he's becoming a priest."

CHAPTER 3

*A*fter an afternoon of driving around the McCullough property with Braydon, Samantha was completely in love with the land. They parked and explored a trail that led to a natural spring and she was stunned when Braydon took a metal cup tied to a post in the ground and scooped out a sample and swallowed it. The watering hole was edged in moss and freezing cold. When he kindly bullied her into tasting it she was amazed at how refreshing the spring water was on her tongue.

They passed a corral by the edge of the five hundred acre property where horses grazed. Braydon informed her that most McCulloughs learned how to ride before they properly mastered the art of walking. Samantha had never ridden a horse before, but was determined to try before she returned home.

There was a cleared piece of land high up on a mountain that had a windmill. She'd always known the contraptions were big, but compared to what she imagined they were colossal. Because windmills were government owned in Center County, this was another source of income for the McCulloughs. All they had to do was sign the papers agreeing that the county could use their property and they were sent a check quarterly for their civic duty.

Growing up in the more affluent suburbs of Pennsylvania and the Jersey areas across the Delaware River where people struggled to obtain even an acre of land, Sam was blown away by how much property the McCulloughs owned. It was too enormous to completely explore in one afternoon alone. It made her sad for the ruthless commercialization that no doubt would someday rob the secret place of its beauty. Hopefully the McCulloughs would never let their land go.

They parked to observe a black bear claw the surface of a small stream for fish when Braydon shut off the truck and gave the engine a rest.

"Will the bear be bothered by us being so close?"

"Not so long as we stay in the car. That's one thing about being this high on the trail. You've got to be real careful about being out on foot. There're all kinds of things bigger than you out here. Not to mention more pitfalls than I can list along the trail. You also have to know when people are hunting on the property."

"Do you let others use your property for hunting season?"

"We have a cabin up that mountain there. It's pretty isolated and primitive. No phones or cable. There's a radio you can call out from in case of emergencies, but that's about it. We let some family friends borrow it from time to time, but other than that, no, we don't let people treat our home as public gaming land."

"When you told me you were from the mountains I never imagined anything as magnificent as this."

The bear, which was hardly more than a partially grown cub, moved down stream toward the rougher waters. Just past the bend of the stream were large moss covered boulders. The incline of the land created a slight waterfall where rapids fell like white foam into the calmer pools closer to where Sam and Braydon watched.

"Do they swim?"

"When they fall in. Sometimes I catch the cubs playing in the shallower parts."

The cub cautiously traveled over the falls, balancing on rocks that jetted out of the surface. His head moved back and forth as he tracked his fast swimming prey.

He was adorable, his big paws swiping deep, the mist coating his brownish nose and black fur. It shook like a large dog trying to dry off. For as cute as the cub was Sam was smart enough to resist the temptation of getting any closer. She'd heard stories of mother bear instincts and even if momma bear wasn't around, baby bear had claws the size of bananas.

Sam gasped as the bear jumped into the water. It looked down for a split second then plunged its head under water and came up with a fish. At first it took the fish over to a rock and held it with amazing dexterity as it flopped back and forth. Once the fish stilled the bear pranced off to dryer land, lunch in its mouth, and scurried up the trunk of a tall pine.

She smiled at Braydon. "That may have been one of the neatest things I've ever seen in person."

"He gave you a good show for a first timer."

He leaned across the seat and kissed her. She hadn't been expecting a kiss, but didn't have the heart to stop him. It was more intimate than a friendly peck, but less sexual than what she expected from him. Again, she wondered at the strange bridge of being just friends they couldn't seem to smoothly cross.

"I'm glad you like it here."

"What's not to like? It's amazing. You're very lucky to have grown up here."

"It was a fun place to be a kid," he agreed. "We better head back if we're gonna make the game. Do you need to grab anything from the house before we head to the field?"

"I don't think so. It's not like I'm playing."

He chuckled. "Fair warning, they're gonna make you play."

THE BASEBALL FIELD was only about a fifteen-minute drive over the mountain. It actually was closer than Sam assumed, but because they were traveling down rough terrain they maintained a speed of less than fifteen miles per hour for most of the trip.

With what she already saw of the McCulloughs, Samantha should've expected a traditional field complete with two dugouts and stadium style bleachers, but she was still surprised when they pulled up.

"Is this still McCullough property?"

"Yup." Braydon parked the truck by the fence facing first base. "We have a league with my Aunt Rosemarie's bar so it made sense for us to have an open field for practice. Colin brings some of the kids from the youth center here from time to time as well."

The mention of Colin brought thoughts Samantha had been ignoring all afternoon to the forefront of her mind.

"How long's your brother known he wanted to be a priest?"

"Since college, maybe before then. I'm not really sure. I was a conceited twelve-year-old when he left for university. I think he told the family that winter when he came home for Christmas."

"Didn't he have to go to a special school for that?"

"Yeah, he goes to seminary at Saint Peter's, not too far from where we are in the city. That's where he lives usually. I think what he's doing now, this Transitional Diaconate period, is like an enforced time of reflection before he takes his vows."

Doing quick math in her head, Sam discerned that Colin was almost thirty. The minute Maureen announced he was becoming a priest Samantha was certain she was going to hell. Not thirty seconds before the proud announcement, Sam was picturing the man naked and begging her imagination to make him drop the towel.

Worse, after the revelation of his holy rank, her dirty mind couldn't help imagining him like a Chippendale dancer, but instead of a bowtie, he wore a priest's collar. Yes, she was definitely going to hell.

They walked through the lot of cars she recognized from the house and some she did not. Katherine was sitting beside her mother and father. Her children were running around on the grassy part of the field. Sam was relieved to see members of the family sitting in the bleachers. Perhaps she wouldn't be expected to play after all.

As they crossed the threshold marked by an opening in the chain link fence surrounding the field, Sheilagh yelled, "Finally, we can pick teams. Jen and I are captains."

Sam turned and started toward the stands when a sharp whistle sounded. She turned to see Kelly yell, "Where you going, Samantha? The field's this way."

She stared back at a gaggle of young McCulloughs and some others she didn't recognize and stammered, "I'm not real good at sports. I'd figured I'd watch."

Kelly gave her a vagabond's smile. "No can do, love. Since Kate's prego we need another player. Come on over so we can pick teams."

Never one to go against the grain, Sam joined the others by home plate. Everyone was dressed in casual clothes, many wearing kelly-green shirts that said O'Malley's Bar and Grill. Sheilagh and a young attractive blonde girl with her O'Malley's shirt tied in a way that showed off her pierced belly button did a quick game of rock, paper, scissors.

The blonde jumped up and down and cheered, "I get first pick! Luke!"

Luke walked over to stand beside the blonde and Sheilagh frowned. "Kelly."

Kelly joined his sister while the blonde eyed the crowd of players. Sam had a flashback to high school and being picked last. She tried not to take the silly fear seriously.

When the blonde's eyes landed on Braydon they lit triumphantly. "Bray."

Braydon left Sam's side to stand beside the leggy blonde. Everyone turned toward Sheilagh. Kelly whispered something in her ear. She smiled. "Samantha." Sam looked around thinking surely there was someone else with the same name.

When no one stepped forward she pointed to herself. "Me?"

"Yeah, you. Come on. Welcome to the winning team," Sheilagh said tugging her between herself and Kelly.

The choosing went back and forth until every player was placed on a team. Jen, the blonde captain, had chosen Braydon, Finn, Luke, her sisters Emily and Taylor, the McCullough's cousin Pat, and another relative named Giovanni. Sam was confused when Kelly informed her Giovanni was in fact related. She wasn't sure where the Italian hailed from in the big Irish family.

For their team Sheilagh chose Kelly, Sam, Katherine's husband Anthony, who everyone called Ant, a cousin named Ryan, a married couple Gina and David, a guy named Tristan, and unfortunately, Colin.

Sam refused to make eye contact with the soon to be priest.

"All right, you picked first so we bat first." After

Sheilagh's announcement, the other team dispersed onto the field while Sam and the rest of her team lined up in the dugout.

As Sam took the last seat on the bench, she frowned. The blonde girl, Jen, was in the field laughing and pressing her palm into Braydon's chest.

Kelly sat down beside her and followed her gaze. "Ah," he said, comprehending what caught her attention. "They used to date. Don't worry. They broke up for a reason. She may look nice from afar, but she's far from nice."

"How sweet."

Kelly laughed but it was a sound lacking merriment. "You say that like you think you should care, but I don't think you really do."

Sam turned a hard eye on Kelly. "What's that supposed to mean?"

"It means you know, and so do the rest of us, that you and Bray aren't anything serious."

"What makes you say that?" The game started. They slid down the bench in batting order.

"I don't know. Maybe the fact you came home with my brother, but won't share his bed. Or maybe it's because I've yet to see the two of you display anything more than lukewarm affection toward each other. But I'm guessing it has more to do with the fact that Bray's a fool who'd pick a girl like you because you fit some concocted bill in his mind rather than actually making any kind of fundamental connection."

"Should I be insulted by what you just said?"

"Absolutely not. I like you, Sam. I like you a lot." That

wicked gleam returned to his eyes. "But don't go getting too excited. I'm just lookin out. I'm not trying to gain a pass at your fanny."

He leaned back on his elbow to watch the game "No matter how sweet I bet it is."

Colin was up to bat. Sam watched as he scuffed his foot over home plate. His T-shirt clung to his tapered waist as he swung the bat back and forth in preparation for his turn. Luke was pitching. His hat was now twisted backwards.

Colin stepped up to the plate and pointed his bat toward the outfield reminiscent of the renowned Babe Ruth.

"Is he good?" she wondered aloud.

Hearing her curiosity, Kelly replied, "Who? Luke or Colin? Luke excels at all sports, but Colin," he laughed, "I have yet to see something Colin isn't good at. Watch…"

The crack of the bat had the rest of her team rushing to their feet. Colin rounded first as Sheilagh slid home. By the time he was passing second, Ant earned their team another homerun. It didn't take long for Colin to get there himself.

He was glorious. The way his limbs carried him around the diamond and back to home plate was something to behold. He smiled and laughed at his brother Luke who obviously expected no less from him.

Sam swallowed a hard lump in her throat as the involuntary yearning to run to him overwhelmed her. He was a priest! Or at least he was going to be by the end of summer. She needed to get ahold of herself and knock off the impure thoughts she was having about the man.

"You're up, love."

Sam turned to Kelly. She quickly stood and climbed out of the dugout. As she was stepping onto the sanded part of the field Colin was stepping off.

A sheen of sweat clung to his skin, but it did nothing to detract from his appearance. Under the thin worn cotton of his shirt she could see his tight abdomen pulling with each breath from his exertion. For a priest he was in incredible shape.

"Pardon me."

Sam jumped out of his way as if he had the plague. God, she was a moron. And the way he apologized for stepping in her way only reminded her of seeing him naked all over again.

Pardon me. I forgot to lock the door.

Maybe a ball would hit her in the head and she'd forget all about what she saw.

She plucked a bat out of a pile lined up against the fence. Unsure if there was a process to selecting a bat, she thought this one seemed fine. Stepping up to the plate she swung the bat a few times before looking at Luke.

"Helmet," he yelled.

"What?"

"You need a helmet."

"Oh." Sam turned and saw the helmet right where Colin tossed it. She scooped it up and settled it on her head. It was warm from the sun and held a heady masculine scent.

"Eeeeeasy out!"

What the hell?

Sam looked toward right field and spotted Jen laughing and looking toward Braydon. He was frowning. Apparently her attempt at being funny didn't impress him.

Sam bent at the knees and faced the pitcher again. Maybe she was good at baseball. Maybe if she kept her eye on the ball and swung real hard she could hit the ball right into right field and into the dumb blonde's head. And it was nasty thoughts like that that were a perfect example of why she should not be around a holy man.

"NICE PLAY."

"Thanks." Colin took a seat next to Kelly and watched as Samantha took the plate. "She any good?"

"I have no idea. She looks nervous," Kelly commented watching the newest player.

Colin thought that was what she always looked like. At least that's how she looked whenever he was around. He felt terrible for not locking the bathroom door this morning. Although it was Braydon's bathroom too, he wasn't used to his brother being home. And he never expected a strange woman to be sleeping in the room next to him. He'd clearly embarrassed her and that was never his intention.

"Helmet," Luke yelled from the pitcher's mound.

"What?" Samantha yelled back.

"Oh boy," Kelly said out of the corner of his mouth. "This ought'a be good."

Colin watched as Samantha fitted the helmet to her head, her freckled cheeks a shade pinker.

"Eeeeeasy out!"

Kelly groaned and Colin frowned. "God, she is such a bitch," his younger brother complained.

"It looks like Braydon's saying something to her now. She has to know he isn't going to react kindly to her disrespecting his girlfriend."

Kelly laughed. "I think you give Jen Miller too much credit where brains are concerned. The woman's a viper."

Colin grunted in response. He watched as Luke threw out a slow pitch. Samantha swung with the enthusiasm and determination of a major leaguer. Unfortunately, she missed completely.

Jen Miller's laugh echoed across the field.

"Take your time, love," Kelly yelled encouragingly from beside him.

Luke threw another slow ball and she swung again, this time without as much zeal.

"Strike two!"

Before he realized he left his seat, Colin yelled, "Come on, Sammy. You can do it!"

She turned sharply to look back at him, a surprised expression on her face. Was she not used to encouragement? She looked back to Luke and adjusted her stance.

Luke opted for an underhand pitch this time, which wasn't allowed, but no one seemed to complain. Colin didn't miss the silencing look Braydon gave Jen when she noticed the exception being made.

When the bat hit the ball Samantha stared as it bounced across the field.

"Run!" the team shouted all at once.

Samantha gave a startled yelp, dropped the bat, and hauled ass to first base. Colin actually heard himself laugh out loud. By the time she was halfway there the other team already fielded the ball and was sending it toward first base. Luckily Braydon was manning the base. When Finn threw him the ball with ridiculously obvious bad aim, Braydon ran in almost slow motion to retrieve it.

"Get the ball!" Jen shrilled.

By the time Braydon had the ball in hand Sam was safe at first. He earned a severe scowl from Jen when he gave Samantha an encouraging swat on the rump. Oddly, the act seemed to startle Samantha as if she were not used to Braydon's touch.

Were they a couple? Had he misinterpreted their relationship? Perhaps they were just friends.

The ball went back to Luke and Kelly stepped up to bat. After Kelly's turn Sam had moved all the way to third. It wasn't until Kelly was actually close enough to whisper in her ear that she realized she needed to move past second, but she made it to third all the same.

She was really quite beautiful. Nothing like what Colin imagined was Braydon's taste. His brother's usual type was Jen Miller, but nicer. Samantha was the exact antithesis of Jen.

Samantha was soft and sweet, an obvious degree of honesty shone clear in her eyes. She appeared up for anything, quite agreeable, and was refreshingly trusting.

She had that girl next-door kind of beauty, yet Colin could think of no one who remotely resembled her. The way her deep brown hair hung and swayed from her ponytail made him want to smile. He liked the way the finest dusting of freckles crested her cheeks, like cinnamon sprinkled over velvety whipped cream. Her lashes were thick and without make up, making them a unique shade of dusty brown.

The sound of the bat cracked again and Colin was distracted from his thoughts. What had he been thinking anyway?

Samantha ran home and Kelly crossed home plate moments after her, colliding with her and practically knocking her to the ground. Sam laughed and Kelly swung her around as they each jumped up and down. Samantha's smile took over her face and Colin felt his own lips curving in happiness.

"I did it!" she shouted, holding Kelly by the shoulders, still bouncing like a child. "I did it! I got a home run!"

Colin regretted being outside of the moment. He wanted to run out of the dugout and celebrate with them. He wanted to swing Samantha around in his arms.

A small shiver of excitement knifed through his stomach, causing an unfamiliar tingle inside of him. What was he doing? Samantha was Braydon's girlfriend and Colin was in seminary. The longing that pulled deep in his body was so unwelcome and took him so off guard he found himself in a panic. Turning his back on his teammates, he quickly said a prayer.

CHAPTER 4

*T*he game ended when Luke hit a home run with bases fully loaded. Sam's team kept up well, but still lost by two points. She thoroughly enjoyed playing with the McCulloughs. The only person she didn't enjoy was Jen Miller.

Jen Miller was one of those girls who needed to constantly be the center of attention. At first Sam was only mildly offended by the brazen way the girl touched Braydon right in front of her. It was unexpected and insulting, as if she were saying *see he likes me enough to disrespect you.*

Sam didn't care if Braydon liked the other girl and wanted to rekindle an old flame. She just wasn't going to stand there and be made to look like a fool. Oddly, the idea of Braydon with another woman didn't bother Sam at all.

It didn't take long to realize the way Jen was acting had nothing to do with Sam personally. By the end of the game Jen Miller had run her hands over Luke, Finn, Pat and anyone else unattached.

Sam didn't miss the growl Sheilagh let slip when the blonde laid her hands on the guy named Tristan. She wondered if Braydon's little sister was sweet on the older man. Not that he was old, just older than Sheilagh's eighteen years. Tristan looked to be in his mid-twenties.

The one thing Sam was grateful for was that Jen never openly flirted with Colin. Sam shouldn't have even been paying attention to what Colin was doing, but she couldn't help herself. Where there were no jealous emotions connected to Braydon, she fought a sickening dread during the game every time the other woman stood anywhere near Colin.

She assumed women saw Colin as taken. Which he was. He was making the sacrament of holy orders. In other words, he was marrying God. Only an idiot would indulge a crush on such a devoted man. Clearly, Sam was Center County's new village idiot.

A loud smack sounded and a stinging sensation radiated from her behind all the way to her shoulders. She turned and Kelly was grinning at her. "Way to go, slugger. Come on. We're going to O'Malley's."

Sam had a moment of displacement as Kelly jogged off to the parking lot. The older McCulloughs were all gathering their items off the bleachers. Katherine yelled for Ant, who was carrying their youngest daughter Hannah out to the car.

Sam scanned the people surrounding the dugout in search of Braydon. For once he didn't have a blonde hanging from his side. She began to head in that direction.

Sheilagh was laughing with her cousin Patrick and when Sam passed them Sheilagh yelled, "Hey Sam, you guys brought the truck, right?"

Sam stopped. "Yes."

"Can you drive a truck? We're trying to figure out drivers for later."

"Drivers?"

"Yeah. Big Irish family going to a pub... My brothers like to drink themselves fuller than a gypsy's bra after a good game. Pat and I can't drink so we'll drive. My mum and dad will likely leave before the others are ready to go. Kate probably won't stay late. Colin won't drink so he can drive, but other than that we'll probably be leaving some cars behind."

"I guess I could drive."

Sheilagh grinned with elfin grace. "Great! We'll see you there." The two teenagers trotted off.

When Sam turned, Braydon was gone. Colin was gathering the bats and other equipment from the empty batting area when he spotted her.

"They all went out to the lot. Luke has a cooler of drinks out there."

"Oh." Why wouldn't Braydon have told her where he was going? She was getting tired of constantly hunting him down.

Colin zipped an equipment bag and slung it over his shoulder.

He didn't look like a priest. He looked like an average guy, an average drop dead gorgeous guy. He cleared his throat.

"Listen, Sammy," he said.

When had he started calling her Sammy? No one had called her that in ten years.

"I wanted to apologize for this morning. If I had known you and Braydon were staying in his room I would've been sure to lock the other door."

"Braydon slept with Kelly. I slept alone."

Why had she blurted that out? For some reason she didn't want Colin to think she was sleeping with anyone. She didn't want him to think of her as a sinner, but deep down she knew it was because she didn't want him to assume she and his brother shared more than they actually did.

"Ah, okay. Still, my apologies. I'll be sure to lock the door next time I shower."

Or not.

She immediately chastised her evil mind. "It's okay. I should've knocked."

"Well, still, I didn't mean to embarrass you. Surely when you came here you didn't expect to be caught in your unmentionables on the first morning."

Sam's face heated and she wanted the earth to open up and swallow her whole. How had she not considered that while she was seeing Colin he was also seeing her? She had stood there, in front of an almost priest, in nothing but a short cotton tank top and a pair of see-through panties. They were probably writing her name in Satan's registration log right that very second.

"I can see I just made things worse. I'll stop talking before I put my foot any deeper in my mouth. I promise it won't happen again. Let's forget about it and start fresh."

He shifted the cumbersome bag and held out his hand. "Hello, I'm Colin McCullough."

She looked at his large waiting hand. His fingers were clean, his nails trimmed neatly. There was nothing sloppy about this man. He appeared deceptively unthreatening, yet Sam had seen the hard muscle and indisputable ruggedness he kept hidden under his plain clothing. She swallowed a dry lump in her throat and took his extended hand.

"Samantha Dougherty."

He smiled. "A pleasure to meet you, Sammy. What do you say we go grab a drink?"

O'MALLEY'S BAR and Grill was only a short drive from the ball field. It was a brick faced building with a nondescript wooden door. Inside, the floor was a black and white vinyl checkerboard and the walls were paneled in honey colored wood. The bar was simple, about twenty feet long with brass handrails and footrest. The countertop was worn so smooth, scrapes and grooves were swirled beneath the flat surface like fossils tattooed over time. The walls were covered with everything from pictures of family and the bar league, to taxidermic game donated by locals.

When they arrived, Sam was introduced to Colleen and Rosemarie, Maureen's sisters and their husbands Paulie and Liam. Rosemarie and Liam Clooney were the owners of the pub. Rosemarie, the youngest of the three sisters, had laid out a feast along the back of the bar for family and friends. Apparently the scrimmage they played at the field was some kind of kick off to summer for the entire town.

She and her husband grew up with Frank, Braydon's father and Paulie and Frank owned the logging business that employed many of the younger men in the family. Turns out, there was a bit of a scandal back in the day when Frank set his heart to Maureen.

She had been seven years his junior and still in school when the twenty-two year old man fell in love with her. Colleen and Paulie had been the first to know about the secret affair, but when Maureen's father found out, he threatened Frank with a shotgun. Sam still wasn't sure if the man actually took a shot at Frank or not. Kelly, who was tending bar, told her his father actually had a scar from his grandfather's gun.

When Frank absconded with Maureen on her eighteenth birthday and returned with his love under the name of Maureen McCullough, her father was furious. It wasn't until Frank built his wife a home that the girl's father actually accepted the union. Legend had it that it wasn't the age or secretiveness that disappointed Maureen's father. It was the fact that they'd been married in a courtroom and not in a house of God.

As Sam listened to the love story, she smiled and stared glassy eyed at Mr. McCullough. He might not say much and appear gruff, but he possessed a romantic soul. Colleen even told her that on Frank and Maureen's first date, he had taken her for a picnic in the woods. At some point during the date he stopped to carve their initials in a tree. It was Katherine who informed her that that exact tree with her parents' initials now rested inside the McCullough walls where Maureen could see it every night before she fell asleep.

It wasn't long before the already rowdy crowd became drunk and unruly. Something called a car bomb was being passed around. Sam wasn't sure of the exact ingredients, but knew it included a pint of black beer and some kind of shot that was dropped in, shot glass and all.

The men dropped the shot and the dark beer faded to a creamier tint as the shot swirled and clouded the brew. They tilted the drink to their mouths as the creamy liquid rose and didn't stop until they slammed an empty glass on the bar.

Once Rosemarie cleared away the food, the older couples said their goodbyes and headed out. Other than a glass of wine, Sam had nothing but soda to drink. The air was on in the bar and her seat happened to be under a vent. Braydon was in the middle of a dart game with Finn so she told Kelly she was going to run out to the truck to grab her sweatshirt.

Everyone seemed to be enjoying him or herself. Pat, Sheilagh's cousin on her Aunt Rosemarie's side, was actu-

69

LYDIA MICHAELS

ally a very sweet kid. She could see why Sheilagh was so close to him. Pat had spent some time talking to Sam about his feelings for Emily Miller whom he assured was nothing like her older sister Jen. While they spoke, Sheilagh was hanging around the guy named Tristan.

When Sam stepped outside she was surprised to see it was already dark. A wide puddle of light poured from above the door, but the rest of the parking lot was blacker than pitch. She quickly went to the truck and grabbed her sweatshirt. It was colder in the mountains than it was in the city or suburbs.

She shut the truck door and paused to slip the hooded sweater over her head.

The clap of the bar door slamming followed by fast moving, heavy footsteps had Sam shoving her head through the neckline and looking to see who was coming.

Through the cars parked in the lot she could only make out the torso of someone tall. The door slammed again and this time Sam saw Tristan come out. She was about to head back to the bar, but froze when she heard the tone of Tristan's voice.

"Luke. Luke, stop damn it!"

Luke stopped, faced Tristan, and placed his hands on his hips. "What?"

"Don't leave. I'm sorry." The other man approached Luke.

Sam remained hidden in the shadows, not wanting to get in the middle of whatever argument they were having. Although she could not see their faces anymore she saw some of the tension leave Luke's posture.

70

"I'm not gonna stand there while you're flirting with my sister. It's misleading and you know it. You wanna play mind games with some girl, pick someone other than Sheilagh."

"I was just having fun with her. I wasn't leading her on."

"You were, and you damn well know it. If you like her, fine, that's a whole other argument we can have. But you and I both know she's not your type."

Tristan stepped closer. In a hushed voice he said, "No, she's not my type."

"Then don't lead her on. She's my sister. She doesn't deserve to get her feelings hurt. She's young."

"I'll be more careful. I'm sorry. Please don't leave."

Sam's eyes were getting tired from straining in the dark. There was a sound of something rustling in the woods behind her and she wanted to get back inside. She heard gravel crunch and looked back to Luke and Tristan. What she saw took her completely by surprise.

Tristan's hand gripped the back of Luke's neck while Luke's hands wrapped in Tristan's hair. They were kissing aggressively. They were kissing with urgency.

Sam covered her mouth in shock. She wondered if the others knew that Luke was gay.

If they did they didn't necessarily know he was involved with Tristan. If that were the case surely Sheilagh would have resigned her feelings long ago. On the other hand, maybe there was nothing here except for—

"Love you."

The whispered statement took away any notions that

this was a one-time thing she was witnessing. They were in love. Their rugged breathing echoed through the empty lot and she noticed they were still standing very close. "Come on. Let's head back in. You go first. I'll follow in a few."

So they were still in the closet with the others. Luke walked back into the bar and a few minutes later Tristan followed.

There was still some crunching going on in the woods so Sam didn't waste any more time following the two lovers. She just hoped they didn't realize she'd been watching their interlude.

COLIN NOTICED Sam return to her seat at the bar and decided to join her. He slid onto the stool beside her and asked Kelly to get him a Coke. When she turned she expelled a breath of surprise. He mentally frowned that she was still uncomfortable around him.

Perhaps it wasn't that they walked in on each other. Perhaps it was the priest thing. Some people weren't always sure how to act in front of him. Knowing a priest outside of church was sometimes like seeing a teacher at the grocery store. It just seemed wrong to admit they were normal human beings like everyone else.

"You know, I'm not going to throw holy water on you and give you penance if you say the wrong thing."

She blushed. The sun had given her cheeks some extra freckles today.

"I'm still just a regular guy."

"Sorry. I guess I just don't know how to be around a holy person in a bar."

He chuckled. "That does sound like a bit of an oxymoron. Thankfully I'm no more holy than anyone else under this roof."

She raised her eyebrows. They were the softest brown he'd ever seen.

"Are you not taking vows to become a priest in a few months? Or is that just what you've been telling the others while you lived the high life off the mountain."

He appreciated her wit. "I'm taking my holy orders on August first, but they aren't vows, just a promise to a bishop to dedicate my life to God's work. Well, that and to be celibate. I'll still be Colin McCullough."

"Can you perform sacraments?"

"Nope. Can't even say Mass yet."

"But you'll be able to soon."

"Yes."

"When you're away at seminary do you dress different?"

"Not really. I usually wear a black dress shirt and pants. No collars or robes yet."

"What made you want to be a priest?"

She relaxed slightly and he was grateful for that. She was still only seeing him as a soon to be priest, but perhaps after he answered all her questions she'd understand he had more than religious interests in life.

"Let's start with this. I'm twenty-nine. I go to church

every day. When I was twelve I began considering priesthood. In the Old Testament there's a line that reads *"there is a fire burning in my heart, imprisoned in my bones; I grow weary of holding it in."* The day I read that was the day I told my parents I was considering joining the church. I met with a local priest and was told that this calling was referred to as Internal Discernment, but I'd have to wait it out to see if it faded.

"I left for college as soon as I graduated high school. I earned my bachelor's degree, took an extra year of theology, and minored in philosophy. What's your major?"

She seemed vaguely taken off guard by his sudden outpouring of personal information, but had no issue keeping up with the conversation. "I'm going to be a secondary English teacher."

"I can see that. What made you choose teaching?"

"My mother was a teacher."

"And she's not now?"

"No. She and my father own a bed and breakfast outside of Lambertville, New Jersey. She stopped teaching when I was fourteen, but they only opened the B&B a year ago after my dad recovered from a massive heart attack."

"I'm sorry. I hope he's doing well now."

"He is. They're very happy with their new business. It was a good thing for them to sell our old home and buy new. It gave them a fresh start that was long overdue."

"Why long overdue?"

"Did you join seminary right after college?"

Her abrupt dodge of his question didn't alarm him.

She just wasn't ready to share certain details of her family life with him, and he could respect that.

"While I was in college I joined something called an affiliation program. It's a group of perspective candidates that can offer support, share discussions, and pray together. That's where I met Father Tucker, my good friend and longtime advisor. After I graduated I spent some time abroad. When do you graduate?"

"I should've finished a year ago, but I took some time off when my father got sick. When I returned the course requirements changed and I got saddled with some extra credit requirements. Graduation was last week. I didn't participate because I'm short two classes. Luckily I can take them this summer and will have my degree by fall."

"Will there be a graduation ceremony at the end of summer?"

"Yes, but it'll be nothing like the spring ceremony. There're only a handful of us graduating late. I'm not sure if I'll even attend it."

"Why not?"

She sighed. "It'll be close to the new school year. If I land a job I'll already be rushing to get things ready for my classroom. It just seems like a lot of unnecessary frills. I mean, I get my diploma. I've already passed the state certification tests. My transcripts and resume have already been mailed. I don't see the point."

"What about to celebrate the conclusion of this chapter in your life?"

She raised her glass and smiled. "All I need for that is some friends and a good bottle of booze."

He saw the moment her words registered with her brain. He definitely had her relaxing, but soon as she remembered who he was her tension returned.

"God, I'm sorry. I shouldn't have said that."

"Call me Colin and, please, it's quite all right. Sometimes a good bottle of booze is just what's needed in life, Sammy."

She looked like she wanted to smile as she eyed him skeptically.

"Do you drink? Sheilagh said you didn't."

"Perhaps she said I wouldn't, but she surely didn't say I didn't. I'm as much a McCullough as the rest of them. The only reason I'm not drinking tonight is because I was asked to be a designated driver. I mean, look at these guys. They're as full as the last bus home."

The lyrical song of her soft laughter caused something inside of him to churn and tighten.

"Where do you guys come up with these sayings?"

"Have you met my grandmother yet?"

"No, I don't think so."

"Oh, you'd remember if you had. She's right off the boat and I swear she's the one who taught sailors to swear."

"Well, I look forward to meeting her. Now tell me, where did you spend your time abroad?"

"Ireland of course! I worked with a Catholic Mission out of Dublin doing social outreach stuff like working with the homeless and mentoring youths. I do a lot of mentoring around here as well. You know, Center County could use some fresh, bright teachers. Perhaps you should send our high school your resume. You seem to be enjoying yourself here."

"I love it here. I never knew places like this still existed in this country. Today we saw a cub catch a fish out of a stream!"

"Did Braydon take you to the falls then?"

"There were small falls. I'm not sure if it was *the* falls."

He wondered if Braydon would mind him showing her the falls.

"You'd know if you saw them. They're stunning. You can jump right off of the mountain ledge into a depthless part of the stream."

Her face suddenly paled.

"What is it, Sammy?"

"I...I don't swim."

"Don't or can't?"

"Both. I mean I used to, but I haven't in over a decade so I guess I can't anymore. How long were you in Ireland?"

Again with the rapid change of topic—Samantha Dougherty sure liked to keep her secrets to herself. The mention of water seemed to terrify her and he was trying to help her enjoy the evening, so he let it go.

"A little over a year. I put in for my candidacy before I left. Mail didn't always get to us promptly in Dublin. Once I received the news I'd been accepted at Saint Peter's I began to wrap up things in Ireland and prepare to return to the States.

"I started seminary when I was twenty-five and earned my graduate degree in social work. I came home in

February for my transitional diaconate. I'm expected to take at least six months to a year to make my final decision. I decided when I was a boy so when my six months are up on August 1st I'll be taking my orders. What's your favorite novel? Mine's *The Catcher and the Rye*."

"Wow, I guess your mind really is made up. Um, I'd have to say J.M. Barrie's *Peter Pan*."

"Really? *Peter Pan*. Well that's one you don't hear too often. Why?"

"Why not? It's brilliant."

He frowned. "Isn't it a children's book? I guess I assumed an English teacher would—"

"Have more sophisticated tastes?" she offered. "Well, I assumed a soon to be priest wouldn't drink or praise a novel written about teenage lunacy and prostitution."

"Touché."

"Besides, I assure you, *Peter Pan* is more than a children's novel. It's perhaps one of the most honest depictions of human relationships I've ever read."

"How so?"

"Well, take Peter. He's an amalgam of every man I've ever met. He wants a mother, yet doesn't want to answer to one. He wants a wife, but also wants her to mother him. He's so in love with himself and his need to have fun, he sometimes loses track of years while having it. It's a constant cognitive battle, the lure of adulthood and the freedom of youth. And then there are the women in his life, each one clawing for a piece of him, yet none of them really understanding a bit of what's beneath the surface. And in the end, because he's too preoccupied with irrelevant titles and meaningless achievements, he'll let it all slip away, because he's afraid of what matters most, letting himself truly love. If ever someone truly understood the male psyche, the part that never grows up, it was J.M. Barrie."

Colin was floored. Samantha would obviously be a phenomenal teacher. He could easily see her taking a group of adolescents and showing them how to love literature. Rather than lie and claim a stuffy classic was her favorite, she admitted to loving a children's novel yet found such depth in the tale where a child would most likely read an adventure without realizing the moral.

As she spoke her eyes lit up. She seemed to find a spark of passion in everything. He swallowed and asked what he knew he shouldn't.

"Are you Wendy?"

She blinked and crinkled her brow. "Excuse me?"

"Are you Wendy? Are you in love with him? The boy who loves himself enough to let life pass by without ever truly risking his own heart. Are you willing to settle for superficial perfection just to pretend at happiness, knowing it may never have depth or be real?"

Her smile faltered. Her lashes fell over her eyes and her fingers toyed with a napkin on the bar. A puff of humorless laughter passed her lips. "You're talking about Braydon."

"I am."

She turned and looked over her shoulder at the man in question. Braydon was sitting at a table with the others.

Jennifer Miller was hanging on his side as they all laughed over something Finn said.

"I suppose I am Wendy in a way. My Pan's certainly overlooked me for an evening of fun and adventure. I suppose that makes her Tinkerbelle."

She turned and faced Colin. "The difference is, Colin, I don't give my heart easily to anyone. I'm not a naive little girl flying off to a fantasy. I know what's between Braydon and me, and it isn't love. I see him for exactly who he is. He's my friend, but little more. I won't give my heart to a man that'll never give his back."

How true her words were. He could see nothing but sincerity in her eyes as she spoke. She was not emotionally invested in his brother. She wasn't hiding the fact either. Braydon, the fool, just wasn't looking. Perhaps she didn't want to address the situation until her time there was done. But was she speaking only of Braydon?

He coveted this woman. He wanted to be the one to make her laugh, wanted to see her eyes light up the first time she saw the falls, watch her run a million home runs, and fall in love with his parents' love story every time she heard it.

He wanted to give her a love story, but he couldn't.

She was meant for a good man who was available to love her with every piece of his honor, while Colin was meant for something else entirely.

For the first time in his almost thirty-years he suffered the disturbing sense of doubt. How had it happened? This slip of a woman without a speck of makeup on her face and a faded Villanova sweatshirt made him feel things he'd never felt before.

He was coveting his brother's girlfriend. Whether Braydon was aware his connection with Samantha lacked depth or not, it wasn't Colin's place to be thinking of her in that way.

He was questioning his vows. He was suddenly questioning the path he'd been on practically his entire life.

CHAPTER 5

*T*he marble steps were drizzled with glossy moisture from a predawn rain. As she approached the landing one hundred pigeons took flight, their wings pounding against their soft sides like the pages of a broken-in bible being turned by an impatient thumb. Samantha looked past the silent parapet where the cavernous bell hung idle, one thousand pounds of steel capable of singing over valleys, past the mountains, bringing comfort to thousands, yet leaving her empty.

Heavy oak double doors, three times the size of any man, stood before her, an architectural feat in beauty and engineering. Enormous stone buttresses countered by delicate brass moldings accentuated the ancient hand crafted windows of martyrs perfected in cubism glass.

An angelic echo of Latin words told her it was time.

Sam's fingers wrapped around the heavy brass knob. The heaviness of the door earned her full attention as she slipped past the fortress-worthy threshold. As her hand released its *burden a grave thud sounded behind her. This was a place meant to welcome, but Sam had no right to be here.*

The chorus of unseen voices rang in slow cadence, intended to beckon, but her heavy bare feet only prodded slowly over the cold ivory slab. It was as chilling as a mausoleum. The pool of holy water to her right was too shallow to bathe her sins in.

Water.

Her unutterable fears set her feet into motion.

Impressive scrollwork had been painstakingly chiseled into the walls climbing to heights meant to humble all men. Dappled colors of sunlight dyed by vibrant glass panes blended to a soft haze of gold and the angels continued to sing in a rhythmic hum of syllables her ears could not decipher.

Like little soldiers, wooden pews stood patiently alone in an unending line. Ivory columns decorated their shoulders like rifles at the ready. Chandeliers sparkled, catching rays of light and propelling prisms over bronze placards marking tombs spaced throughout the granite walls. An intricate scene of heaven graced the cathedral ceiling seeming so real a child would believe it a secret passage to paradise.

Two cents to pay the toll.

Her feet carried her for an eternity, all the while her mind reached for forgotten words. Prayers were like pledging the flag; sometimes they needed to be said in a tune to acquire the next line. How did the Act of Contrition start?

Oh my God, I am heartily sorry...

Beyond the altar stood soundless pipes stacked a hundred in a row, but they only played for those willing to atone. She heard nothing.

A marble table decorated in holy cloths claimed the focus of the grand and forgotten place. The golden tabernacle secured with a delicate lock hid treasures below a sculpture of the Madonna on the right. A candle that never extinguished burned to the left. And above all else, hung Jesus on the cross.

Oh my God, I am heartily sorry for having offended thee.

Sam should leave. She did not belong in this place. She tainted it by simply being there.

The clap of a door shutting echoed from the left followed by the click-clack of sure footsteps upon the ivory floor. Her eyes darted to the shadows in hopes of finding a place to hide. She could not be seen here.

I detest all my sins.

"Sammy?"

Sam turned to the beckoning voice. Colin stood, formally attired in a long black robe, black satin buttons ticking from collar to hem. He looked right. His perfectly combed hair and clean-shaven face a beautiful match for such a pure starched white badge upon an expanse of black.

He smiled and placed something on the altar as he approached. "How are you? You look well."

Sam said nothing. His calm manner disarmed her. When he stood just in front of her she finally said, "You've made your vows."

"I have."

"I thought..."

He tilted his head, his soft eyes wondering at her surprise. "You thought I wouldn't?"

"No, I mean..." *her words felt clumsy.* "I don't know what I thought. I should be going."

He placed a gentle hand on her arm. "Did you come here for the sacrament? Would you like a blessing?"

Her eyes clouded with tears. She was so stupid. "No. No, I cannot take sacrament. I'm not worthy."

"We are all worthy."

"I'm not," she choked.

He hushed her sob and whispered confidentially as if the idols had ears, "Would you like to make a confession?"

"I can't."

"Something is obviously bothering you. Let me take away your sins."

"You can't."

She stepped back, needing to put some distance between them. Slowly she raised her fingers and touched the patch of white showing on his collar. "This suits you, Colin."

"Father McCullough," he corrected. "Would you like to join me in saying the rosary, Sammy?"

"I don't pray those prayers anymore."

"But you used to."

"Yes. A long time ago. I stopped after..."

"After what?"

"After I lost my faith in God."

"We all misplace our faith from time to time. God is patient. He waits for us to find Him again. Come. Let's pray and see if we can reacquaint the two of you."

He reached for her arm, but she shied away from his touch.

"What are you afraid of, Sammy? God is forgiving to all who are repentant."

"I'll never be deserving of forgiveness. Even now, I'm accumulating more sins from my impure thoughts."

"Tell me what you have done, Sammy."

"No. I don't talk about her."

"Who?"

"My sister."

"Meghan," he offered compassionately and she blinked in confusion. How did he know?

"Yes." Samantha could no longer stem the tears filling her eyes. They trickled hopelessly over her lashes.

"You are not to blame, Sammy." Again, she was taken aback by his knowledge. The place she was standing began to flicker and dissolve, hazing over like a dream slipping out of her grasp. This wasn't real and she had no business dreaming of him.

She tried to force herself to wake up, but she failed. Frustrated, she looked for an escape. The doors were too far away now, an illusion she couldn't reach. She turned to him.

"You know nothing," she accused. She didn't deserve his empathy. The angelic voices suddenly silenced and Colin looked over his shoulder at the cross. When his eyes returned to hers they were set in shrewd certainty.

"You think you are the only one who struggles with sin. Do you know your Act of Contrition?"

She shook her head. *"I've forgotten it."*

He ran a hand over her hair, his fingers holding the ends. He smiled, then let go. The severe set of his eyes was at complete odds with his gentle, longing touch.

"'Forgive me my sins; the sins of my youth; the sins of my age'. You were a child, Sammy. Let God take away your pain. Let Him end the suffering."

"He can't. I tried."

"You do not believe He's your Savior?"

"I don't believe I'm worthy."

"Oh, beautiful Samantha, you're quite worthy. You are 'the sins I have kept concealed for so long.'"

"What comes next?"

"And which are now hidden from my memory."

"So have you forgotten me, Father McCullough?"

"I try every day."

Sam pressed her lips together and gave a tight nod. The fact that she'd been worked out to be some sort of dirty thought stung.

"I'll go now."

"Don't stay away too long, Samantha. I'm running out of time."

"Time for what?"

"Until it all becomes real." *Father McCullough pressed his lips gently to hers and whispered, "Go now, before the temptation becomes too great."*

SAMANTHA WOKE UP WITH A START. Her body thrummed with a sexual pulse that should've never stemmed from such a dream. She was in Braydon's bed, yet she dreamt about his brother, as a priest! She was going to Hell.

She needed to put a stop to these thoughts once and for all. Her best course of action would be to avoid Colin as much as possible for the remainder of her time at the McCulloughs'.

She sighed. It was Sunday. She had nineteen days left.

Samantha stood and frowned at the door to the hall. The absence of children squeaking and galloping up and down the hall had her wondering what time it was. She found her cell phone and checked the time. Nine thirty; compared to the day before, she'd slept in.

Setting out her clothes for the day, she faced the bathroom, pausing to look for any show of light seeping from the crack beneath the door before she knocked. No answer.

Sam eased the door open to find only a dim, empty room. Her eyes dwelled on the opposite door.

That would be Colin's bedroom. She looked to the floor and noticed there were no lights flooding under the crack from that room either. She was tempted to peek into his private space, but the idea of him catching her snooping was humiliating enough to stave off her curiosity.

Pulling the shower curtain aside she had a flash of Colin, stunningly naked, soaping up his deliciously hard, muscular body. She moaned as she imagined trickling beads of water forming slow rivulets over his abs.

"Bad Samantha," she mumbled as she turned on the water and adjusted the temperature.

For the next thirty minutes Samantha chastised herself every time she thought about Colin. Instead she tried to occupy her mind with thoughts of the upcoming day. Perhaps she could find someone to show her the orchard. Maybe try her hand at horseback riding. Maybe Colin would show her how to sit properly on a saddle. Maybe help her stay balanced by sitting behind her, his thighs tightly encasing hers so that her bottom rested flush against his solid—

"Bad!" she hissed as she tied her sneakers and adjusted her tank top. She took one last look in the mirror. "That's as good as it's gonna get."

As she headed down the steps the house still seemed unusually quiet. It was only ten in the morning. Surely everyone hadn't already eaten and left to start their day? She acknowledged that Braydon wasn't the best at playing the host, but he wouldn't have made plans without even telling her. Chances were he was sleeping off a hangover.

As she reached the bottom of the stairs she looked to her left. The den was empty and dark. Frankie, Skylar, and Hannah were nowhere to be found. Had Katherine returned home last night?

She turned into the quiet kitchen and smiled with a sense of relief.

"Good morning, Kelly."

"Good morning, love. Sleep well?"

He was sitting alone at the long farm style table, sipping coffee from a steaming mug, and reading the newspaper.

"Fine. You?"

With Kelly she had already formed a type of unspoken and completely nonthreatening camaraderie for which she was extremely grateful. She went to the cabinet and searched for a mug. After two tries she found the shelf where Maureen kept them and pulled one down. Pouring a cup of coffee she asked, "Where is everyone?"

"Church. They should be back soon. Bray's still in bed if you want to go wake him up sweetly."

She scrunched up her face and frowned into her coffee.

Kelly chuckled. "What is it with you two? I have to admit I've never seen one of Braydon's girlfriends that weren't forever trying to be the center of his attention. You act like you couldn't care less."

Samantha moved to a seat opposite Kelly and shrugged. "I'm not going to follow him around like some lost puppy. If he has other things to do…it's his vacation too." She certainly wouldn't be following him around when Jen Miller already had the job covered.

"And what about you, Sam? What do you hope to get out of this vacation?"

"I don't know. Some time to relax, experience the mountains, meet new people."

He nodded almost theatrically as if he were someone wise and not a wild disheveled man sitting shirtless in a pair of Scooby Doo pajama pants and nothing else. He reminded her of a rebel leprechaun. The way his hair spiked in clumped points, this way and that, almost gave his ears and eyes an elfin quality. Like the rest of them, he was beautiful in his own unique way.

As he took a large bite of his kiddy cereal and slurped back a dribble of milk that ran down his chin, his eyes crinkled merrily. They looked at one another for a long, silent moment, the ticking seconds each passing with a loud crunch of cereal.

Her gaze quickly darted to his unclothed chest. He, like Luke, had Celtic tattoos, but somehow Kelly's seemed a bit more menacing. Gaelic verses wrapped his arm like a tribal brand. Maureen was right. He was a rogue.

Kelly's spoon clanked onto his empty bowl and Sam's gaze returned to his and away from his body.

"What?" she asked accusingly as if she wasn't gawking at him.

"Ah, my dear, no need to be ashamed. Look to yer' fill. If you like, I'll drop me drawers and show you where the real treasures lie."

"You're an ass," she mumbled, drowning her laugh in her coffee as she hid behind her mug.

Kelly smiled knowingly and stood. As he walked past her he playfully tugged her ponytail.

"Try all you want to deny you were eyein' me goods, but there's no denyin' that blush turning yer cheeks pinker than a misbehaving youngster's bum."

She pressed the back of her fingers to her skin as the truth of his accusation burned under her touch. Kelly dropped his dish in the sink and stretched loudly beside her, his fingers locking and pressing far above his head as his torso lengthened, dropping his loose Scooby Doo pajama bottoms down another inch.

"Rut-row, almost gave you that show you were wantin'. Better get dressed before you come after me lucky charms."

She still found it amusing how being in this house somehow altered their dialect. Anyone who didn't know they were all American would've assumed they had come right off the boat from Ireland.

Gravel crunched and Kelly peeked out the window.

"They're back," he casually announced as Braydon made an inelegant entrance into the kitchen.

"Morning," he mumbled. To who, Samantha wasn't sure.

Bray only had eyes for the coffee pot. He clumsily poured a cup for himself as more cars pulled up and car doors opened and slammed followed by the slow build of McCullough voices.

"Fuck. They're all comin' aren't they?" Braydon mumbled.

Kelly slapped his brother on the back and gave an overzealous squeeze which caused Braydon to wince. "Yup. Better take your woman and your coffee and hide now if you want to escape them. Once the Grans get here there'll be no getting out."

Like the slow moan of thunder produced by a thousand hooves in an approaching stampede, the McCulloughs rolled in. While most were just beginning their day, Maureen looked as though her day was at its peak. She entered the house as if she had been there all along. Walking into the kitchen in the midst of a story being told to whoever was trailing behind, she somehow managed to tie an apron around her sturdy waist while lighting the burner, heating a pan, and shuffling an exorbitant number of eggs from the refrigerator.

Frank came in silently holding a brown paper bag stuffed with something. He placed it on the counter next to Maureen while she continued to chatter without pause and crack egg after egg into an enormous skillet.

"...And I'll tell you something else that Francine needs

to watch. She looks as though she's loosin' a pound a day. I'm thinkin' I should send over a few baskets of food, Frank. Lord knows her boys aren't lookin' after her the way they should. A damn shame, boys with a mother who did nothin' but worry over them for decades and now they're all too busy to help her mend after such a fall. Bullshite is what it is!"

Sam found it amusing the way Maureen frequently dropped names into her dialogue as if she were having a conversation with a specific person when really she was addressing the room at large. Frank nodded, but remained silent as he poured himself a mug of coffee. Braydon's mom needed no acknowledgement that he'd heard her. She just continued on.

"Perhaps I'll make her some soup and a nice apple pie. You know how people love my pies. Good mornin', darling," she said without breaking her momentum as she passed Braydon. "I'm going to have to take a trip into town to get her a bag of paper goods too. Francine doesn't need to be standin' 'round at the sink doin' dishes on her cast. Kelly, take this out to Rufus," she instructed passing a large bowl of something that resembled canned meat to Kelly and bustling back to the stove to stir her eggs.

Kelly opened the door and Finn walked in, appearing harassed as a little old woman with short orange hair and soft, but sharp wrinkled eyes the color of sea glass followed. The woman chattered in an accent so thickly Gaelic it first seemed she was not even speaking English. It took a moment for Sam to realize this was Mary

O'Leahy, Maureen's mother and Braydon's grandmother, or Morai as he referred to her.

Finn looked at Braydon, rolled his eyes and shook his head as if the tirade he was suffering had been going on for hours. Braydon laughed into his coffee and moved to greet his grandmother.

"Mornin', Morai."

The tiny woman squealed in the middle of her diatribe and roughly pinched Braydon's cheek.

Knowing he was hung over and that pinch must have felt more like a fork in the eye than an expression of affection, Sam smiled sympathetically at him. His grandmother pulled him down to her height and kissed him right on the lips.

"Me beautiful boy! Yer mum tells me yer here with us fer a few weeks, aye?"

"That's right, Morai."

In a louder than usual conspirator's whisper she said, "And she tells me you've brought a lassie home with ye?"

Smiling he turned to Sam and said, "Morai, this is Samantha. Samantha, this is my grandmother, Mary O'Leahy."

Sam stood and held out a hand. "It's nice to meet you, Mrs. O'Leahy."

She took her hand, but eyed Sam as if she were hiding something from the rest of them. Sam fought the urge to squirm under her scrutiny. Finally Braydon's grandmother said, "Aye, she'll do." And then turned to help Maureen at the counter.

Braydon leaned in as if to reassure her, but was interrupted when Sheilagh blew in like a tornado followed by Luke's much more subtle entrance.

The McCullough women were all a bit scary, Sam decided.

Sheilagh snatched an apple out of a basket and wiped it on her shoulder before taking a large snapping bite out of it. Juice dribbled down her chin and she caught it with her thumb as she climbed into a chair at the table and tucked her feet onto the seat. "Luke, you wanna go to the lake today? Pat and Ry are going."

"So really," Kelly butted in, "you're planning on displaying your jiggly bits in a bikini for Tristan, is what you're saying."

Sheilagh lobbed her half eaten apple at him and Kelly laughed as he caught it with surprising reflexes then, as if he'd just been given a gift, he took an appreciative bite of the fruit.

Luke looked at Kelly. Sam wondered if Luke suffered from guilt for his secret affair with his sister's crush.

"I think I'll hang back today. I have some stuff to get done," Luke said with transparent insincerity, yet no one seemed to question him.

Sheilagh shrugged as if his attendance were inconsequential. "How about you, Samantha? Wanna come to the lake?"

"Uh..." Sam fought the cold dread that swamped her belly at the thought of being near water. "Is it a beach?"

"Yeah."

"Okay, but I'll have to just hang on the sand. I didn't pack a suit."

Of course she didn't. Sam didn't swim, so had no reason to own a suit.

"You can borrow one of mine," Sheilagh offered.

It would probably fit, but Sam would rather avoid having to make excuses throughout the day when asked to swim. "You're smaller than me."

"Hardly. And besides, it's a string bikini. You can adjust the hips and neck."

Sam jumped when Braydon hugged her from behind. It was always awkward when he displayed affection in front of the others.

He pressed his face into her neck and whispered, "Come on Samantha, let's do the lake today. You'd look great in a bikini and you know it."

Although the others probably couldn't hear his comment she blushed anyway. He smelled of coffee laced with whiskey which she knew was left over from the night before.

The kitchen door swung shut again. At the sight of Colin dressed in a formal button down and dress slacks she tensed. Suddenly very uncomfortable with Braydon's position, she eased out of his embrace and stood.

Sheilagh's brows lowered the slightest degree as if she noticed Sam's sudden change of disposition. The sharp redhead looked to her eldest brother and Sam feared she'd detected her impure thoughts, but then Sheilagh's nose crinkled as if the whole idea of seeing Colin as anything other than a holy figure was ridiculous. Her expression showed she'd dismissed the entire byplay as meaningless.

"Come on, Samantha, come to the lake. It'll be fun to have a girl there for once."

As if drawn by her name, Colin watched her as he poured coffee into a mug. Never taking his gaze from hers he somehow managed to pull the pot away without spilling a drop just before his cup overflowed.

Unaffected by her withdrawal, Braydon took a seat along with everyone else, sans Colin and Maureen, who was placing a heaping pile of home fries on the table followed by a steaming plate of eggs. Feeling more the center of attention by standing, Samantha quickly dropped back into her seat and looked at her plate.

Sheilagh was still watching her, but Sam couldn't expend the energy to care because she was too focused on ignoring Colin's penetrating stare.

"We should take the boat out," Braydon suggested as he piled food on his plate. "Samantha would probably rather go tubing than sit on the beach all day."

The blood drained from her face and her stomach flipped horribly at the idea of being dragged behind a speeding boat on a tube whipping over water. Suddenly, a day with Sheilagh on the sand sounded perfect.

"I think I'd rather go with your sister if you don't mind."

He shrugged as if how she spent her day made no difference to him.

"That's fine. We'll probably all meet up there at some point anyway."

Colin took a seat in her peripheral and unbuttoned his collar and rolled up his sleeves before reaching for a dish.

He seemed oddly comfortable within any setting. This aggravated her. She had some preconceived notion that he should appear more proper than the rest.

She froze mid-nibble when he asked, "Do you like boats, Sammy?"

Placing her fork on her plate she wiped her mouth on her napkin and looked into those piercing green-blue eyes. The rest of the family, including Sheilagh, was busy eating and chatting without the courtesy of eye contact. It was as if they were standing above the rest on a cloud of privacy.

"Not particularly."

He nodded as if he understood there was more to what she said than was actually spoken. She frowned at him and he silently laughed. Her stare shot back to her plate and spent the rest of the meal avoiding his gaze.

An hour later she was staring in the mirror, tugging at her cotton shirt, frowning again. Sheilagh wasn't kidding when she said her suit had strings. That was pretty much all the bathing suit consisted of, strings and a couple small patches of navy blue nylon.

Her body was incredibly exposed even with the cover of her shorts and shirt. One wrong move and a nipple would fall out. There was no way she was taking off her shirt at the lake. Her underwear and bra would've been a more decent cover.

When there was a knock at the door she turned. Braydon walked in before she could answer.

She scowled at him, wondering what he would've done if she were indecent. Not that he seemed to even look at her. He marched over to his dresser and grabbed a key attached to a spongy keychain from a dish then went to the closet and retrieved a pair of flip-flops. It was his room, but she still bristled when he intruded on her privacy without apologizing.

"Are you gonna drive over to the lake with Shei?"

Sam sat on the edge of the bed and watched as he removed items from his pocket and sorted through them as if taking inventory then returned the items to his pockets in a more organized manner. Good thing she wasn't an overly sensitive girl or an attention whore, because his disregard for her was starting to get really old and she considered herself a rather tolerant person.

"Sure."

"Good." He glanced at her as he was about to leave then paused. "Did you get a suit?"

She nodded.

"Can I see?"

"I'm not planning on taking off my shirt."

He walked over to her and tucked a strand of hair behind her ear. His fingers reached for her hand and tugged her to her feet. He was going to kiss her. There was that odd change in the atmosphere that told her so.

Standing, she looked him in the eye. He smiled and she knew he was feeling tickles of emotion that were absent from her.

"So modest," he commented softly as he touched her bottom lip with his thumb. She somewhat resented that her body couldn't produce even the most mediocre reaction to his attention when he gave it. It was as if her rational conscience was too involved around him to ever let her forget herself.

His lips touched hers and slowly coaxed her mouth open. The kiss was pleasant, but nothing more. His hands rested on her hips, softly massaging the slight curve. As his tongue slowly played with hers he moaned and pulled her closer. He was slightly aroused, but nowhere near fully.

How could he be satisfied with this lackluster chemistry? There was something about their interactions that made Sam believe it would never be anything more, and anything appearing as more between them would be completely artificial.

She pulled back. "Braydon, I think we need to talk."

He looked down at her with lowered lashes. "About?"

"Us."

"What about us?" He attempted to kiss her again and she turned away. He frowned. "What, Sam? Just say it."

She really wanted to avoid setting him straight until it was time for her to leave. There was nothing fun about having to awkwardly be a guest in the house of someone you broke up with, especially with his entire family there.

Once she finished college she'd probably acquire more of a social life. She never really dated seriously. It wasn't that she wasn't sexual. She simply led a more pragmatic life. Always crossing point A to get to B, all the while remembering she'd soon be approaching point C. Apparently, losing her virginity was on a whole different end of the alphabet.

She was an excellent student. School had been an

amazing distraction for her when life was simply too hard for her to cope. She invested all of her energies in her studies rather than examining her fear and regret. She never allowed herself to surrender to the pain that would swallowed her whole. Instead, she put all her energy into school and became a straight A student, but now that school was ending she'd need something else to occupy her time. Perhaps she should start on her Masters.

"I don't think this is working."

His mouth opened and she suspected this was coming out of left field for him. They really were on two separate wavelengths. "Sam, you haven't given us a chance."

"I have. I like you, Braydon, but I'm not sure us dating is the best idea."

He stepped closer, placing his hands on her hips as he looked into her eyes. "Why? We're good together. We have fun."

What fun? They'd barely hung out. "I just…" The sound of someone clearing their throat and a soft knock on the door had them breaking eye contact.

When Sam saw that it was Colin she jumped away from Braydon so fast she nearly stumbled, but Braydon caught her by the elbow and steadied her.

"Bray, Luke's waiting for you in the truck."

Braydon turned and retrieved the key he placed on the dresser again then quickly kissed her cheek. "Thanks. I'll see you later, Samantha."

She looked down at her bare feet as he left and waited for Colin to follow him.

He didn't. She felt him watching her once again, knowing he probably saw them kissing.

"Are you about ready to go to the lake?"

She looked up at him and felt some sort of invisible barrier between them as if he were hiding an emotion he didn't want to share. Suddenly swamped with guilt as if she betrayed him, she nodded. He was dressed in loose fitting swim trunks and an old faded O'Malley's T-shirt, this one kelly-green with a washed out shamrock on the chest.

"Aren't you going with the guys on the boat?" she asked.

"I was going to go to the lake, but I…I just remembered I have something I need to do."

It was a poorly disguised lie, but Sam was grateful for it. "Oh."

His gaze left hers and traveled over her body from her shoulders to her feet. The dark triangles of Sheilagh's bikini were visible under the soft cotton of her shirt. By the time his stare wondered over her exposed thighs a second time she couldn't help the chill that ran up her spine. Her nipples tightened.

"Right," he said meeting her gaze once more. "Well, have fun, Sammy."

He turned and walked to his room, the soft but final click of his door closing behind him filling her with ominous regret and shame.

CHAPTER 6

The lake was peaceful. It was different than a Jersey shore beach. The sand was coarser, the water browner, and the atmosphere lighter. Although it was private property and only the McCulloughs and close friends were there, there were enough of them that it reminded Sam of a 50's styled resort. If she looked hard enough she could probably find a log bridging over a creek to dance on.

The warm sun caressed her skin, countering the cooler breeze as it danced across the land coming off the lake. It was a great body of water that curved and wrapped around pine trees and mountains in the distance. Although she couldn't see Braydon and the others at the moment, she could hear the boat speeding and chopping through the surface.

There were no waves like in the ocean. Although the lake had a gradual incline from the coast, it was calm enough to spot ripples when a beetle landed on the surface.

In the distance about fifty feet out from the coast was a small square dock. Tristan had swum out there earlier and had been napping there ever since. Sam knew from watching him go that after about twenty feet the lake floor became untouchable. There'd be no going in the water for her.

Sheilagh lay on her belly across a bright orange beach towel facing Patrick as they played Gin Rummy. A small radio broke the silence and Sam softly tapped her foot in the coarse yellow sand to the beat.

"Gin!" Sheilagh declared.

"Finally! Come on, I'm sweating. Let's go in the water," Pat said as he stood and stretched.

"Race you to the dock?"

"Yeah, because that's not obvious," Patrick teased and Sheilagh shoved him as she darted into the water.

She seemed to have no issue with running around in nothing but Lycra strings and patches. "Wanna come, Sam?"

She stood and shaded the top of her sunglasses and looked up at Patrick. He was a sweet kid and Sam really appreciated the way he always included her in whatever else the others were doing.

"No thanks. I think I'm going to take a nap."

"Okay, suit yourself. You may wanna put on some more sun block though. Your nose is getting red."

He ran off and Sam took his advice and rubbed in a bit more sunscreen. It wasn't long before she was peacefully lounging in one of the abandoned chairs on the cusp of sleep, basking in the warmth of the sun.

A while later as the distant voices and splashing from the water faded into white noise, the chill of a shadow passed over her as if the clouds were momentarily blocking the sun. The thud of something hitting the sand made her realize it wasn't the clouds blocking the sun, but a person casting shadows.

She opened her eyes and stilled at the sight of Colin. Grateful for the veil her dark glasses provided she watched him unfold a beach chair and remove his shirt. Knowing her voyeurism was wrong, she covertly kept her lashes lowered in case he looked her way and saw through her lenses.

She wasn't prepared when he paused before seating himself to boldly stare at her. Suddenly very aware of her body, his gaze a caress upon her sun kissed thighs, she fought the urge to fidget. Her fingers, although completely still, felt as if they were slightly twitching along with her toes.

What was he looking at? His gaze roamed over her knees and down to her ankles.

"You better put sun block on your feet. They're burning."

She tensed.

Should she quit her campaign to feign sleep and admit she was watching him too, or continue on with her see-through ruse for self-preservation's sake?

Damn it! She was such a crappy liar. She lifted her

glasses and smiled. "Thanks." Reaching into her bag she pulled out her sun block.

"How's the water?"

"Uh, I don't know. I haven't been in."

She avoided looking at him by taking an extra-long time rubbing the milky sunscreen into her arches and making sure to get deep between her toes where sun would likely never touch.

Sheilagh's laughter traveled to them from far out by the dock. Patrick was wading in the water close by as Tristan tickled her. Sam wondered if she had somehow misinterpreted his sexual orientation the evening before. What he was doing with Luke's sister was unmistakably flirting.

"What's wrong?"

She turned to Colin and again was reminded of how devastatingly handsome he was. "What?"

"You're frowning. Is something wrong?"

"Oh. No, I was just watching them."

Colin looked to the dock and sighed. "I should worry that a man seven years older than my baby sister is touching her that way, but Sheilagh's a force to be reckoned with. She won't let him take things too far."

While that may be true, Samantha disagreed. She could already tell that if Tristan were open to more intimate matters with Sheilagh, all he would need to do is say so and the girl would be agreeable to anything he wanted.

They watched the two play a moment longer when suddenly Sheilagh lost her footing and stumbled off the dock, arms pin- wheeling as she fell.

Sam gasped and sat upright, alarming Colin in the process. When Sheilagh finally surfaced Sam gave a sigh of relief and sat back again, but her shoulders were uncomfortably knotted with tension.

"You don't like water do you, Sammy?"

She turned sharply to Colin, prepared to deny such a silly fear, but when she saw nothing but compassion in his gaze she relaxed her defenses.

"No."

"Why?"

She looked at him, knowing it was a normal question, but still resenting the breach of privacy. "I just don't."

"Did something happen to you?"

Fuck you, she wanted to say, but knew that was cruel and unjustified and definitely not the way one spoke to a priest. "I don't like to talk about it."

"Don't like to or don't?"

"Don't."

He nodded with understanding. "Fair enough."

Colin leaned back in his chair and shut his eyes. Samantha continued to watch him a few moments longer before doing the same.

Normally okay with silence, Sam was uncharacteristically at odds with the quiet. Unable to tolerate it a moment longer she said, "I thought you had other things to do."

The moment the somewhat snarky comment left her mouth she regretted it. Not only because it could be taken as rude, but because she also realized she might've disturbed him from taking a rest.

"Sorry."

"No need to be sorry," he said sitting up and draping his tanned arms over his knees.

How did a priest get so many muscles? He removed his glasses to look at her and Sam found the action unnerving. "I know I should've done what I intended, but the draw of sitting in the sun with friends and family was all too tempting." His voice was so deep and soft at the same time.

"What did you have to do?"

He pressed his lips together as if he didn't want to answer. After hesitating a moment longer he said, "I needed to get over myself, basically. Sometimes it's confusing, approaching a change you've been preparing for practically your entire life. I guess you may be going through a bit of the same thing with graduating this summer and finally becoming a teacher."

She could understand that. "It is a bit surreal."

He nodded. "Surreal, yes, that's a good word for it. I suppose it's natural to feel suddenly insecure about something you spent years convincing yourself you were certain of. Did you ever want to be something besides a teacher?"

"A figure skater," she whispered as the sense of a ghost passing through her sent chills up her arms. Why had she just admitted that?

"Really? That's different. I used to want to be a firefighter, but my mother would've shot me first. Why did you change your mind?"

"I grew up."

He frowned as if not understanding her answer. She wished he'd stop giving her that analyzing look. "Skating isn't a fantasy job. There are plenty of adults that do it and make a living of it. Would you have wanted to compete in choreographed skating or in more of an athletic capacity?"

She snorted. "You've seen my athletic skills. Definitely not someone who excels in agility or grace. It was just something I dreamt of when I was a girl. Nothing more than a daydream."

"Why dismiss something you're passionate about?"

"Because I'm not. I was, but not anymore. Like I said, I grew up." She sounded defensive, but she really wanted him to drop it.

"What made you grow up, Sammy?"

Her heart started to pound and she felt like she couldn't breathe. Why was he being so persistent? Her forehead beaded with perspiration that had nothing to do with the heat of the sun. He seemed to notice a change and began to look around for something. What, she didn't know.

He reached to the opposite side of his chair and faced her again with a water bottle. He handed it to her. "Here, have a sip of water."

She took it from him and wanted to scream when she saw how badly her hands were shaking. *Fuck!* Her fingers reached to unscrew the lid and accidentally dropped the cool bottle into the sand, the grains immediately gluing to the condensation.

"Goddamn it," she hissed and then realized her

mistake. She looked at him apologetically, but the moment she opened her mouth to say sorry her lungs took it upon themselves to gulp down a much needed breath of air. Her chest tightened painfully as her heart raced like she'd just sprinted a mile. Her eyes blinked rapidly as dizziness threatened to make her faint.

Damn it, she was having an anxiety attack. She hadn't had one in almost ten months. She really thought she was over them.

"Shit," Colin muttered and quickly got out of his chair and knelt in front of her. He turned her face toward him and instructed calmly, "Sammy, look at me. It's okay, just breathe."

He reached for her fisted hand and unclenched her fingers, placing her open palm on his chest directly over his strong heartbeat. His skin was smooth and warm. "Breathe with me."

She looked into his blue-green eyes. They were so close he only managed to take her breath away once more. She watched him inhale and the warmth of his breath caressed her cheek as he slowly exhaled. Unbelievably, calm washed over her and her panic receded as her breathing slowed.

Never seeming to blink or break eye contact, he nodded and slowly smiled. "That a girl. You got it. Just breathe with me."

His hand somehow managed to find the back of her neck. His thumb drew careful circles over the fine baby hair that never quite made it into her ponytail. When her breathing returned to normal he still didn't let her go.

Realizing their proximity, Samantha knew she should extricate herself from his hold before someone approached and misinterpreted their position. It was crucial that she avoid having to explain what just happened. But something held her there, something stronger than Colin's touch.

Similar to the shift in the air she felt earlier when Braydon was about to kiss her, the air shifted again, only this time the shift was something more, something potent as if creating a vortex that would swallow her whole if she allowed it to touch her.

Was he going to kiss her?

They looked at each other, their faces so close she could actually see the tiny flecks of gold in his irises.

"That's it, Sammy," he whispered. "Breathe."

She wondered if he realized she was fine now. If he was only pretending she still needed him so that he didn't have to let her go. They each leaned closer and she suddenly didn't care about who might be watching. She wanted him to kiss her more than she wanted her next breath. Her lashes slowly lowered and his palm slid to the side of her neck, his thumb caressing that soft spot below her earlobe and her jaw. She leaned into the caress. His hand cupped her face, but didn't stop her. As a matter of fact he seemed to follow the movement by sifting his fingers gently through her hair.

A whispered sigh passed her lips that somehow carried the weight of a siren.

Colin's hand was immediately withdrawn and he was on his feet. Jarred by the sudden movement, she looked up at him. He seemed to be the one having trouble breathing.

She shook her head as if to tell him nothing would have happened, but they both seemed to know that was a lie not worth being uttered.

Apparently desperate for an escape, Colin did the safest thing to assure she didn't follow him. He turned without a word and didn't stop moving until he dove into the safety of the water.

CHAPTER 7

$\mathcal{T}$he following day was peaceful. It was Monday so many of the McCulloughs were at work. Even Braydon decided to pick up some extra money and help out his family as they worked logging in the nearby woods. Sam was enjoying the day with Maureen and Mary, who insisted she call her Morai, which was pronounced *Morree.*

She hadn't seen or spoken to Colin since their encounter on the beach. He considerately avoided her by swimming to the dock and remaining there until she and Sheilagh left the beach. She wasn't sure if he was even in the house.

Sam woke up early in the morning to the sound of the shower running, and once she realized he was naked on the other side of the door it became impossible to go back to sleep. Tossing and turning until sounds of the rest of the family awaking broke the silence of the house and she finally showered and dressed.

There had been something so peculiarly intimate about showering in the same place he had recently been standing, both naked, water from her body mixing with the water that had sloshed off his skin...that was the pathetic route her thoughts had taken the entire day.

After she'd dressed, she ventured to other parts of the house and found Maureen working on something in the kitchen. Needing the distraction from her thoughts, she offered to help. They were making up a basket for a woman in town named Francine who had recently fallen down the church steps and broken her foot.

Maureen was one of those impressively talented chefs that knew recipes for anything by heart and could measure accurately with nothing more than her fingers or palms. She directed Sam without overtures or requests. Her directions could offend some, but Sam was not insulted. She found it flattering that Maureen had enough faith and confidence in her skills to simply assume she could do any task well. Her high standards only made Samantha want to please her more.

As she plugged apples into a hand cranked peeler bolted to the counter she continued to wind the mechanism as long strands of green apple peels spiraled into a brown bag resting on the floor. Maureen filled the silence with chatter from everything about the town gossip to stories of her children's youth. It seemed the woman knew there was no future for Samantha and Braydon, yet still spoke to her as if she was meant to stay.

This confused Samantha, the way Maureen invested in sharing with her personal antidotes that were a prerequisite to becoming a member of the McCullough clan, but she was enjoying herself too much to ask Braydon's mother why she bothered.

Around four o'clock Colleen, Maureen's older sister, came in looking flustered, but still in good spirits. Samantha understood her mood the moment a little old woman followed her into the kitchen rapidly speaking in...Italian?

Colleen rolled her eyes and mumbled, "Jesus, Mary, and Joseph, somebody hand me a drink or a shotgun. This has been going on for over an hour."

As if this were a common occurrence, Maureen finished washing her hands at the sink and reached to the cabinet below, just beside the window cleaner and dish detergent, and pulled out a bottle of Irish whiskey.

Colleen found a cup quickly and filled the glass with two fingers then threw it down the hatch. "Christ that's good."

"Hello, Mary. How are you today?" Maureen shouted at the small Italian woman.

The little woman, whose hair was blacker than onyx turned to her sharply and said, "Do you believe the doctor still cannot find a damn thing wrong with me?" She told Maureen, outraged. "I have been through a'fifty-five exams and they cannot find a damn thing."

"Be grateful for your health, Mom," Colleen groaned.

"Health! What health? I wake up feeling as if I have

been dragged by a pack of mules. What healthy woman wakes up a'feeling like a'that?"

"Yer not ill. Yer old!" Morai snapped, appearing equally as irritated as her daughter Colleen.

Samantha actually shied away when she saw the look the little Italian shot Morai. "Who are you calling old?"

"You! You got bollocks in your ears?"

The other woman shouting a stream of Italian at Morai and Morai, appearing to understand every word of it, puffed up her chest and shouted back, "Sod off! Yer older than me, ye'are. Look at ye, visitin' every chemist in town tryin' to ken the antidote for agin'. I'll tell ye it now, Mary, like I've told ye before. It's grace and ye got about as much in ye as a stone. Quit yer bellyaching and get on with it like the rest of us and stop actin' like a gobshite!"

"Oh dear," Maureen muttered, reaching for the whiskey her sister was still holding.

"*Vaffanculo!*" the Italian woman shrilled.

Samantha wasn't sure what the word meant, but she knew it was bad.

Luckily, Colleen stepped forward calmly and said, "That's enough now. Mum, go back to what you were doin' and Mary, why don't you start heating the gravy?"

Mary the Italian pressed her red lips together and pulled in a tight breath, but reached into the bag Colleen carried in with her and yanked out an old apron, the kind that looked like a smock and buttoned up the shoulders.

The angry Italian continued to mutter in disgruntled Italian, but pulled a large pot from the cabinet to cook with. She seemed to be playing the martyr, commenting here and there about what a bother it was to cook for a bunch of unsophisticated Irish palates, yet needing to provide her services so there was something decent for everyone to eat.

Sam stood watching, afraid to move and perhaps be noticed by the angry woman, as she lifted a huge jar of red sauce onto the counter and began spooning it into a large pot.

"I'll tell you what the problem is, I'll tell you," Italian Mary mumbled. "You are just bitter, Mary, that Arthur sat next to me in church."

"Sat next to ye, aye? Are ye out of yer bloody mind? Ye gave him no choice shoving yer boney arse down the pew until he was wedged against the rail. Arthur is a gentle man and ye frighten him with yer pushy ways."

"You gotta' know how to treat a man. That's your mistake. Men like being a'told what to do. And I'd rather be boney than built like an ox!"

Colleen and Maureen fit unbaked piecrust to two pie tins and were having their own conversation as if the women were not about to kill one another again. Morai came over to where Sam was sitting and began collecting the peeled apples and slicing them precisely with nary a look to where the blade landed.

"I may be built like an ox, but yer the one who acts like ye were raised in a barn."

The sound of a metal spoon being forcibly dropped onto the counter filled the kitchen. Mary the Italian turned, mouth open, prepared to fire at Irish Mary, but suddenly stilled when her gaze fell on Samantha. *Not good.*

"Who are you?" She pointed accusingly at Sam.

Maureen dusted off her hands on a rag and came to stand beside Sam as if her presence could somehow protect her. "This is Samantha, Mary," she shouted. "She's Braydon's friend from college."

Italian Mary frowned as she thought about Sam's orientation to the family and then her expression changed entirely, morphing into a painted red smile and glad eyes. She clapped her hands together happily, her knotty knuckles decorated with fancy ruby rings and gold bands.

"Braydon's friend you say? How a'wonderful! Come here child and let Nonna have a look at you!"

"Better go," Colleen mumbled and Sam stood to slowly walk to the little woman.

Italian Mary clasped her hands in her own, her jewelry clacking together like teeth.

"Aren't you just beautiful!" she said in a thick Italian lilt.

Sam smiled, but regretted the moment she let down her guard. One of those heavily jeweled, knotty knuckles came up to her cheek and pinched so hard tears immediately filled Sam's eyes.

"You be sure to a'be good to my Braydon. He needs a fine woman to look after him. Are you planning on a'marrying him, dear? Oh, it will be a fine Catholic wedding from the looks of you!"

"She's not marrying Braydon," Morai corrected. "You're about as sharp as a bloody ball."

Sam wasn't sure what to make of that comment. Did

everyone get that she was barely invested in her relationship with Braydon?

Her concern for herself escalated abruptly when Italian Mary turned her dark eyes on her.

"Why don't you a'want to marry my Braydon?" she asked accusingly.

"Um…"

"You think you can do better than him?"

"No, I just…we…"

"Oh, leave her alone," Colleen snapped, physically turning her mother-in-law back to the stove and shoving the ladle into her hand. "Stir the gravy."

Morai whispered, "Don't mind her, lassie. She's as thick as manure, but only half as useful. She doesn't understand shite about the way of things. Now come on and peel those last three apples and I'll show ye how to make a pie that men will be fallin' over ye fer."

The rest of the afternoon passed at turtle speed, Samantha afraid to breathe within Italian Mary's earshot. When the boys started filing in for dinner she snuck away to her room for a few moments' peace.

Shutting her door she went straight to the bathroom. When she shut off the faucet after washing her hands she heard something that made her still. It was Colin's deep voice. Slowly, she approached the adjoining bathroom door and listened.

"Of course," Colin said then was quiet for a moment.

Was someone with him? She heard nothing but an echoless silence on the other end of the door.

He cleared his throat. "I don't want to wait. That'll only

confuse me more. It's already June. I have less than two months. The sooner I take my vows the sooner I'll be feeling more like myself again. I'm sure it's just anxiety as time is closing in."

He was quiet for a moment then, "It has nothing to do with that. Yes, I'm sure. How would her being here matter anyway? She's here for my brother."

He seemed to finish the end of his statement with a tinge of hostility and—dear God, was he talking about her?

"I spent all morning in the chapel and then ran six miles. This anxiety needs to be dispersed so I can put myself back to right and focus on what I'm here to do. I despise feeling so distracted. I'm not normally like this."

He seemed to be listening to the person on the other line. She had no doubt at this point that he was speaking on the phone. Was she the cause of his distraction?

"Yes. I know that. I know what you had with Amelia and that you'd choose another day with her in a heartbeat over a lifetime dedicated to God, but I'm not you, Father Tucker. I've never cared about those things. Whatever this is, it'll pass and it's wrong of me to make her think any different. I think it's best that I return."

Sam placed a hand on her chest as chills raced up her spine.

"It should be my choice when I return. I understand I can't take my vows until August first, but I see no reason why I have to be forced out of my home."

Was he planning on leaving his family because of her presence? She felt like an intruder in the worse way.

"I know this is my home, but Saint Peter's is my home too. If I wish to return early I should be permitted to do so."

Samantha couldn't listen to another word. She blinked back tears and swallowed against the hard lump forming in her throat.

Quickly, she went to the opposite door and made the bed and began tossing her clothes onto the covers. She needed to leave. There was no way she could be held responsible for ruining Colin's last stay with his family before he became a priest.

She should've never come here. It was the idea of returning to her parents' empty home that had her sniffling and wiping back tears. What was wrong with her?

Going to the closet she saw someone moved her suitcase to the top shelf. She stood on her toes and tried to latch onto the handle with her fingertips. When she had a mediocre grip she yanked and the case came tumbling down with a thud.

What she wasn't prepared for was the heavy trophy that followed and slammed into her shoulder then landed on the floor with a bang.

The sound of movement had her looking up from where a mark was already forming on her skin.

"Sammy, are you okay?"

Shit. She let out a breath and the last of her composure slipped. With slumped shoulders she slowly turned and faced Colin. The moment he saw her face she knew there was no hiding the fact that she was crying. *Damn fair Irish skin.*

He still held the phone to his ear, but his eyes were held wide on her face. "I'll have to call you back," he said, shutting the phone and tossing it on the bed.

"You're bleeding."

"What?" she looked at her shoulder and sure enough there was blood. "It's just a scratch. A trophy fell on me."

He frowned examining her arm. "How did that happen?"

She wiped her eyes, hoping she'd seen the last of her tears. "I was trying to reach my suitcase."

He looked at the bag on the floor and to her clothing piled on the bed. "Are you leaving?"

Better me than you. "I have to go. Something's come up."

"Is everything okay? Your family?"

"They're fine. I just…I need to be getting home."

He gave a silent "oh" and looked down at the carpet.

He was again in casual clothes. He looked as if he had run very hard that afternoon. Lengthening shadows from the fading sun brought her attention to his sneakers. The man looked perfect in just about anything, even ratty old Nikes.

"I suppose Braydon will be going too, then."

"What? No. Braydon can stay. I can even take a train back. I just need a ride to the station."

"Does he know you're planning to leave?"

Tell me to stay, she thought yearningly and grew even more frustrated. "What?"

"Braydon. Does he know you're leaving?"

"Oh. No, I just decided."

He thought for a moment, that introspective look in

his eye again. Then he looked back to the bathroom and down at his phone on the bed and back to her. Shit. He suspected she had been eavesdropping.

"Sammy—"

"Don't. It's fine. This is your home. I don't want to cause anyone to be uncomfortable in their own home."

"It isn't like that—"

"It's not a big deal. My parents will be glad to have the time with me anyway."

"I thought Braydon said they were away."

Damn it! "They cut their trip short." *Nice. Lie to the priest.*

It didn't matter anyway. He looked at her and she knew he didn't believe her. He pinched the bridge of his nose as if he were getting a headache. She took the opportunity to retrieve her bag from the floor and carry it to the bed, careful not to get too close to him.

Ignoring Colin, she began unzipping the case and refolding her items before packing them away. When he grasped her arm she froze.

"Sammy, don't. Don't go because of me. Please. You have as much a right to be here as any of us. You're Braydon's guest."

She shook her head sadly. "He wouldn't know the difference if I stayed or left. You all are reading way too far into our relationship."

A beat of silence. "Look at me."

She hesitantly did as he asked and turned to face him, wrinkled t-shirt still in hand. His gaze searched her face.

All she knew in that moment was that the touch of his

skin to hers, no matter how casual a grip he held on her arm, it somehow managed to send more of a shock to her core than anything else ever had. Why? Why this man?

"Do you love him?" he finally asked.

She pressed her lips together in irritation. "I told you I don't. We're friends."

"But I saw you kissing him."

"You saw *him* kissing me," she corrected. "And people kiss all the time. It doesn't mean they're in love."

He looked as though he wanted to say a hundred things in that moment, but all he said was, "I can't, Sammy."

"Can't what?"

"This…the way you make me feel. He's my brother and I'll be a priest in less than two months."

She wanted to kick him. How dare he assume that she was giving him an invitation to turn down? She knew what he was! She wasn't some Mary Magdalene trollop hoping to throw him off his path to God. She resented the fact that he thought she could be so uncaring about his commitment.

"I never asked you to be anything more than his brother, Colin."

He dropped her arm and took a step back. His Adam's apple moved under the shadow of his jaw as he gave a tight smile, but his eyes remained unmoved.

"My mistake," he said gruffly. "Anyway, please stay. I'm sorry if I've made you uncomfortable, but there's no need to go. I'm leaving in the morning."

She imagined the entire family sitting around questioning each other why Colin left when he was supposed to be there for the summer. They'd eventually figure something out. He didn't lie, she assumed, and feared he would confess it had something to do with her. Being held accountable for his leaving would be utterly humiliating.

She was angry that he'd put her in that position. Getting home to some Ben and Jerry's sounded all together great. "Don't bother," she snapped and turned to continue packing.

She gasped when he reached for her again, this time with more force, and spun her around. His soft lips landed on hers and she squeaked in surprise. He held her just below her shoulders and she wasn't sure what to do. Surely he'd come to his senses in a minute.

She stood there, eyes open, and waited. His mouth never opened, only pressed to hers dryly, lips to lips.

When he pulled away he was visibly shaking. He shook his head and attempted to say something, but no words came out. He turned, but then faced her again as if he wasn't sure what to do. The palm of his hand gripped the back of his neck in a show of irritation. She hadn't a clue what to say. He wasn't looking at her and she knew he was having some sort of internal argument with himself.

"I can do better than that."

When he reached for her the second time she was again shocked.

Her hands went to his chest and he wrapped his arms around her torso arching her back. He was practically holding all of her weight, pulling them pelvis to pelvis and lifting her to her toes.

His mouth coasted over hers and at the first touch of his tongue she felt some sort of pent up release deep within her belly and her panties suddenly flooded with desire. Never in her life had she had that sort of reaction to another person.

"Kiss me, Sammy. Show me how to kiss a woman."

Her mouth slowly opened and he found his way inside. If he was any sort of novice there was no telling from his kiss. Slowly, his tongue tickled hers and her hands glided up his chest, across his warm and stubbly neck and into his soft dark hair. He pulled her close so that her belly pressed to his and it was perhaps the most sexual position she had ever been in with a man.

He moaned into her mouth and slanted his lips over hers, taking control of the kiss. A storm of fluttering tickles unleashed in her lower abdomen. She met him with every lick, nibble, and caress.

"God, you taste good."

The mention of God had her cowering in shame. She gave him one final stroke with her tongue then carefully extricated herself from his embrace. On shaky legs she moved across the room so that the bed separated them. She couldn't help but admire the waist of his shorts and notice his erection pressing against the back of his zipper.

She was a horrible, horrible person.

"Sammy—"

The wanting that burned inside of her became almost painful. Impossible to satisfy. "Don't, Colin. It means nothing. I'm leaving tomorrow so you might as well stay."

"Please don't go. I just...I never needed to kiss a woman like I needed to kiss you then."

"Well, that moment's over now and I'm still here with Braydon and you're still going to be a priest. I need to leave. It's wrong for me to stay here and lead your brother on. And I couldn't live with myself if you left your family because of me or if I..." He obviously figured out she'd been listening to his conversation. "...If I caused you any more distraction."

"Talk to Braydon. He doesn't have to know about this, but tell him how you feel. I know him. He'll want you to stay. *I* want you to stay. I know what I am and I know this can be nothing more than what we just shared. It won't happen again and I'll leave you alone. Please. My mother and sister and the rest of my family are enjoying your company. Stay. Don't go home to an empty house. You're welcome here. If you stay, I'll stay."

"And if I go?"

"I'll leave as well."

She shut her eyes and sighed. "Fine."

"Good."

He took her suitcase and lifted the clothes out of it. He carried it to the closet and seemed to think twice about putting it back on the shelf. Rather, he stowed it on the floor next to Braydon's shoes, picked up the trophy from the floor, and placed it on his brother's dresser.

Without looking at her he said, "Dinner's probably ready."

He left the room the way he came, this time securely shutting the bathroom door behind him.

The moment she was alone she dropped to the bed and let the severity of what happened consume her. Wrapping her arms protectively around herself, she began to tremble, but she refused to let herself cry over her own stupidity. Her head hurt, where she scraped her shoulder burned, and her eyes stung with the tears trying to break free, but she would *not* cry.

CHAPTER 8

*D*inner was delicious, but awkward. Braydon kissed her cheek when she returned to the kitchen then proceeded to ignore her as he regaled the others with stories of the day. Sam kept her nose down and avoided eye contact with all of them.

After Colin left she allowed herself only a few moments of self-pity then told herself to grow up and get over it. He was going to be a priest and she couldn't mess with that. Even if she could sway him otherwise he'd only end up resenting her in the end. And for what? A few measly kisses. Sam had no business interfering with his plans.

As much as she wanted to leave she wanted to stay. Katherine and Anthony and the kids had come to dinner and after the women were finished tidying up the kitchen, Sam sat on the floor of the den with Frankie and Skylar playing *Trouble.*

Braydon and his brothers sat out front drinking and telling old stories they each heard a hundred times, but still found as amusing as the first telling. Colin left after dinner. Sam was curious about where he was going, but told herself it was none of her business and she'd be better to stop thinking of him so much.

She needed to talk to Braydon, but could tell by the course the evening was taking that tonight was not the night for a serious conversation. Around nine o'clock Katherine gathered up the kids and said their goodbyes. Italian Mary was already asleep on the recliner, but when Katherine considered out loud about letting her stay rather than waking her, Frank jumped from his seat on the couch and offered to carry her out.

Anthony ended up waking his mother and shuffling a sleepy and much more docile Italian Mary out to the car. Once the kids were gone Maureen and Frank made their excuses and headed up to bed.

Sam stood by the door for a few minutes debating whether or not to tell Braydon she was going to bed. Their drunken merriment echoed off the trees as their words slipped clumsily out of their mouths and slurred together.

They were all piss drunk.

Sam wondered what it was like to be so uninhibited. She doubted she could ever let go that much. Feeling like an interloper, she decided to let the McCullough siblings have their fun and simply head off to bed.

Her mind was restless. The house was quiet aside from the occasional rowdy peal of laughter that reached her window. She'd been lying still, staring at the ceiling for at least an hour when a soft sound jarred her from her thoughts. Sitting up to investigate the sound she wandered to the window. The boys were all exactly where she had left them.

Suddenly there was a clatter and a moan coming from the next room. Without thinking, Samantha followed the sound and entered Colin's room through the adjoining door. The room was dark, but from the moonlight spilling in she could tell it was utilitarian and precisely the way Colin preferred it.

There was a thud and she quickly searched for a light. Unable to find a switch on the wall she stepped in and tried to see what the sound was.

"Colin?"

The only reply she got was raspy laughter. Following the sound, she found Colin lying on the floor beside his bed in nothing but briefs in a fit of laughter. "Are you drunk?"

"Guilty," he admitted with a ridiculous smirk.

"What is it with you Irish? I always thought the drinking thing was a stereotype."

"Oh, it tis, my love. This is purely a McCullough thing."

"How much did you drink?"

He shut one eye and pressed his finger and thumb together. She looked down at him in exasperation.

"A smidge doesn't do this."

"Aye, but a smidge a dozen times can be a powerful thing. It ganged up on me and now I've gone and fallen on me arse! But it isn't all bad, you see, because now I have a beautiful lassie looking over me." He laughed, "And now I'm spoutin' poetry. Do you like poetry, Sammy?"

She rolled her eyes. "Here, let me help you up."

She held out her hand, but rather than reach for it, he said, *"Oh Sammy dear, I'm down here, lying on me back. What keeps me here is the beer, a beautiful woman, and the fact that I'm a wreck."*

"Lovely."

But he wasn't finished. *"When we drink, we get drunk. When we get drunk, we fall asleep. When we sleep, there's no sin. When we commit no sin, we go to heaven. So, let's all get drunk, and go to heaven. But in heaven there is no beer so let's drink it up while we're here!"*

She frowned. "What is that?"

"An old Irish toast."

Rolling to his side, Colin tugged his jeans over and rifled through the pockets. He pulled out a flask and frowned when he put it to his mouth and nothing came out.

"You don't need any more of that," she said taking the flask out of his hands and yanking him off the ground.

He was unsteady and she was glad the bed was there to catch her before he knocked her on her ass. However, when he practically fell on top of her she wasn't sure it was such a good thing. The heat of his body singed through her clothing and she quickly scrambled out from under him.

She sat up and tried to steady him beside her.

"How's your shoulder, Sammy dear?"

He moved her hair away from her shoulder and eyed

her scratch from earlier. It really was just a scratch. His thumb gently traced the curve of her shoulder as he watched the movement, transfixed.

He whispered, *"Here's to temperance supper, with water in glasses tall, and coffee and tea to end with—beautiful Sammy, and me not there at all."*

He took a deep breath through his nose. "Why do you smell so good, Samantha? Better than any flower or meadow, nothing like any other woman I've ever been in the presence of."

She looked down unsure what to do. She should stand, but she wanted to stay. His hand slowly lifted to her chin and turned her to face him. His eyes looked as though he had been to hell and back.

"You're a temptation I cannot seem to outrun, Samantha. And now I'm going to kiss you again. Tell me I can kiss you one more time."

She was suddenly very aware of her body. The weight of her panties, the fact that she'd come into his room in nothing but a tank top, the pull of her breasts against the ribbed fabric of her shirt as her nipples chafed with each pull of her lungs, the spot where his naked thigh touched hers, and the way he looked into her eyes and saw a part of her everyone else seemed to somehow overlook, it was all too much.

"Colin—"

"Please."

She knew it was wrong, but what was she supposed to do? She wanted him to do it! Slowly she nodded.

He leaned into her and captured her mouth as if he

had been waiting to do that since the moment they last broke apart. His hands found her hips and coasted across her back as his chest pressed into hers and he lowered her to the bed. Her mind cried danger, but her hormones didn't seem to care.

He kissed her like a man starved for the affection. His mouth tasted of sweet liquor and that earthy flavor she associated with him and him alone. It was nothing like the first kiss or even the second for that matter. He got better by miles with each intimate second.

Her legs reflexively curled closer to her chest as she pressed her thighs together. He licked at her mouth, whispering words of pleasure with each couple of breaths. The heat of his palm coasted back to her hip and stopped just over the cotton band of her panties. His fingers slid under the fabric and touched her hip there.

"So soft you are, Samantha. I had never imagined you would be this soft."

The bulge of his erection pressed into her side. Never in her life had she experienced something so erotic. She feared she would burst if he stopped. It was wrong.

She was about as clueless about this stuff as he was, but she didn't care. On a prayer that she not embarrass herself —yes, she realized the irony that she was praying to a God she was taking from and betraying—she prayed Colin wouldn't be disgusted by her brazenness. She took his hand from her hip and slid it to the front of her panties.

He stilled and Sam feared she had ruined everything.

She shut her eyes unable to see his rejection and worried she was seconds away from tears. Why did she do that? He only wanted to kiss her. He stood and she slowly sat up, guilt weighing her down, still too chicken to face him in her embarrassment.

The door clicked and she crumbled inside. He left her.

The sudden caress of his fingers upon her cheek shocked her.

Her eyes flew open and she looked at him.

"I just wanted to lock the door, Samantha. Do not be ashamed of what you did. You're beautiful."

Like a cat, she pressed her cheek to his palm and sighed in relief. He reached for her hand and helped her stand. Reaching down he pulled back his covers and waved her to get into the bed.

Sam had no idea what was happening or about to, but she did exactly as he asked.

He slowly moved toward the other side of the bed and paused by the bathroom door.

"Is your bedroom door locked, Sammy?"

"Yes."

He nodded and continued to his side of the bed. Pulling the covers back he slid in beside her and pulled her close. They each lay on their sides, knees to knees, nose to nose. Simply gazing at one another for the longest time, occasionally kissing, but nothing more.

The quiet consent was mutual. They explored each other with soft touches and gentle glances. There was no excuse for her allowing him to touch her other than the tidal wave of desire she seemed to be drowning in every time she felt his caress or stared into his blue-green eyes.

His hand eventually worked its way to her breasts. He

held her there, yet still seemed to be following some code of restraint. His knuckle coasted over the stiff tips of her nipples, but nothing further. His control made her want him all the more. She was balancing on a sharp blade of sensitivity, where every tiny movement of his had her sucking in a breath or aching for some sort of release. It was divine torture.

If not for her panties, her thighs would have been damp. Colin was completely erect, yet seemed not at all concerned about that.

"You're so incredibly beautiful, Samantha," he whispered.

"No, I'm not."

"Yes, you are. It's such a natural beauty. It's as if it comes from hidden deep inside, safe, so that no one can mimic it. I've thought about you since the moment I first saw you."

She smiled, the heat from her blush making her skin even warmer. His thumb dragged across her lower lip as his fingers slowly ran through her hair.

"I've never been this close to a woman before. I never wanted to be, but with you...with you I only seem to want. I want to make you laugh. I want to talk with you, touch you, smell you, and taste you."

"What happens tomorrow, Colin? This can't change anything. You are who you are and I'm not meant to be a part of that."

His eyes shut as if he could hide from the reality he was fighting so hard to keep at bay. "I wish I could tell you this changes things, but it doesn't. I already belong to

God. It's what I've always wanted, planned on. My vocation defines me and without it I'm lost."

For some reason, rather than rationalize the whole thing or beg for what she craved, what she needed most in that moment was to comfort him and take away the confusion in his eyes. "It's okay, Colin. I know who you are and I respect you for it."

"I'm sorry."

"Please don't apologize. I want to be here with you even if it's just for tonight. I've thought about you too. You seem to be all I can think about anymore."

He kissed her then, soft and slow. It wasn't long before they were each breathing heavily and holding onto each other as if they could somehow make this moment last. He never removed her clothing and barely touched below her shoulders.

As he rolled her to her back and fit himself on top of her, their legs tangled and glided over each other in all the right places. They fell into a rhythm and his erection nudged her sex through the cotton of her panties. They each tipped their heads back and moaned.

"You feel so good, Samantha. I could kiss you like this for days."

He nudged himself into the cradle of her sex again and something coiled deep inside of her. She wrapped her legs around his hips and pressed her body into his. It wasn't long before they were each highly sensitized and grinding against one another as if they could somehow break through all the physical and mental barriers that separated them.

LYDIA MICHAELS

The bed slowly rocked and quiet squeaks filled the room. She prayed no one overheard. She sighed and pressed her mouth into his shoulder to muffle her cries of pleasure.

Deep guttural moans built in his chest and vibrated against her breasts. Their skin was damp causing them to slip over one and other. Closer, closer her body pulled toward something unknown. She wanted to run there and at the same time hold whatever it was back so that the moment never ended.

"Samantha," he breathed as he kissed her bare shoulder.

"Oh, Colin, please."

"Yes, Sammy, yes."

She could sense he only needed to hit that spot a couple more times and….Her mind stepped out as her body came alive and locked. It was as if she were momentarily dying, or flying, there was nothing but peace.

Her limbs twitched and her flesh covered with goose bumps. Her neck arched back and her body bowed off of the bed into him. He continued to grind into her and he appeared to suffer the same release. His arms trembled as they held his weight over her. Neck arched, his head fell back as he moaned long and hard.

Sam could feel warm moisture between them and knew it was their climax. She'd had her first real orgasm and he never even penetrated her or removed her clothing.

When he kissed her he did so with such affection. The distance she knew would come with the next day made

Samantha ache. She wondered if allowing herself to get this close to such an incredible man was really worth it after all.

She'd never been so attracted to another person, never experienced such acute desire in her entire life. It was as if he fulfilled her so much all the empty places of her soul no longer pained her.

She realized since entering his room hours ago, she hadn't thought of Meghan once. He made her pain go away and he was the first person to ever give her that peace.

Damn her for loving one more person who would be irrevocably ripped away from her. Resentment toward God suddenly choked her. It was as if she were the same helpless little girl who just lost her sister all over again. Only this time when she cried, she had Colin there, holding her tightly. She wasn't sure if his presence made it better or worse in the end, but the fact that he patiently allowed her to cry without asking for explanations was a blessing.

CHAPTER 9

*O*ver the next few days Colin did his absolute best to avoid Samantha. The morning after she'd come to his bed, he awoke to the soft click of the bathroom door shutting sometime around dawn. She didn't return.

That day, and the days following it, he spent at the youth center working with local teens on a project to redevelop the local park. He hadn't returned home until late in the evening and only saw Samantha in passing. She was occupied with others and unable to speak to him about what happened.

He hated that he was possibly hurting her with his avoidance, but he didn't know what else to do. He wanted her with a fierceness he'd never felt before and yet he could never completely have her. They hadn't slept together, but in some way, what they had shared seemed all the more intimate.

Not only was he becoming a Diocesan Priest, he was a practicing Catholic to the bone. He believed in abstinence until marriage. Unsure if Samantha still held her virtue, considering otherwise was altogether intolerable, but he was as inexperienced as they came. Never before had he kissed another being so intimately, touched another's flesh so personally, struggled with temptation so intensely. He needed to keep his distance or once again risk losing control.

Colin didn't know if Samantha talked to his brother. Braydon would no doubt feel the sting of rejection, but his younger brother had to know Sammy was not invested emotionally in whatever they shared.

The day he saw Braydon kissing her...he never in his life suffered such aching jealousy. It was a hybrid reaction created from envy, anger, and many other sins. He was breaking a commandment and coveting a woman who belonged to not just another man, but his brother.

He tried to stay away, realizing he was only hiding from his fears. Attempting to brush off the attraction, he followed the others to the beach. He intended to leave her be, but for some reason he found every word she said fascinating. And then she suffered a panic attack.

Colin wasn't sure what triggered her reaction. They had been speaking of childhood goals and suddenly she was paler than a ghost and struggling to breathe. His fear for her in that moment was completely irrational and inappropriate, but so very, very real.

It aggravated him that Braydon had been neglecting her, yet it irritated him to see his brother with Sammy.

What've happened if Sammy had another episode like the one on the beach and no one was there to help her come back to herself? Damn Braydon for being too selfish to not give her the time he owed her and the company she deserved.

By Friday Colin was running out of errands and places to hide. He awoke thinking he'd visit the church and see if they had anything that needed tending. Perhaps there was a senior who needed a ride to a doctor's appointment that would take up the majority of his day. Pathetic. Was this how he was going to ride out the next week?

Samantha was supposed to be staying with them until the seventeenth. There was one week left. As much as he wanted her to go he wanted her to stay. How would he survive the next week without being able to touch her, laugh with her, hold her in his arms? Never before had the idea of celibacy terrified him so. Even the temptation to bring himself to release while thinking about her in the shower or in the privacy of his room was novel. He'd never been one to masturbate, but since meeting Samantha he struggled to withstand the temptation.

It was lust, he told himself repetitively. Samantha was a lovely woman, easy to care for, a pleasure to spend time with. Any man with eyes and a brain would undoubtedly feel the same way. He was merely one victim in the long line of men that would someday lose their hearts to Samantha Dougherty. But if that was true, and what he was feeling was simply lust, why would this impatient yearning for her not fade?

The scent of home cooked breakfast filtered from

below and he wanted to be out of the house before everyone rose for the day. Grabbing his phone and keys, he quickly left his room. He paused when he caught Braydon knocking on Sam's bedroom door.

"Hey, Col, you taking off again today?"

Colin stuck his items in his pocket and tried not to appear as guilty as he felt while looking at Braydon. "Yeah. I need to head down to the church to help out with some things."

"Oh yeah? What's goin' on down there?"

Before he could answer with a lie Samantha opened the door. Her hair was damp and her clothing was somewhat clinging to her skin. She'd obviously just gotten out of the shower when Braydon knocked.

"Braydon." She looked to her left and saw him. "Good morning, Colin."

"Good morning, Samantha. Did you sleep well?"

Her cheeks flushed and she looked to the floor. "Yes."

"My mom and the aunts are going antiquing," Braydon cut in. "I wanted to see if you wanted to hang with them or come with me today."

She looked up at him. "Where are you going?"

"I was gonna go pick up some bait for tomorrow and then get stuff ready at the lake for tonight."

"Tonight?"

"Yeah, it's our annual bonfire at the lake."

Colin watched as his brother gave Samantha a coy smile and fingered a strand of her damp hair.

"You and I snuggled up under a blanket by the fire..."

Colin fought the urge to smack his brother's hand

away from her. He should go, but he couldn't stop watching her, nervous to see what she'd do.

"After everyone leaves we could sneak out to the dock and do some night swimming, just the two of us."

Colin's gaze tore from Samantha's beautiful face as he stared at his idiot brother. Did he not realize that in the whole week she'd been here, not once had she gone near the water? It didn't take a genius to figure out that she had some deep-seated fear of water.

He turned back to Sam and all remnants of her earlier blush washed away. Her cheeks looked bloodless and the narrow column of her throat worked as she repetitively swallowed.

Sam stepped out of Braydon's reach and his brother's fingers released her hair. "A fire sounds nice. Will everyone be there?"

"They should. You're going, right, Colin?"

Colin remembered the last time he'd been at the lake with Samantha. He wondered if somehow her panic attack had to do with the fact that they were at the lake. Why had he not considered that? Although he planned on avoiding anything to do with Samantha, he worried that she may need him in case she had another episode. Lord knew Braydon wasn't the best at detecting her discomfort.

"Yes, I'll be there."

She looked at him sharply, clearly not expecting his attendance.

"So you wanna go with me or the women today, babe?"

Colin gritted his teeth at his brother's term of endearment. She'd obviously not spoken to him about their relationship yet. He was angry that in three days and nights she hadn't taken an opportunity to clear the air with Braydon, but then again, her breaking up with his brother would change nothing about Colin's situation.

"I'll go with you. I just need to pull up my hair and grab my Chap Stick."

Before she turned back into the room Colin caught a look at her mouth. Her lips were red as if she had been biting them. God he wanted to kiss and soothe those soft lips.

"I got to go," he practically barked and turned toward the stairs.

"Hey, you all right, bro?"

"Fine," he lied without looking back.

COLIN ARRIVED at the lake shortly after suppertime. He dined at the rectory and spent most of the day painting the parish's school hall. He figured he needed something to eat up his free time, so he volunteered for the project that morning and was elbow deep in eggshell paint by noon.

As he parked his Jeep he gripped the wheel and took a calming breath. He could do this. When he felt centered and in control he left the Jeep and headed toward the lake and into the limpid twilight. As he crested the bend of evergreens he could hear his family's rowdy laughter. Just another bonfire like they had been having for the past twenty-nine years of his life. But his feeling of control was short lived.

Before his relatives even came into view he heard her. She was laughing at something with undisguised amusement. Her voice lilting from octave to octave like a bird song so pure it could be called a lullaby.

When he spotted her he regretted his presence immediately. This evening was guaranteed to torture him and test him in ways he'd never been tested.

She was with Kelly. Did all of his brothers have to touch her? Kelly had his arm around her shoulders and was speaking close to her ear as she looked forward as if imagining whatever he was describing and she smiled. She continued to laugh as his vagabond brother went on with an anecdote about God knew what.

She literally took his breath away. Her faded jeans showed off her long tapered legs. He loved the way she could look stunning in casual clothes. The temperature was dropping as darkness approached and she wore a dark blue Villanova hooded sweatshirt. Her feet were bare and the only thought Colin could process was *I wonder what color her toenails are painted?* He would bet either clear or a shell pink that was as close as one could get to clear.

He was so consumed with imagining her dainty feet he barely heard Luke and Tristan approach.

"I told you I would, babe. I'll head to town tomorrow and pick it up and get it done this week."

"Thanks. I'd do it myself, but I gotta get—"

The sound of footsteps halting had him shaking his head and peeling his eyes away from her.

"Oh hey, Colin. I didn't see you standing there. What are you doing?"

Colin supposed he did look a bit odd standing in the approaching dark watching the others, but for some reason Luke's question struck him as overly anxious. "I was just heading down there. Hey, Tristan. How ya' doing?"

"Good, man. You?"

Tristan was a fairly new arrival to their circle. He moved up here after being their cousin's roommate in college. Tristan and his brother Luke had hit it off immediately and Colin was glad his brother had such a friend to bring him out of whatever dark place he had been heading toward.

"Good."

Luke looked as though he wanted to ask something.

"What's up, Luke? You look like you're about to be sick."

His brother gave an uncharacteristically fake laugh. Nervous was something Luke rarely was. Something had spooked him though.

"Uh, nothing. I'm gonna head down to say hi to the others. I'll catch you later, Tristan. Colin."

Colin looked at Tristan who appeared fed up. What just happened? "Is he all right?"

Tristan shook his head, but continued to watch Luke go. "Yeah, he's just...Luke."

Colin shrugged and headed toward the others.

It proved fairly easy to avoid Samantha with a group the size of the McCulloughs, but his traitorous mind continuously sought her out against all odds. By eleven, he sat brooding in a chair, nursing a beer that was piss warm, and watching her on the other end of the fire wrapped under a blanket with his brother Braydon. He ignored the sound of someone plopping down in the chair beside him.

"Hey, bro. What's got you so down?"

He looked over at Kelly and knew his demeanor was the farthest thing from welcoming, but as always, Kelly was undeterred. He took a sip of his tepid beer.

Kelly gave a long ominous whistle. "Wow. Don't usually see you in this mood. What happened?"

Colin ignored him as a fire raged in his chest when Braydon tried to pop a hot puffed marshmallow in Samantha's mouth. She dodged his finger and took the morsel into her hands to eat.

"Colin?" The serious note in Kelly's voice had him turning to face him. "Seriously, you okay?"

"I don't know, Kelly. I don't know what I am."

Kelly eyed him with all seriousness. "What happened?"

He gave a deprecating laugh and shook his head. "I can't talk about it."

"You sure? You could tell me anything, Colin, and I'd never betray your trust or judge you. I love you, man."

"Thanks. I love you, too. But this is something I need to figure out for myself."

Kelly nodded solemnly. "Okay, but the offer still stands. You know, no one expects you to get it right all the time. You may be taking your vows, but you aren't JC. No one's perfect. It's human to be unsure."

"Thanks."

About an hour later Colin had taken all he could take. Samantha dozed off, looking all too comfortable with her head resting on Braydon's shoulder. He stood and went to say goodnight to his parents and the rest of them. He debated not saying goodbye to Braydon, but knew that was wrong. Steeling himself, he walked over to him and Sammy.

"You takin' off, Col?"

"Yeah. I'll see you in the morning."

When Braydon reached up to shake his hand he jarred Samantha and woke her up. She sat up, looking groggy and stiff and frowned. As she turned her head she winced.

"I'll see you, man," Bray said.

"Are you leaving?" Samantha rasped in a drowsy voice that seemed to go right to his heart and other inappropriate places. *Whoa.* He needed to stop. His thoughts were getting worse by the day. By the hour.

"Yeah. I've had enough."

She stretched. "I think I've had enough too."

Braydon pouted. "Really? The nights just getting started."

"I can give you a ride back if you want," Colin suggested, sounding all too eager to his own ears. Samantha eyed him skeptically. "That way Braydon can stay as long as he wants."

She looked at Braydon. "Do you care?"

"Nah, do what you want, babe. I'll be fine. Go home and get some rest."

"Okay."

Samantha stood to gather her belongings. Colin stepped away so as not to hover or seem anxious. He waited by the trail back where the cars were parked and watched her.

Her ponytail had come partially loose and hung cock-eyed. She still looked half-asleep. Rather than put on her sneakers, she carried them in her hand along with the bunched up fleece blanket she'd been resting under.

He was suddenly very frightened about what he'd just gotten himself into.

CHAPTER 10

Colin drove back to the house with more precision than he used when taking his driver's test as a sixteen year old boy. His knuckles gripped the wheel so tight they were bloodless. Samantha sat quietly beside him and not once did his eyes leave the road.

As he pulled into the empty driveway he looked up to the dark house and his heart clamored so fast and hard within his chest he feared he might actually pass out. He shut the car off and neither of them moved or said a word.

After looking out the windshield for another several minutes he finally said, "I'm sorry I haven't been around the past couple of days."

He glanced at her and she looked as though she had been watching him all along. Her expression was blank and her eyes shone in the moonlight. "I figured it was for the best."

She didn't nod or reply. They sat, separated by the

console, and simply stared at one another in silence. Like horses lined at the gate propelled into motion by a shot, they each suddenly lunged at each other, mouths slanting over mouths, teeth clacking together, hands squeezing flesh and pulling hair. He wanted to inhale her.

Her tongue passed his lips the same time his passed hers. She was breathing roughly, but so was he. It was as if they were in a race and the finish line was the difference between life and death. He squeezed her shoulders through her sweatshirt, ran his fingers through her hair dislodging her ponytail completely. She moaned into his mouth and pulled her body up so that she was kneeling in the passenger seat.

Fingers forked through his hair sending chills over every square inch of his chest. Dear God, he was so aroused he feared he would come just from kissing her. He needed to get control of himself. He fought for control of the kiss but she seemed determined not to relinquish it. He slowed his tongue's onslaught of her mouth and slid his palms down the side of her neck, his thumbs rubbing soothing circles on either side of her jaw.

"Samantha," he breathed as he slowed their kiss.

As their need faded from a volatile eruption of desire to smoldering embers she pulled her mouth away and pressed her forehead to his. Her eyes were squeezed together so tight she looked to be in pain. Colin shut his eyes as well, simply holding her for another moment before he had to let her go again.

When he finally pulled away he noticed the glass of the windshield was humid and starting to fog.

"We'd better go inside."

Her eyes opened and she looked at him questioningly.

He should have worded that differently. "Samantha, I can't."

She nodded solemnly and he knew if he wanted her in that moment she'd be his. "I'm sorry."

He turned and exited the car. By the time he reached the passenger side, she darted towards the house. He missed his chance to kiss her one last time.

The loss of that one last kiss was crushing. Screams of frustration stuck in his throat. For the first time since childhood, he wanted to cry. He needed that kiss and he'd never have it.

As she climbed the front steps in her bare feet he wondered if the pain of not having her would ever go away. If for the rest of his life he would always long for that last kiss, that extra caress, that final look back. She wouldn't look at him now.

She waited by the door for him, head hung, gaze averted with a curtain of hair preventing him from reading her expression. It wasn't fair for him to keep doing this to her. He was killing himself, but the idea of hurting her made his actions a thousand times worse.

He opened the door and flipped on the hall light. Slowly, she marched up the steps and he followed. Not a word was spoken. The air was thick with longing and regret. Enough. It had to be enough.

Her heart was something sacred that should not be abused. There was no excuse for hurting her anymore. It was obvious what this was doing to her—to them. No matter how much pleasure they drew from one another, there would always be a goodbye. And soon that goodbye would be final.

He stood at his bedroom door and she stood at his brother's.

"Goodnight, Samantha."

"Goodnight, Colin."

He thought he heard tears in her voice, but by the time he looked back at her she was already in the room with the door closed. He sighed and went into his own room and shut the door behind him.

Tossing off his shirt perfumed by the smoky scent of campfire he forked his fingers through his hair and pressed his palms into his desk. Leaning over the surface, he played back the last half an hour in his mind and berated himself.

He tried to think back to his theology courses for the slightest anchor that would remind him of who he was. He fought to recall the way he felt the day he received his letter of acceptance into the Affiliation Program, but could not recreate the feeling of elation.

His mind recalled the first day he met his good friend and mentor, Father Tucker, but the memory played flat. The pride and satisfaction he experienced while in Dublin working as a missionary was still very real, but any man could do community service. He was not to be any man, but a holy man, yet he could not grasp the feeling of sacredness.

He allowed himself to become a profane example of all that he stood for and believed in. And the worst part was that he recognized his complete lack of concern for what was happening to him and didn't know how to alter his perception, how to get back those old ideals.

"Fuck!" He shoved the desk against the wall and stood.

He paced for a few minutes and then decided that while he couldn't correct all his faults at the moment he could at least calm his inner being and eradicate temptation with a cold shower. He went to the bathroom and opened the door and came up short when he saw Samantha, towel in hand, and face pink, with wet tracks of tears running down her cheeks.

Shit.

He suddenly thought of a verse from the Old Testament. *Like a fire burning in my heart, imprisoned in my bones; I grow weary of holding it in.* It was the verse that helped him recognize his call to the church, only now it had taken on new meaning.

She had become the fire burning in his heart, trapped by his bones and scalding every last bit of common sense and devotion to his cause from his mind. He was so, so weary of holding his desire for her in. He simply wanted to surrender and let it all out. To be freed, once and for all, of this agony.

She met his gaze and swallowed as if about to say something, but then came up short.

God, the pain was clear on her face.

He had done that to her and he was a bloody selfish prick for playing with her emotions. She shook her head and looked down. Another tear glided past her spiked lashes until it disappeared beneath her jaw and diluted to nothing upon her slender neck. Those tears should not be wasted.

Watching them fall was as sacrilegious as watching one dump holy water. Both, sacred waters wasted.

As they stood, facing off in silence, her arm dropped as if too weak to hold itself up anymore. The folded towel unraveled and touched the floor. Her fingers loosened and the cloth feathered out of her palm and to the ground beside her feet. And that was the moment he truly became undone.

Perhaps it was witnessing her complete surrender to sadness. Or perhaps it was that one lone tear. He would never know for certain, but he was pretty sure he realized he loved her the moment he spotted the polish upon her toes, pale pink, almost clear, like the inner soft side of a seashell.

He took two steady steps toward her and ignored her surprised gasp as he scooped her into his arms and carried her straight to her bed, hesitating before lying her down. The room was too much his brother's. There was simply too many signs of Braydon there for him to face at the moment.

He turned and carried her back into his room and shut the bathroom door with the heel of his foot. Much better. He looked around, not quite sure if he should lay her on the bed or let her stand. Unsure of himself he looked down at her face and saw she was leaving all decisions up to him.

Right. The bed then. No, the floor. The floor is safer.

She must have realized his indecision because he heard

her giggle and looked down and saw poorly disguised amusement dancing in her eyes. He would take her laughing at his expense any day before tears.

Feeling foolish, he finally admitted, "I don't really know what to do here."

She laughed. "Why don't we talk?"

"Okay. Where?"

She looked around. Other than his desk chair there really wasn't anywhere else to sit. "The bed?"

It seemed so final to go to the bed. They could sit there and talk. They'd just have to keep things within their control.

He quickly played through a list of what if's and the pros and cons of the bed versus his lack of other options until finally, completely disgusted with himself, he mentally called himself a pussy—which oddly made him feel more like a man and less like a priest—and sat her on the bed.

He pulled the desk chair over and sat across from her. Now what?

After a moment she made an adorable face that he interpreted as her mentally saying, well, this is awkward.

They both laughed uncomfortably. Someone needed to say something, so he figured he might as well be the one to break the ice.

"I'm sorry."

All amusement left her face and was replaced with fear. "Please stop apologizing," she whispered.

"But I am—"

"I know. But every time you apologize you say goodbye."

"Oh."

He wanted to say sorry for that too, but figured it best if he refrained.

"I'll try not to do that anymore."

She blushed. He loved the way that behind all that assumed confidence and American girl charm there was something definitively demure lurking.

"Are you a virgin?" He had no idea where the question came from, but couldn't regret asking it, even when he saw he had shocked her. Her blush moved from soft pink to crimson.

"I...well...I'm twenty-four."

"And I'm twenty-nine."

"You're different."

"So are you. Answer the question, Sammy. I'm not going to ask you to say a Rosary."

"Yes. There was one guy, but he wasn't right for me and we broke up before it got that far. Since then I've dated, but not really ever felt serious enough about anyone to go that far."

The relief he felt that she had definitely not slept with Braydon was immeasurable.

"You are too, right?"

He laughed. "Being that I had my first real shot at making out the other day, what do you think?"

The side of her mouth kicked up, forming a small dimple in her cheek. "Good."

He sobered for a minute. "You know I can't."

He regretted that his words caused her smile and dimple to disappear. "I know. We shouldn't anyway. It isn't right."

"Don't think I don't want to, Samantha. I look at you and feel as if I'll crawl out of my skin if I don't touch you. You make me feel things I've never felt. But my path was chosen years ago. It's all I've ever wanted and I'm only months away from getting there. I cannot...It would confuse things, that's all. And it would be wrong for me to take something that's meant for your husband."

"I'm not a virgin by choice, Colin. It has nothing to do with religion or God or anything other than I never met a man worth giving it to."

He wanted to know if she'd give it to him if he asked, but knew that would only be inviting trouble.

Instead, he inquired, "Why do you dislike the church so much?"

She laughed without humor. "If there is a God, He's cruel and selfish and no friend of mine."

His heart ached to hear such disdain for the one ideal his life had been dedicated to. She wasn't the first to express such views to him, but for some reason it made him feel like he had even less of her approval he assumed he had a moment ago.

"God loves us all, Sammy."

"Do not speak pious platitudes to me, Colin McCullough. You have no idea what my life was before I came here."

She was right. He was only being given this small snippet of her and he wanted more.

"Tell me."

"No."

"Why not?"

"Because you'll comfort me and I'll only love you more fiercely for it and in the end I'll be destroyed all the more."

He stilled. Did she realize what she just said?

She looked up at him, a frown crinkling her brow. "What?"

"Did you hear yourself, Sammy? What you said?"

"That I'll only love you more? Yes. I know what I said."

He wanted to convince her it wasn't so. Somehow persuade her so their separation wouldn't be as monumentally heart wrenching in the end. He took both her hands in his.

"Sammy, what this is, what you feel for me, it isn't love. You're just infatuated right now."

"Do not presume to tell me how I feel, Colin. I know my heart. People assume it takes years and months to love someone and that our affection must be rationed to only the best of the best. Well, I think that's bullshit. Life's too short not to tell those we love that they mean something to us. What I feel for you…you may never be my husband, or my lover, or even my friend, but there is a very real part of me that loves you. Maybe it's because of the way you are with the others, maybe it's the way you helped me when I lost it at the lake, or maybe it's because I'll never completely have you, but whatever it is, it's real and you will not take it away from me because it makes this more difficult for you."

She was right. He loved her too. Still, he wanted to

convince her otherwise. How had things gotten so out of control? "Who did you lose the chance to say I love you to?"

She looked down and he tipped her chin back up gently.

"I'll never have the pleasure of being all those things to you, Samantha, but let me know you. Give me something of yourself I'll never lose once I take my vows. Something to always hold onto. We're friends."

Her gaze lowered as if she were suddenly engulfed in sadness, an abyss of memories only she could see.

"My sister."

His blood turned to ice at her words.

"She was twelve. I was fourteen. I could've saved her. Do you know what it feels like to know you had a chance to make everything different but you made the wrong choice and let it all slip away? It's an unrelenting guilt that never leaves, a daily reminder that your life should have been different and will always be a little duller, a little less happy, always halfway full. And when you try to convince yourself it's time to let the guilt go, something reminds you of all the others you hurt by choosing wrong, and you sentence yourself to a million more years of guilt and know it'll still never be enough to reverse what's been done."

"I'm so sorry, Samantha. I had no idea."

Her eyes shimmered with unshed tears, but he could tell she was working very hard not to let them fall. Was that part of her sentence? Did she take away her right to cry for her own pain over losing her sister?

He moved to the bed and pulled her into his arms. His soul needed to comfort her. Needed to hold her. This was what she was afraid of, him doing just that and making their situation all the more complicated. He should have just let her muddle through, but he couldn't. He was a selfish bastard.

His lips kissed her temple and breathed in the clean scent of her hair laced with traces of smoke from the bonfire. Somehow their bodies twisted and settled so that his back rested against the headboard and her head rested on his chest. He continued to run his fingers over her hair, his palm over her shoulders, touching her anyway he could, as she spoke.

"It was winter and so cold even the Delaware had partially frozen over. Big blocks of white ice floated on the surface and all the foliage along the banks was temporarily frozen in place in the direction of whatever way the wind had last blown.

"We grew up between the creek and the river. Whenever it was cold enough we'd skate on the canal. That was the coldest winter I had ever seen. One morning, Meghan and I decided we'd go down to the canal to see if it was ready. My parents told us to wait for them, but I was fourteen and in no need of parental advice. We bundled up, grabbed our skates and headed across the frosted yard and into the woods. The canal was on the perimeter of our property, but still a ways from the house.

"As soon as we got there we smiled. It was a perfect canvas of untouched ice. We laced up our skates and tossed our shoes to the side. Meghan was the first to hit the ice. I was still lacing up my one skate as I watched her wobble through the dried decaying autumn leaves and down the bank. She stepped onto the ice just as I was standing and I rushed to catch up to her, afraid she'd hog all the fun and mark the ice before I had a chance. We liked to try and write our names in the surface with the blades of our skates and see who could make the best figure eight. She laughed as she coasted onto the ice and I told her I was going to race her to the bridge and win.

"When my foot first touched the surface there was a weird sound in the distance. When ice breaks, it doesn't sound like you think it should. It isn't loud, or rolling, it's soft, like a cloud breaking off and floating to a different part of the sky. I didn't know what I heard, but I looked anyway. There was a layer of frost on the surface so it was difficult to see any fractures. When I heard the sound again it was followed by Meghan's squealing laughter as she raced down the canal toward the bridge. That was when it hit me and I realized what the sound was.

"I screamed her name as hard as I could and rushed to go after her, but before I even had both feet on the ice she'd disappeared. I never felt so alone in my entire life. Everything was silent. There wasn't a splash or a creak or even a whisper in the empty woods. It felt like an hour, but I could've only been standing there for a minute. I didn't understand why she didn't just climb back out. It was a shallow canal. In the spring it barely reached our knees.

Once I realized she was trapped under the ice I didn't know what to do. I thought to skate over to where she fell through, but hesitated; afraid I might fall in as well. I wanted to run for help, but with my skates it would've taken to long and been too late. The only thing I could think to do was trudge across the bank and get to where she had fallen. I kept talking to her as if she were right beside me the entire time, 'It's okay, Meghan. I'm coming, Meghan. We'll get you out and Mom will make cocoa and let you use the heated blanket to get warm again.' I think I even made a joke that while she was being babied I would be grounded for life for not listening to our parents.

"By the time I reached the hole in the ice I was flushed and sweating. I bit off my mittens and carefully crawled toward the opening. For a minute I thought she somehow tricked me. The hole seemed too small for her to fit through and there was a branch sticking out which told me the water was really shallow where she'd gone through. I actually looked around to see if she was hiding somewhere and considered that the entire thing was a dream, but then I saw her hand. It was already turning blue.

"I crawled as close as I could to where she was and began clawing at the ice. I must have been screaming because at some point my mother and father were there. My dad was in his slippers still. I watched him step into the water and try to break away the ice. He eventually got through it with the use of a heavy branch, but it was too late. Meghan drowned."

Sam lost the battle with her tears. Warm wet puddles gathered on his chest. He held her and rocked her and thought of all the things he'd been advised to tell grieving family members who had lost loved ones, but none of those words seemed good enough for Samantha.

Eventually, she sat up and looked at him. Her hair was a mess and her eyes were red and puffy, yet she was still more beautiful than any woman he'd ever seen. He brushed her hair away from her face and tucked it behind her ear.

"I'm so incredibly sorry you had to suffer through that and that you're still struggling with grief. Your loss is…it's something no one should have to cope with. I'm sorry, Sammy."

"Since then I've been terrified of water."

He understood that without explanation. "Is it something you're okay with or is it something you wish you could conquer?"

"I don't think anyone likes feeling afraid or weak. But it's my kryptonite. Whenever I'm close to water I become crippled with fear. I've tried hypnosis, therapy, meds, nothing helps. If I push myself I eventually shut down and have a panic attack. You saw how lovely they can be."

His fingers softly pinched her chin. "You're too much in your head. You need a distraction. I bet if you were able to let go and forget about what happened you would actually be able to swim quite well. You have to trust yourself."

"I can't swim. I haven't done it since I was thirteen. Besides, I think it would be impossible to swim while hyperventilating which is exactly what would happen if I tried."

"And that's why you need to be distracted."

He kissed her lips softly, unable to resist the temptation.

"I sometimes fill in as a lifeguard at the youth center. I'm certified in CPR and even competed on the swim team in high school. If you'd like, I could teach you. I'd never force you if you were afraid, but I could go to the lake with you or to the community pool and we could try some techniques out, see how close to the water you can get. The moment you feel a panic attack coming on, you tell me and we return to dry ground."

"I couldn't go to a pool. It's incredibly embarrassing when I lose it. I'd be humiliated if I broke down in front of all those people."

"What about in front of me?"

"No. Not in front of you. Besides the fact that you've already seen me lose it, I trust you, Colin. I know you'd never judge me or make fun of me. I also know that you'd never let anything harm me even if it meant getting yourself hurt in the process."

To hear someone say those things about his character, actually about him, not about his vocational worth or intent, was incredibly moving. So many others saw him as a figure in a gown, although he had yet to earn that robe. The moment he announced his intentions of becoming a priest, people began treating him differently. From that moment he had always felt a little bit farther away, on the outside looking in. Even his family sometimes held him at arms' length as if he couldn't possibly understand what everyday life involved.

Not Samantha, though. She made him feel as if he

belonged. Had a place right by her side where he would always fit in. Until she left and he took his vows that was.

"What is it?" she asked curling up on her knees more.

"What?"

"Your expression just turned so sad."

"Oh, I was just thinking."

"About what?" She ran her fingertips lightly over his chest and he wondered if she was even aware that she was touching him.

"My fears."

"What do you fear, Colin?"

"Losing you."

Her hand stilled. She glanced at him as if weighing his sincerity.

He was being completely genuine. In ten years he had been unwavering about his purpose in this life, yet since meeting Samantha, he began wondering if there was a path that led to a more rewarding life. A life by her side.

He wanted her, but he'd always heard that love fades. He loved God and the church. His vocation was like a burning in his bones, but now a new burn had started to grow and he wasn't sure what to do anymore. The reality was that he'd never be brave enough to throw it all away on a whim. It would make a mockery of all his hard work and sacrifice thus far and if he made a mistake, it would be Samantha who would take the brunt of the consequence.

"You'll be an incredible wife someday to a very lucky man, Sammy. Perhaps you'll ask me to perform the ceremony."

Coldness settled in her eyes and he wondered if he

said too much. He was only trying to ground them both with a dose of reality, but she clearly didn't appreciate it.

"Don't try to push me away with passive aggressive comments, Colin. If you want me to go, I'll go, but at least have the courage to ask for what you want."

She was right. It was a cheap shot intended to cut, but again, he wounded her in the process. He was about to say sorry, but didn't want her to misinterpret it as goodbye. "You're right. I shouldn't have made such a comment. It was insensitive and I was only being spiteful at myself, but unintentionally hurt you. I'll try not to do that anymore."

"Well, after all that now I feel badly. Just be honest with me. Don't patronize me or try to pretend this is leading to a place that it's not. I understand what the reality is. I'm a big girl. But you need to be honest with me or things will only get more confusing than they already are."

"You're right."

She settled back down by his side and he held her close. They continued to talk for several more hours about everything from how they spent most of their days as children, to what their kindergarten teachers' names were, to whom they took to the prom. With every word Colin recognized they were only making the inevitable harder on themselves, but neither one of them seemed to care.

By four a.m. the others had all come home and they laughed as they heard them stumbling down the hall. Sammy had grown sleepy and was only speaking in one word answers that didn't always match the questions he asked.

He needed to say goodnight, but he hated the idea of letting her go. When she didn't answer his last question or reply, he softly whispered her name. Carefully, he sat up and lifted her into his arms. She grumbled and cuddled closer to his chest.

He carried her through the bathroom and into his brother's room, holding her in one arm and pulled the covers back, careful not to jostle her too much. When he laid her down he saw that she was once again awake.

"Will you hide from me now?"

"No. I'm through hiding."

She shut her eyes and smiled. "Love you, Colin McCullough."

He fought so hard to not say the words back. Pressing his lips tight, he kissed his fingertips and touched them to her forehead. Her breathing settled and she had once again drifted off.

"Love you too, Sammy."

CHAPTER 11

*W*hen Sam awoke on Saturday half the house was empty. Frank and the majority of his children and his nephews had gone on a fishing trip. With all that they had discussed the night before, Samantha wasn't sure what Colin's plans were. She didn't have to wait long to find out.

As she sat on the bed tying her shoe there was a knock on the bathroom door. She stood and reached to open the door. Colin stood in the doorway holding her shampoo.

"Hey," she greeted.

"Hey," he said, leaning around the doorjamb as if he was looking for something. "I ran out of shampoo and was wondering if I could use some of—" Satisfied that they were alone, he tossed the shampoo onto the counter and tugged her against his chest then yanked the bathroom door closed. His lips found hers and her body thrilled at the way he kissed her. How cute was he making up stories about shampoo so he had an excuse to knock on her door?

"God, you taste good." He said as he plopped her bottom onto the counter.

He leaned into her and her knees came up, clamping around his hips. Holy shit, he was kissing her like a mad man. Her body was already trembling, her sex moistening, and her breasts heavy and wanting to be touched. In a moment of pure blind courage she grabbed for his hand and slid it under the hem of her t-shirt.

His fingertips burned against the flesh of her belly and thankfully he didn't break their kiss or pull away. However he also didn't go to her breasts. His hand curled around her waist and squeezed her in a way that had her sex weeping. His mouth ripped from hers and began to kiss her neck.

When his mouth latched onto the lobe of her ear and he sucked, his breath tickling and sending shivers racing down her spine and across her nipples, she moaned. "Oh my God, Colin."

Teeth nipped at her neck and licked up to her jaw. *Holy mother of God.* Never before in her life had she felt like this. She rocked against him and loved the feel of his arousal bumping her sensitive clit. She finally understood so much about things that had always been a mystery to her before now.

Suddenly he stood to his full height and in one swift move he pulled her shirt off of her body as if he were skinning a rabbit. His eyes lit at the sight of her breasts and his breathing grew deeper. Watching him, although his gaze was on her chest, she sat up and unsnapped the center clasp at the front of her simple cotton bra. The cups sprung apart, but clung to the inner curve of each mound. His eyes widened in fascination as she leaned back onto her palms and waited for him to make the next move.

He glanced at her, then back to her breasts, then back to her face. She gave him a tilt of her head that told him it was his call. Slowly, reverently, he reached forward and nudged the cups away from her breasts exposing two tight brown nipples.

He audibly sucked in a breath and touched the underside of her breast with the back of his knuckle. "Jesus, Mary, and Joseph, Sammy, the more I see of you the more perfect you appear. God is surely testing me."

She didn't want him to talk about God now.

"Touch me, Colin. Please."

He looked at her, a battle of emotions playing in his eyes.

"I'm not sure I know how. I've never done anything like this before. I knew it would only tempt me to read about it, so I'm sadly ignorant. I wouldn't want to do something you didn't like."

"I'll tell you if you do something I don't like. Honesty, remember? Just do what you feel. What your instincts tell you is right."

"I'm afraid I won't ever want to stop touching you."

God, that would be nice. "It doesn't matter. We only have this time. Don't make me wonder for the rest of my life what your touch would've been like. Please, Colin. I've never wanted like this before."

He looked to the door as if checking to see if they were closed. When he seemed satisfied that no one would come barging in, he reached forward with both hands and gently pinched her nipples. Calloused fingers curved around the weight of each breast. She arched into his touch, wanting more, and moaned.

"Does that feel good?"

"Yes, hold me there, Colin."

His large masculine hands cupped her soft skin. He held her heavy breasts in his palms and coasted his thumbs over her nipples. With each touch of his flesh over hers, her sex tightened. She wanted more.

As he played and experimented with different ways to touch and hold her there, she began to undulate and squirm. Her body was needy and she wanted to tear off his clothing and pull him down to her so his flesh pressed into her, forming pockets of heat in between them until they clung together and could only be peeled apart.

She eyed the bulge straining behind his zipper and knew he must be painfully aroused, yet he seemed completely unconcerned with his own comfort and satisfaction. The male organ had always intimidated her, but the thought of seeing Colin there, completely naked for her, was likely the most erotic thought she'd ever entertained. Samantha reached for him and his arm shot out and caught her wrist.

"No." He looked terrified as if she were going to cut it off.

She had obviously gone too far.

"O-okay, Colin."

She tried to retrieve her hand but he held it tight.

He looked at her with such desperation she didn't understand what he wanted.

His voice was a rasp, a caress over her senses. "If you touch me it will all be over. I won't be able to stop."

Like a bucket of ice water, reality crashed over her once again. This was all they would ever have, satisfaction that ultimately left them unfulfilled. Her spine curled and her shoulders drew in to try and shelter herself while he still held her wrist. A sense of shame for being a fool knifed through her. He pulled her hand to his mouth and kissed the backs of her fingertips.

Did he want her to leave? Should she stop? She didn't understand where he was at that moment and didn't want to push him or make him feel guilty.

"What do you want, Colin?"

"All of you."

He shut his eyes for a moment and released her wrist. When he opened them again his gaze locked with hers. His sapphire eyes turned a deep shade of emerald. She loved seeing them change like that.

"I want so much, Sammy, I don't know how to hold it all in."

She shook her head in sympathy. At what point did a sacrifice become worthless? How much more would he deny himself? There was a good possibility that this was all they would ever have, a few stolen kisses and secret moments of heavy petting.

"Then let some of it go, Colin. Let it out. You told me you were first a man before all else. Let yourself be a man."

His eyes hardened as if she somehow offended him. He looked at her challengingly and she wasn't sure what she said that triggered that reaction. She hadn't meant to insult him or question his manhood. She only meant to repeat the words he'd said to her earlier that week.

He swallowed and stood a little taller, suddenly seeming bigger, greater, and more confident. The change was not subtle. As a matter of fact, it was so obvious she felt as though gentle Colin had suddenly left the building and a stranger now stood across from her.

Before she understood what he was doing he had her wrist again and tugged her down from the counter. The moment her feet hit the tile floor he spun her around to face the mirror. His hands glided down her arms and placed her palms on the edge of the counter. He gave her a little press as if that would keep them there.

"Don't move."

Perhaps she should've been worried about the change in his disposition, but she was too turned on and caught in the moment to process what she should and shouldn't be feeling. He kicked her feet apart and her stance widened. Colin stepped close behind her and his length pressed against her back.

"You tell me if it's no good, Sammy, and I'll stop."

She looked at him in the mirror, catching a glimpse of her own body braced before him, breasts full and swaying with tightly pulled tips, and nodded. His hands first touched her hips, massaging and feeling their way into a comfortable niche. Once he found his hold he tugged her against him with both hands. The clash of his body crashing against hers made her moan. She wanted him to do it again.

Soft lips found her shoulder and he kissed and nibbled her there. Her head lolled to the side and against his muscled chest. He continued to rub himself against her bottom as his hands slid over her hips and circled her belly. His mouth kissed a trail from one shoulder, across her back, and to the other then down her spine.

Sam's knees quivered, ready to give out. Her panties were so wet the fabric buckled below her moist folds.

When he kissed his way back up her spine her body was so sensitized anything harder than a feather light caress would make her shatter. His hands glided up the front of her and cupped her breasts tightly, practically pressing them into her. The pressure was divine. He melded her to his form and held her body in place with his strong hands. She moaned, breathy and long. Strong fingers squeezed as he continued to kiss her neck.

His hands slowly released hers only to adjust so that his fingers could pinch and pluck at her nipples. Oddly, the firmer he grasped her sensitive tips, the more pleasure she derived from his touch. He rocked against her so much that her pelvis was now against the hard edge of the counter. She shamelessly began to use the edge to create friction where she needed it.

When Colin realized what she was doing he yanked her back against his hips cutting off all contact with the counter aside from where her hands still held. His sea colored eyes shot her a reproving look in the mirror and then his hand reached between her legs and gripped her sex over her khaki shorts.

It was too much. Her legs crumbled, but he banded an arm around her ribs and held her up. His hand massaged over the crease of her shorts. When the curve of his hard fingers pressed against her wet panties, separating her, and rubbed against her hard needy clit she cried out. He bit down on her shoulder and sucked at her flesh as she came.

When her body finished climaxing she was a quivering mess. Colin kissed her gently and turned her to face him. He held her close and kissed her on the mouth until her equilibrium was somewhat restored. When they pulled apart she was still seeing stars.

He gazed at her through thick lashes and whispered, "I always want you to see me as a man first, Samantha. When I'm with you, I can shamelessly think of nothing else."

SAM WAITED in the kitchen for Colin and helped Maureen snap green beans for dinner. The woman never stopped. It was nice, sitting with her, idly chitchatting about everything and nothing at all.

"And what are you up to today, dear?"

"I was thinking about going to the lake," Sam said as she tossed a few more snapped beans into a large faded plastic bowl.

"Oh, that should be nice. You didn't want to go on the boat with the rest of them?"

"I'm not really a boat person."

Maureen gave her a dubious smile and stage whispered, "Neither am I, but don't tell Frank that. I much prefer to keep my feet on the land where my cheeks are rosy and not faded kelly-green."

Sam chuckled and stifled her excitement when Colin walked into the room. His hair was wet from the shower he insisted he needed after their time in the bathroom earlier. He walked over to his mother and placed a smacking kiss on her cheek.

"Mum," he greeted and she tapped two light smacks on his cheek before he could pull away.

"Yer awfully pleasant this morning, Colin dear."

"And why shouldn't I be? It's a beautiful day and I'm off to the lake to relax and embrace the lazy days of summer."

"Oh, Samantha's heading there, too..." Her words faded off and she looked toward Colin. Sam thought she saw her fingers tremble as she continued to snap the beans. "Yer brother'll be wantin' to know where you've all gotten off to. I'll be sure to let him know where you are when he returns."

Sam looked at Colin, suddenly fearful that his mother had come to the true conclusion of what was happening between them. He didn't notice her concern, or at least pretended not to.

He only smiled at his mother and said, "Good. I haven't

seen enough of Bray since I've been home. Tell him I said to come find us when he gets back."

Maureen seemed to sag in relief, her shoulders deflating as some of the tension left her. "Of course, my dear. Now you two run along and have a good time. I'll finish up here, Samantha."

When they arrived at the lake all was quiet. Sam supposed that was the glory of owning your own private beach.

"Did your family make this lake or is it natural?"

"It's man made, but not from us. We've expanded over the years. Our property line's slowly grown and we've accumulated quite a few of other people's plots. This belonged to our neighbors. They headed farther north and gave us first dibs at their spread. We'd always swum here as children so it just seemed right that we own it. Who knew if other buyers would've let us continue to swim here?" He placed their chairs on the sand and leaned in to kiss her quickly on the mouth.

She pulled away and looked around. "Colin, someone might see."

"There's nobody here, Sammy. It's just us."

"But you told your mom to tell Braydon to come down when he returned."

"Yes, and if I know my father and the rest of them, that won't be until dinner. You can relax. No one will sneak up on us."

She relented and spread her towel over her chair. Colin took off his shirt and sat in the chair beside hers. He spread lotion over his arms and shoulders. She was so mesmerized by his body, she may have stopped breathing for a moment. Feeling suddenly brazen, she pulled off her own t-shirt and dropped it into the bag.

"You better make sure you put some block on. The sun's—" He stuttered when he looked up at her and Sam fought a smile at having such an effect on him. She held her hand out for the lotion and he handed it to her as if he were a wooden puppet with only his arm tied to a string. "I didn't expect you to own a suit like that."

She laughed. "I don't own anything like this," she said looking down at the narrow blue patches held together with floss. "This is Sheilagh's."

"I have to have a talk with that girl."

She looked up from rubbing lotion on her chest. "Why? You don't like it?"

"I like it very much. On you. On my baby sister...not so much."

"Well, that's a double standard."

"If you knew what I was thinking right now you would understand."

She smiled and then let the topic drop as she applied block to her legs and feet. They sat for a couple hours just talking. Every once in a while they'd simply sit in silence. Colin's hand would find hers and their fingers would link between the arms of their chairs. It was silly to get such a rush from such simple contact, but to Sam it was one of the most intimate experiences of her life.

When the sun became unbearably hot she considered suggesting they head back, but bit her tongue because she didn't want the day to end. Once they were back at the house there'd be no holding hands or personal talk.

"Come on," Colin said, standing from his chair. His skin glistened with perspiration.

She looked up at him and squinted. He was so tall his body faded into a silhouette blurring with the backdrop of the blazing white sun.

"Where are we going?"

"We're going to walk down and put our feet in the water."

COLIN LOOKED DOWN at Sammy shading her eyes from his view and hoped he was doing the right thing. He didn't want to push her too fast or too hard. They'd been at the lake for quite a while so she had some time to adjust. He hoped she was ready to take this step.

"Just our toes, Sammy. You don't even have to get your ankles wet."

He followed her gaze toward the lake. It was calm, mirroring the trees and mountains like a second escape into a beautiful underground world. He waited.

He knew she was warring with herself and her fears as well as her desire to not let him down, but this wasn't about him. This was about her letting go of the pain associated with losing her sister Meghan.

He glanced around to try to see the world the way she saw it. To him, the land was beautiful, breathtaking, serene, but to her it was likely frightening, powerful, and superior in an intimidating way.

He pointed to a scrubby patch of trees forming a hedgerow at the edge of the beach. "Let's walk over to those trees and back."

She followed his finger to where he pointed, actually having to turn her head in the opposite direction of the water because the trees were that far from the bank. He saw the moment her flaccid confidence grew into unthreatened surety.

"Okay."

He helped her up. Her skin was warm and slightly pinker then when they first arrived. They strolled along the beach with slow steps and watched as their feet kicked up little grains of sand.

"What classes do you have to take when you go back?" He could have asked about her parents or something more personal, but he wanted to keep things general and loose, all thoughts away from the past.

"Classroom Management and I need three more credits in Spanish."

"You speak Spanish?"

She laughed. They were halfway to the grove. "Not really. I can decipher it enough to figure out the general message if it's written down, but I'm awful at speaking it."

"*¿Y qué sucede cuando alguien habla español para usted?*"

She stopped walking and grinned. "You speak Spanish?"

"*Sí.*" He reached for her hand, giving a soft tug for her to keep walking.

"Well, I have no idea what you just said."

"Then you answered my question."

Glancing sideways at him, she asked, "What did you say?"

"I asked if you could understand the language when someone speaks it aloud to you."

She giggled. "No."

They approached the thicket of trees and the sand became coarser with each step. He spotted a few bramble branches and burrs hidden in their path and decided they better not get any closer in bare feet. Colin casually turned them back toward the lake.

"What kind of stuff do you learn in Classroom Management?"

"Strategies and techniques for keeping students in line and not letting them run you out of the classroom."

Colin tried to imagine Samantha in front of a schoolroom of young, boisterous teenagers. He couldn't quite meld the soft image of her with a severe governess type persona he guessed she'd sometimes have to employ.

"Are you nervous?"

"Yes and no. I've already done my student teaching so a lot of my apprehension has been put to rest. I'm more concerned I won't have time to find a job by September or not have the time to get my classroom together."

They'd passed their chairs about twenty feet from the bank.

"Have you sent out resumes yet?"

"Yes. When you get a degree in education you have to keep a portfolio. It's this big book of all your philosophies and samples and pictures from your experiences as well as all your transcripts. I have that done, which is good, because I actually have a few interviews lined up for July."

"Are they in the city or closer to home?"

"For now they're closer to home. I'll have to give up my apartment because it's considered student housing. I really don't want to look for a place to live and start a new career at the same time, so I figured staying with my parents until I get my feet on the ground is better."

She gasped. Speaking of feet, theirs just touched the water.

The cool water skimmed his arches. He wanted to keep her distracted.

"Do you think you'll miss the city?"

"Yes and no."

He pulled her close and wrapped his arms around her waist so that her back was to his chest and his chin rested on her warm, soft hair. They simply swayed together and he gloried in how wonderfully she filled his arms.

"There are a lot of things I despise about the city."

"Like?"

"The noise, the pollution, the people who are perpetually rude like it's their birth right."

He chuckled and moved them forward a smidge. Her shoulders tensed, but he didn't acknowledge her apprehension. His arms crossed over her bare belly, his left hand resting on her right hip and vise-versa. He massaged her skin lightly.

"Was the school you student taught at in the city?"

"Um..." She answered as if it were a difficult question, likely she was having a hard time with their position. The

water crested their feet and was now just below mid-calf.
"I...what?"

"The school you did your student teaching at, was it in
the city?"

"Oh. Yes."

"Where about?"

Her breathing became slightly labored but nothing like
the other day when she suffered a panic attack. With
every brush of his fingertips along her skin, her body
seemed to relax into his by small degrees.

"With traffic it was about twenty minutes from
campus."

"And how far is campus from home?"

"About forty minutes. It's mostly highway, but then
you get into the city and it takes forever."

He nudged her forward a step and asked, "Are you
considering applying to that school?"

"Yes. They already have my resume and I have a good
rapport with the faculty there."

"How far would a commute be from there to home?"

"Probably about thirty minutes, because it's not as
ensconced in the city as my apartment."

A light breeze danced across the surface. Branches
swayed slowly and he was mesmerized by the way Samantha's skin prickled from her shoulders to her neck leaving
a dusting of goose bumps. The water was warmer than
most times of the year, but still cool over their skin. He
kissed the side of her neck.

"I think you'll be a wonderful teacher."

She grew quiet and he wondered what she was thinking about.

Finally she said, "And you'll be a great priest."

His mouth opened and he hesitated. Shutting his eyes, he said, "I hope so."

"You will. You have this calming quality about you. It's enchanting. Between that and your looks I imagine your female parishioners will be so up in arms it'll be worse than the tales of Father Ralph de Bricassart from the *Thorn Birds*."

"And are you to be my Meggie? The woman that haunts my dreams and owns a piece of me God will never have?"

She stepped out of his embrace and turned to face him. "No, Colin. Meggie led a tragic life and I won't sentence myself to such a fate. She was the thorn bird that sang only once then bludgeoned her heart as a price for that short song. When you give yourself to the church, give all of you. It's torture to emotionally be in two places at once. True love is a complete surrender without regret or ever looking back. You'll be marrying the church and that's where your heart must lie, same as I'll someday give my heart over to my husband without reserve. I'll never forget our time here, but I plan to work damn hard to. I can't put myself through a lifetime of wanting what I'll never have. I will not 'pierce my breast for the glory of one song' that'll never be sung back to me."

He brushed a wisp of hair away from her face. She was so reasonable yet somehow had an incredibly romantic soul.

"I'll always envy the man that marries you, Sammy. I'll confess it first among all sins until the day I die. I know I shouldn't, but the heart is a muscle with reflexes of its own that we have no control over. You will always be my one thing left unfinished, the masterpiece that slipped away."

She gazed up at him with slightly trembling shoulders. He wondered if she shook, not because of her fear of the water, but because the reality of his words. He hadn't lied. He'd never forget her. She was the first and only woman he had ever cared for to such a degree. He needed her then in such a way it shook him to his core.

Slowly leaning down, so not to break the emotionally laden moment, he pressed his mouth to hers. Their bodies touched only at their lips as he sipped from her. Her small tongue skated over his lower lip and he smiled. He had never imagined kissing to be so intoxicating.

Slowly, she took a small step closer to him and her breasts pressed into his chest. Under the inconsequential scraps of fabric, her pebbled nipples gently stabbed into his skin. His arms wrapped tightly around her and the kiss intensified, picking up speed and overflowing with need.

Her body tipped back as he deepened the kiss. He somehow managed to lower her to the ground and settled himself on top of her. She gasped. Cool water crossed their sun kissed thighs and electrified his senses. Her shorts became wet, forming a film over her skin, and sand clumped to their flesh like grits of glue. They were only at the bank, sitting upon the water's edge, so when he eased her back the ripples of the lake lapped at her hips, but left her shoulders dry.

Dark hair spiraled around her face like a dark halo, small flecks of yellow sand interrupting the solid chestnut sheen. He tugged at the string around her neck and watched as her top came loose. Raising her arms above her head, she knotted her fingers together and rested them in the sand. He pulled both sides of the string toward her belly, flipping the cups covering her breasts back, exposing two tightly puckered nipples.

In her position, her breasts appeared less full then they had earlier that day when she'd leaned over the counter of the sink. They seemed smaller, but still magnificently feminine. He brought his hand to her flesh and cupped her breast, granules of sand creating a friction that wasn't there before. Instinctively he bowed his head and sucked one tight nipple into his mouth.

Samantha moaned and arched farther into his touch. She tasted fresh yet salty. So close to her skin he could smell the fragrant lotion she had used earlier. His other hand found her other breast and cupped it firmly from the soft underside. He dragged his thumb back and forth over the turgid tip.

Sucking her nipple deeper in his mouth, he lightly held it between his teeth as he drew his tongue back and forth over the fleshy nub. She squirmed beneath him and he switched his attention to her other nipple.

Colin kissed and suckled and licked at her flesh until she was a fury of confused moans and movement. Sammy's slow motions became frantic as though she longed for that satisfying end, but also didn't want the pleasure to stop. Garbled words of love left her lips.

His body heated to such degrees he could no longer feel the heat of the sun. He was the sun, a fire burning so intensely for this woman beneath him he feared he'd burst into a million pieces and never be able to put himself back together again. She was changing him and once changed, certain parts of him would never be the same.

His mouth crashed down upon hers and he kissed her with the magnified intensity of a million emotions colliding into one. He loved her. He loved her in a way that rivaled even his love for the Holy Father. His body shook, and she suddenly pushed against him and he rolled onto his back.

With quick little movements she climbed upon his body and straddled his hips. Her mouth found his again and their potent kiss continued. As her knees sank firmly into the sand on either side of him, their bodies molded to one another's. She rocked her hips over him. Their bodies were sealed so tightly together, that if not for their clothing, he would be inside of her.

At the thought of entering her, his entire being shivered. Would she be warm? Soft? Wet? She rode him as she kissed him with so much passion it was as if she could no longer contain it all.

A fire in my heart, imprisoned in my bones; I grow weary of holding it in.

As she dragged her pelvis over his, something shifted inside of him. It was as though she cradled his erection in her hands, every movement sending sensations splintering through him, igniting every nerve. Her touch singed him in such an addictive way he never wanted her to stop. The warmth of her core penetrated her shorts and his. Like tiny fingers tickling his shaft, squeezing, pressing, dragging, she gripped him with her core. He was going to ejaculate. He should stop her, but all common sense vanished.

He gripped her hips so tight he feared he'd leave bruises. His eyes rolled back as he dragged her faster and faster over his hardness. Her head tipped and she sat taller, allowing just the right amount of pressure to give him the most pleasure. He moaned and she cried out. Their breath had become a tribal beat building in tempo and pitch, a ceaseless tattoo, escalating to introduce some grand moment.

Through half closed eyes he watched her heavy breasts sway with each move and it was that vision that threw him over the edge. His muscles locked as his shoulders rose off the sand beneath him. Warm jets of semen poured out of him and coated his thigh. Samantha cried out again as she too found release. Their bodies trembled as one and she collapsed across his chest as breath sawed out of his lungs and blood rushed like wind in his ears.

After a few minutes of simply basking in the afterglow of such an intense climax, she finally admitted, "That was the most incredible experience I've probably ever had."

He kissed her temple. "You're stunning when you find release. So open and free. It's what I imagine bliss looks like."

She smiled, her lips pulling against his chest. She

placed a kiss there. "I hate to say it, but I think the others will be getting home soon. It's almost time for dinner."

He sighed. "We should probably start heading back."

Colin didn't want to go back. He didn't feel like being around his family. He only wanted Samantha, in his arms, touching his body, conversing for hours on end about nothing and everything under the sun. Damn it all, that their clandestine relationship had to be hidden. Colin wanted to have the right to shamelessly touch her and kiss her whenever the need struck him.

They would return to the house and pretend they were nothing more than polite acquaintances. His brother would have more right to touch her than he. He was suddenly furious with their situation. Not wanting Samantha to detect his stormy mood he nudged her to his side and stood.

"I'm going to take a quick dip to clean up. I'll be right back."

The water cooled his temper, but he still wasn't looking forward to joining the others. As he strode out of the water he caught Sammy with a peculiar grin on her face. Her smile, whatever it was for, was infectious and lightened his mood substantially.

"What are you smirking at?"

"This," she said sitting on her bottom, feet directly in front of her, and her knees drawn up to her chest. Her palms pattered the shallow inch of water beneath her making soft splashing sounds. She had remained in the water while he swam.

Colin's grin grew to a full, proud smile. "Well, look at you."

"I didn't even realize I was still sitting here until you were gone for about five minutes. Then out of habit I prepared to stand up, but I realized I wasn't feeling scared or panicky so I stayed and watched you swim."

His heart pinched with pride. "That's wonderful, Samantha."

She grinned at him and they had a moment of quiet reverence for the small, yet enormous accomplishment she'd made. To an outsider it would appear meaningless and laughable, but he knew to Samantha it was like a wall coming down. He understood she'd done more today than she'd been able to do in the past ten years and he was immeasurably proud of her small but incredible victory.

CHAPTER 12

*A*fter returning to the house Colin and Samantha slipped passed the others somewhat unnoticed. Luke and Finn were cleaning fish out front while the others helped with other preparations for dinner or disappeared upstairs to get washed up. Colin offered to let Sammy shower first while he remained in the kitchen small talking with his father about the fishing trip and cleaning corn. A while later he went upstairs to shower as well.

As he was drying off he heard the rumble of a masculine voice coming from Samantha's room followed by her softer tone. He paused to listen and realized it was Braydon.

"I'd rather not put myself through another night of Jen Miller giving me the stink eye as she hangs all over you," Samantha said.

"She probably won't even be there, Sam. Come on. We

always go to O'Malley's on Saturday nights. Everyone's going."

"Including Jen Miller."

"Don't be jealous. I know we haven't had a whole lot of time together, but you could've come on the boat today."

She scoffed. "Braydon, I am *not* jealous. I just don't like being made to look the fool."

"Well, you could always keep me company so that Jen doesn't get the opportunity to sneak in," his brother said in a cajoling voice that made Colin frown.

There was some shuffling around and Colin scowled at the door.

"Braydon, don't," Samantha said in a patient but stern voice.

"Come on, Sam. We barely spent any time together since we got here. There's still a while 'til dinner. Let's enjoy it."

Colin pulled in a furious, tight breath and ground his teeth together. He considered busting into the room and interrupting them, but he was still in his towel and his near naked appearance in front of a guest would make Braydon suspicious.

"Braydon, I said I don't feel like it."

His brother sighed. "Fine. Will you be upset if I go out tonight?"

"Do what you want. It's your vacation too."

"Are you mad at me? Did I do something wrong?"

Samantha sighed. "No. I'm just tired. I didn't sleep much last night and I'm cranky. Go to O'Malley's tonight. Have fun. We'll catch up later."

A few minutes later when Colin heard the bedroom door click closed and the sound of Sammy's soft footfalls moving around, he tapped on the bathroom door and peeked in. She was standing in the center of the room with her head flipped over, tying her hair into some sort of knot.

"Hey," he greeted softly so not to startle her.

She stood, her hair flipping back in an arc of brown. When she smiled at him he fought the urge to kiss her. It would be wise to avoid contact with the family so close by and dinner only a few minutes away.

"Hey."

"You okay? I heard you and Braydon talking."

She made an expression that told him she found the whole situation unfortunate. "Yeah. I should really talk to him, I tried, but he doesn't seem to be listening. There's this part of me that knows whatever we have going will fade by next month with him here and me back at school. Come fall he'll be back in class and I'll be teaching my own. I don't see the point in hurting him and it isn't like I can use you as an excuse."

No, it would be best if she kept his name out of it. Their situation was temporary, but the others were not. They all saw him as a son, a brother, and a priest devoid of any sexuality. It would confuse his family to imagine him as anything else. If his mother found out, she would second guess his path, and he knew he was doing what he needed to do by joining the church. The energy it would take to explain this thing with Samantha to all of them and convince them he was still intending to take his vows was a daunting hypothetical he preferred to avoid.

Rather than say as much, say what she already knew, Colin said, "I think Bray understands how you feel more now than he did yesterday. He's still your friend, Sammy. If you wanted to go to O'Malley's I would understand." But he wouldn't enjoy her being there with Braydon instead of here with him.

"I know, but I don't want to go. I meant what I said about seeing him with Jen. I swear I'm not jealous, but because I'm here with Braydon and he does nothing to stop her, he makes me look like a fool. He can do what he wants, but I'm not going to come out with claws over a boy I'm really not interested in, nor am I going to sit there and look like a pathetic doormat. He can take her to bed for all I care, so long as he isn't flaunting it in front of me and the rest of the family."

"They have a past, that's all, Sammy. He isn't doing it to be hurtful or disrespectful."

"I know. Maybe their history isn't as much in the past as they thought. Maybe they need to work some things out. I don't want to stand in the way either. If he likes Jen he should go after her."

"Are you always this level headed?"

She smiled. "I giggled like a toddler in a tub today because I sat in two inches of water. You know I'm not of complete sound mind in all matters."

"You should have giggled. I wanted to. It was a great thing you did today. Don't minimize it by acting like it wasn't. I'm proud of you."

She blushed. "Thanks."

Like two silly teenagers they watched each other with bashful modesty.

Finally Samantha said, "You better go get dressed. It's almost time to eat."

Later that night after the others had gone off to O'Malley's, and Maureen and Frank disappeared to bed, Colin sat in the den forcing himself to read one more chapter of a book he was too distracted to even remember the title of. It was all gibberish to him anyway.

Sammy was tired. After dinner she had helped the others straighten up and then grabbed a book off a shelf in the den and said goodnight, claiming she had a bit of a headache. Colin's mother doted over her for a few minutes and then left her to rest. He'd given Samantha a look that promised he'd be up to wake her once the others were all occupied elsewhere. His parents were likely settled in bed by now and the house was quiet, but he needed to wait a little longer.

After fighting back his impatience and rereading the page he was on three more times, he finally closed the book and stood up to stretch. Colin climbed the stairs quietly and entered his room, careful to lock the door behind him. Cutting through the bathroom, he found Sammy curled up under the soft covers and sleeping soundly in the dark.

Without hesitating, he slipped his arms under her body and scooped her up carrying her to his bed. She stirred when he placed her under his covers. Her eyes were soft slits fringed with dusty brown lashes that watched him intently.

Colin removed his shirt and jeans and stood before her in only his briefs and crucifix. She rolled to her back and smiled. Crisp white cotton panties rode low on her abdomen and accentuated her hips. A simple pink tank top covered her upper body, but he could see her nipples pebbling under the worn fabric.

He climbed in beside her.

"How's your head?"

She giggled. "You know my head is fine."

He kissed it anyway for good measure. "Are you still tired?"

She made a soft purring sound only a woman would know how to make. "Yes, but I'll wake up."

He pulled her to her side. "Don't. I just want to hold you. We don't need to talk."

Her body snuggled in close to his and he reveled in the soft warmth of her in his arms. How would he ever sleep alone again without feeling like something was missing?

He watched her in the low light seeping from the bathroom. She was so incredibly attractive. There was not a bit of makeup marring her face. Her soft brown hair was natural and healthy. With his face so close to hers he could count every freckle that crested her nose and cheeks. They reminded him of sprinkled cinnamon, and he recalled a Natasha Bedingfield song.

He watched her until his eyes grew heavy and he no longer could keep them open. Pockets of warmth filled the hidden places between their curves. The last thing Colin thought before he drifted off to sleep was that he would probably die an old man and still recall exactly how she smelled and felt in his arms.

Colin's mind roused when he heard a sound, but he didn't open his eyes when he felt Samantha's warm body still curled next to his. He pulled her close and nestled his face into the curve of her shoulder and breathed in the soft scent of her hair.

It was his brother's voice that had him coming fully awake.

"Jesus fucking Christ," Braydon hissed and both he and Samantha jolted upright wearing matching expressions of apprehension and guilt. "What the fuck's going on here?"

"It's not what it looks like, Braydon?" Colin said quickly blocking Sammy's partially dressed form from his brother's view.

She must have forgotten to lock her door.

"What the fuck is it then? Jesus Christ, are you fucking my girlfriend?"

Before Colin realized what he was doing he was out of bed and grabbing Braydon by his shirt.

"Show some respect!" he seethed, giving him a hard shake. "I told you it isn't what it looks like."

"Then what is it, Colin? Because to me it looks like *my* girlfriend's in bed with *my* brother who is about to become a *priest*!"

Colin loosened his hold of Braydon's shirt and stepped back. "We aren't sleeping together," he admitted quietly. "Sammy's a virgin and so am I."

The personal detail about Samantha's virginity seemed

to shock his brother, but he quickly recovered and Braydon's look of surprise returned to a scowl.

Colin looked back to the bed to check on Sammy. She was sitting up and appeared extremely uncomfortable with the situation. Her cheeks were crimson red as she averted her gaze and clutched the covers to her chest.

"Is this what you've been doing? Why you haven't wanted to spend any time with me?"

Colin was about to answer, but realized his brother was addressing Samantha. She looked at him and anger glinted in her dark eyes. "Don't act like I've been neglecting you any more than you've neglected me, Braydon. Since the moment we arrived you had no apprehension about leaving me to entertain myself."

He scoffed. "That's not true." Braydon's posture turned defensive. "I invited you tubing, to swim in the falls, fishing. You're the one who refused to spend time with me."

She looked away and Colin softly confessed, "She's terrified of water, Bray. She can't do those things."

Braydon looked as though that was the most ridiculous excuse in the world. "Well, you could've told me that."

Sammy scowled at his brother with big eyes, her lips firmly pressed together in irritation. "Would it really have mattered, Braydon? Be realistic. You regretted asking me to come the morning after we arrived. I love it here, but all I'm doing is interfering in your free time. We enjoy different things."

Braydon looked at her, his expression appearing vulnerable and unsure. Both characteristics Colin did not normally see on his sought after brother's face.

"That's not true," Bray whispered. "I like you, Sam. We're good together. I didn't know about the water thing. I'll stay away from the lake for the rest of the week."

Thankfully Samantha halted him from making more unrealistic promises.

"No, Braydon. I like you too, but as a friend. I know what you're looking for and I'm not it."

His brother appeared bewildered by her rejection. Braydon had always been the golden child of the McCulloughs, the one chased after by every beautiful girl in the county. It wasn't often he was turned away.

"I'm sorry," Samantha whispered.

When Braydon raised his head all vulnerability was safely hidden away. He glared at Colin. "Is this because of you? Are you even taking your vows now?"

"Braydon, don't say something you'll regret," Colin suggested. "This isn't personal. It isn't about you—"

He gave a sardonic laugh. "You think? She was my guest, Colin, and of all people I never thought I had to watch my back around my brothers, let alone you."

The accusation stung, but Colin took it. "I'm sorry. Please don't make Sammy feel bad about it though. I take full responsibility."

Bray let out a dry, low laugh. "Sammy is it?" He shook his head as if still struggling to believe what he'd walked in on. "Well, you two enjoy each other. I'll be sure to stay out of your way. I wouldn't want to ever be accused of poaching from my own family."

Shit. This was really bad. If anything his family was

always loyal to one another. Before Braydon could leave Colin reached for his arm, "Bray…"

He stopped, but didn't look at him.

"I need to know you won't say anything to the others. Samantha's going back to school at the end of the week and come August I *will* be making the sacrament of holy orders. Nothing's changed."

"For you," he said under his breath.

"Please, Braydon. She doesn't deserve to be dragged into the middle of all this in front of a family she's just met. I understand that you're angry at me. Be angry for as long as you need, but don't hurt her in the process."

Braydon looked up at him with such a penetrating stare Colin feared he could see right through him and see how he truly felt about Samantha.

"If anyone hurts her, Colin, it won't be me."

CHAPTER 13

True to his word, Braydon did not breathe a word about what he had seen. While the morning after he struggled with looking Samantha in the eye, the tension quickly faded and he was once again acting as her friend. There was still, however, tension between him and Colin.

The days passed faster than Sam was prepared for. In the mornings she would usually spend time with Maureen and sometimes the aunts and Katherine, while Colin went to the Church to work on painting the school or other things that needed tending. They found it easiest to stick with the rest of the family in the afternoons, and in the evenings they had fallen into the routine of sneaking off to the lake to see how far Colin could distract Sam into the water.

She had made it up to her ribs and Colin was immeasurably proud of her.

The water became less of a fear and more of a need to please him, to show him that she could handle anything. She craved that look of pride he showed with each little bit of progress she made. Her apprehension of even being near the lake had faded in ways she couldn't process. On Wednesday they had been so elated at her progress they could barely keep their hands off each other.

There was something sacred about their time at the water, something that was theirs and could never be shared. It was her memory, her secret kiss tucked neatly in the corner of her smile that no one else could ever lay claim to. With each passing night she fell more and more in love with Colin McCullough and her fear of the coming Saturday became more paralyzing than all thoughts of water.

Thursday night came and they waded into the lake, its silver moon shadows sparkling like tiny diamonds along the surface. Colin held her securely by her hips and walked backward, holding her with her back to the shore until the ground fell away and she floated in his arms. It was a terrifying and euphoric feeling wrapped into one.

He instructed her how to move her arms and legs to bob in place. Only the mildest panic crept in when small spatters of water crested her shoulders and splashed her face. He held her and whispered words of encouragement and her anxiety faded. It was surprisingly peaceful, floating with her shoulders under the warmth of the water. When her legs grew tired she wrapped them around Colin's hips.

His laughter slowed and he looked at her with such a

serious expression. His blue-green eyes looked almost golden in the darkness.

"I love you, Samantha."

"I love you too, Colin."

They kissed in the water for a long while, their bodies heating and coiling with each breathless moment. His arousal pressed so close to her center she felt naked. She wanted to pull her suit aside and touch him to her, flesh to flesh.

She broke away from their kiss and breathed, "Colin, let me touch you. Please, I want to feel you."

He pressed his forehead to hers. She knew he wanted to say yes, but there was still that part of him that wouldn't give in.

"What do you need, Samantha?"

"You. I need you inside of me."

His hand coasted over her hip and his fingertips grazed the soft patch of skin between her belly button and bikini bottom. Slowly, his hand moved lower. She let her body become buoyant, loosely wrapping her legs around his hips, and keeping her hands where they held her at his shoulders.

Fingers trailed down the front of her bikini and pressed lightly into the crease of her sex. He moved his fingers slowly up and down over the fabric as if orienting himself with her shape.

"I've never touched a woman here."

She looked at him but said nothing, simply waited to see what he would do, hoping he would truly touch her. After a few moments of him petting her there, a hollow ache built inside of her, screaming to be filled. What had always been simply anatomy was now an empty void connected to every nerve of her body, every muscle, to her mind, and most of all, to her heart. She was a puzzle piece missing its complimenting half. Colin's half.

When his fingers breached the cool wet fabric of her suit and teased at the soft patch of hair the material hid, Samantha struggled to remain still in his arms. She began to panic when his fingers pulled back up before ever making contact with her sex, but then relaxed when she realized what he was doing.

His fingertips rode the inner hem of her suit like a track until they came up to the knot tied at her hip. Her heart raced as his fingers tugged the soft string causing the bow to come loose.

The two strings fell away from her hip and Colin pulled the front away from her body until her sex was bared for his touch. The forgotten suit wrapped one thigh. He looked into her eyes, and his fingers coasted toward her folds.

They feathered back and forth there for a moment, building her anticipation to a fever pitch. He was unintentionally teasing her and she never wanted it to stop, yet at the same time she wanted to scream at him to do more. Finally his fingers fell away and his palm cupped her wanting core.

Samantha's eyes rolled back and a guttural groan left her throat. Colin was breathing so hard his shoulders seemed to inflate with each breath. Her eyes shut, but she could feel him watching her. The broad tip of his middle finger separated her folds and she begged him to keep going. He breached her opening and slid in to the third knuckle, his other fingers still cupping her from the outside.

The sensation was incredible. Right. Her body lifted, the water easing her movements and keeping her almost weightless. His left arm wrapped around her lower back as she continued to lift her body up and down shamelessly upon his hand.

"What does it feel like, Samantha?" His voice was a mere whisper falling in between her labored breaths and the slight sloshing of the water against their skin.

"Good. It feels so good, Colin."

He pressed the heel of his palm against her clitoris and she purred deep within her throat.

"There?" he asked.

"Yes."

He continued to rub as she rode his finger. He turned his wrist slightly and another finger trailed along her labia.

"Can you take more?"

"Yes."

The other finger slipped inside, lining up beside the other. The fullness was splendid. She became disoriented by the sensuality of it all. Pulling herself up by his shoulders, she pressed her face into his neck making throaty sounds of pleasure.

He dragged his fingers out and slowly glided them back in. Her body opened for him the more he slid his fingers in and out. Her channel became as slick as her skin that was fully submerged in the water.

Colin increased his rhythm and touched an extremely sensitive spot deep inside of her that made her hiss.

He stilled. "Sorry."

"No, it's good. Don't stop."

He pressed again, finding that soft place hidden deep within her sex. She could tell the tissue there was softer, slightly more tender and sensitive than the other parts of her sex. Whatever it was, Samantha wanted Colin to never stop touching it.

A third finger played at her opening but didn't quite fit with the others. The more he reached for that spot inside of her, the closer his thumb came to her clitoris. His motions grew more confident that he wouldn't hurt her and pumped his fingers in and out of her sex with a little more force and speed.

When his thumb pressed directly on her sensitive bud, she cried out. He understood this was one of the most sensitive places on her body. He tried touching her there a few different ways, but couldn't seem to keep any sort of rhythm with his thumb while his fingers pumped in and out of her.

Finally he grunted and shoved his fingers deep into her sex. They found that soft inner spot and pressed into it. His thumb then clamped down on her clit and rapidly strummed her. His touch caressed her most sensitive flesh both inside and out. She heard her voice echo around them as she came and cried out his name. Her body tensed and locked so tightly around him her abdomen lifted out of the water.

As her locked muscles unraveled and she came back to earth Colin suddenly began to pound his fingers in and out of her once more.

"Again," he grunted, holding her tightly to his hip.

She looked at him about to tell him she couldn't possibly when another climax tore over her like a tsunami washing all doubt out of its path. The inner walls of her sex fluttered and pulsed around his fingertips, as there was a heavy release of moisture from within her.

Her entire body shook as he cupped her weeping sex, his touch remained tucked deep inside of her. She was tired and disoriented. In that moment she would be incapable of even spelling her name. The only thing she was sure of was that she loved this man and letting him go would be the hardest thing she'd probably ever have to do.

Colin kissed up her neck and found her mouth. He seemed torn between wanting to kiss her thoroughly and wanting to whisper words of love to her.

His mouth opened and closed over hers. "So beautiful." He licked at her bottom lip. "So soft." He nibbled along her jaw. "Never have I seen something so breathtaking as you letting go." His mouth sealed over hers and his tongue stabbed past her lips. He devoured her mouth and sent her senses spiraling once more. She became a body without bones.

When his fingers stirred within her she moaned tiredly. "Give me one more, Samantha. I know you can take it. Let me feel you one more time."

She didn't stop him from touching her, but she couldn't seem to muster any more enthusiasm. She was rung out, spent, completely and totally sated. Her body jerked when his thumb coasted over her clit. She was so incredibly sensitive there. Pleasure became almost painful to endure.

Suddenly his fingers slipped out of her, causing her to feel incomplete and bereft, then they were moving toward the shore. Her body shivered as he carried her to shallow ground and the coarse sand pressed into her back. Colin's weight settled on top of her.

He kissed her lips, her neck, the curve of her breasts. The sopping inconsequential weight of her bikini bottom wrapped around her knee vaguely registered.

"I can't stop yet. Forgive me, Sammy, I can't let you go just yet."

She exerted too much energy in order to lift a hand to the side of his face. He raised his head from where he was kissing her stomach and gazed at her. So much pain and anguish and need in those deep ocean colored eyes. Her mouth was dry and her eyes could barely stay open, but she managed to form words. "S'okay, Colin. I'm yours."

His shoulders dropped as if hearing her acceptance was an enormous relief. He laid his cheek upon her belly and whispered, "I love you." She was too tired to say it back.

Slowly he scattered kisses across her skin, upon her belly, down her thighs, at the backs of her knees. She lay supine beneath him allowing him to touch her freely as he pleased.

Come the end of summer he'd take his vow of celibacy and never touch another woman again. She supposed she had it easy, knowing her body was the only one he would ever know. He, on the other hand, had to accept that she would someday have a husband.

Her mind returned like an explosion playing in reverse. Her body became revived with each caress. The sensation of Colin's warm tongue licking up the crease of her sex had her propelling forward. She must have startled him, because he jumped back. His expression was that of a little boy spying on his friends older sister getting dressed, seeming contrite but still willing to do it again.

"Should I not do that?"

She loved how this big confident man was so unsure when it came to matters between man and woman. She didn't know what to tell him. No, you don't have to? Yes, please lick me there until I come again? It seemed so personal. Sinful. Dear God, he would be a priest soon and he wanted to put his mouth between her legs.

Something about imagining him in his Godly clothes filled her with such resentment toward the church. Damn God for taking another person from her. Well, He could have him, but she'd have him first!

Her legs spread wide and she spread her arms out in complete submission. It was the most wanton display she'd ever even contemplated let alone attempted.

"Do it again," she tempted and Colin seemed torn between looking at her face and her glistening pink sex.

He swallowed and then dove between her legs. He licked and kissed and fucked her with his tongue. His fingers came into play and although she was slightly sore, she wanted him to keep going. The third climax she feared was now something she needed immensely.

Her knees pulled back and her toes dug into the wet sand. He gripped her ass cheek hard enough to leave a handprint. His arm drew back as his fingers lanced in and out of her. She panted with each up stroke, her voice growing needy and higher pitched the closer she came to her release. His tongue licked over her sensitized clitoris, up and down, up and down, and then he did something marvelous.

His lips closed over her clit and he sucked hard, much like he had done with her nipples. Her mind zinged and her nerves zapped like a string of lights sparking at each bulb. She shouted and wrapped her thighs around his broad shoulders. He didn't let her go. His hands slid under her bottom and lifted her more to his mouth.

Tighter than a bow, her body finally collapsed. He licked at her slowly and softly as if cleaning her up. His cheek pressed against her thigh and he turned his face to lay a kiss there upon her tender flesh.

She wondered if she should go ahead and join a convent, because after what just happened, she was pretty sure he had ruined her for all other men.

CHAPTER 14

Friday morning at breakfast, Samantha had a difficult time eating. Tonight would be the last night she spent under the McCulloughs roof. Maureen had already extended several invitations for her to return and Sam knew they would apply with or without Braydon's company. Sam also knew she would never accept her invitations.

Her time here was over. It would be too painful to come back and face all the memories she and Colin had created here. And God forbid she ran into him again after he took his vows. Seeing him dressed and marked, as a man of God, would be too real, too painful. She'd rather never lay eyes on him again than to see him that way, as a man she would never completely have.

Sam pushed her eggs around on her plate and pretended to eat. She did her best not to look at Colin,

knowing he was feeling much the same way and afraid
that seeing her moroseness mirrored in his eyes would be
her undoing. Kelly was relentlessly teasing Sheilagh and
Luke was once again absent. Finn and Braydon were
discussing their plans for the following week.

Braydon looked up, startled, when his mother said, "I
was thinking. Wouldn't it be a fine thing if you were to
take Samantha to that new fancy restaurant at the end of
town for her last night here? I know it's nothing like those
posh places you kids have in the city, but it's the nicest
place our town's ever had to dine at. Isn't that a wonderful
idea, Braydon dear?"

Uncertainty crossed Braydon's face.

Sam chanced a glance at Colin to find him also
watching his brother. Would he tell them that they were
no longer an item? That Sam had spent the last two weeks
corrupting Colin, tainting his impeccable record on his
way to sainthood.

Braydon hadn't spoken to Colin since catching them in
bed together. He hadn't told about what he saw, but most
likely because there had never been an opening big
enough for such a bomb to be dropped. Would he drop
that bomb now?

She gave him a pleading look. *Please don't ruin this for
Colin.* It was difficult enough without the rest of them
judging him.

Braydon looked at first her and then his brother. He
cleared his throat. "Um, that sounds nice. What do you
think, Sam?"

"Sure."

She wanted to spend her last night with Colin, but she had to go along with this ruse or else risk the others' suspicions.

"Wonderful!" Maureen cheered and everyone went back to eating.

Sam looked at Colin, her apology pouring from her eyes. He smiled back at her, looking disappointed, but knowing it was not her fault and that there was really no other option.

Out of the corner of her eye she saw Kelly watching them. She turned quickly but her mistake was already made. Guilt flooded her as the blood rushed from her face.

Kelly's eyes, usually so full of merriment and sarcasm, appeared completely serious, as they bounced from her to Colin and back again. He looked to his older brother with unguarded concern. At that moment, Colin's expression also seemed to register that Kelly had put two and two together.

Sam began to panic. Everything was getting ruined. It was her last day, and she just wanted to enjoy it with Colin, without the others finding out about them. She had the rest of her life to mourn his absence. She wasn't ready to relinquish him now. Her heart began to pound and she felt as though she was going to be sick.

She wouldn't get to be with him one last time.

She wasn't ready to say goodbye. Was this what tomorrow would feel like? No, tomorrow would be worse because it would be final. Permanent. There wouldn't be the remote chance that she might pass him in the hall or catch him sneaking into her room to steal a kiss.

Her chest hurt.

Everyone's voices blended together until they formed a loud obnoxious hum that deafened her to all other sound.

As the fleeting thought that she was having a panic attack occurred, she looked to Colin and saw mirrored fear in his eyes. He stood and everything went black.

SAM OPENED HER EYES, her vision winked from flurry to fuzzy to clear and she saw Braydon and Maureen looking over her. She must've passed out because she was lying on the kitchen floor.

"Mother of Christ, thank God you're awake!" Maureen cried when she opened her eyes. "Have you ben drinkin', love? It's nary ten o'clock. Or maybe a drink is just what you need. Sheilagh, grab my whiskey under the sink, next to the Windex."

"Are you all right?" Braydon asked his tone soft and genuine.

Her head hurt. Had she fallen out of her chair and hit her head? How embarrassing. The sharp, humiliating sting of tears prickled her eyes. She looked at Braydon, wishing he were Colin. Maureen continued to fuss and chatter to the others.

Braydon leaned close to her ear and whispered, "He's right there, behind me. Look over my shoulder. It's killing him not to be able to hold you and check if you're all right. Be a dear and give him a nod so he can relax."

She looked over his shoulder and saw Colin. He was standing with his back practically to the door and his expression restless. When their gazes locked she gave him a shake of her head telling him that aside from being humiliated, she was fine.

After breakfast, Sam had to down a shot of whiskey just to get Maureen to relax and stop fussing over her. No one understood what had happened and she didn't want to explain her history of panic attacks. Realizing she wasn't going anywhere, Colin left but never said where. She needed to get a grip. How did the saying go? *An hour of love is better than a lifetime without it?* Well, her hour was about up.

When she returned to her room to wash her face and get over her bruised pride, Braydon knocked at the door. It wasn't closed so he pushed it open. "Hey, can I come in?"

"Sure." She waved for him to enter. It was his room after all.

"You okay?" He pressed the door closed and sat on the bed.

"I'll live. Just embarrassed."

"There's really no need to be embarrassed. No one's making fun of you. We were all worried."

She plopped down on the bed and sighed.

"What happened, Sam?"

Resigned, she admitted, "I have anxiety attacks. I've had them since I was a kid. They don't come as often as they used to, but when they do come, they can sometimes cause me to black out. What you just saw was a pretty bad one."

"Is it Colin? Is that what you're stressed out about?"

She looked at him. He didn't seem angry or to be judging her, only curious. "It's a lot of things, school, my parents, graduating, job hunting...Colin."

"What's going on between the two of you? I know it's more than friendship, Sam."

She pressed her lips together and refused to cry. Barely whispering she said, "I love him."

"Does he love you?"

She nodded.

"So he's not taking his vows?"

She shook her head. "He's still becoming a priest. He never led me to believe this would change anything and I knew it changed nothing going in."

COLIN MARCHED a long way from the house and when he'd gone far enough he roared at the injustice of the world, angrily forking his fingers through his hair and kicking a rock into the distance.

"You got it out now, buddy?"

He spun on his heel and found Kelly watching him.

"Go back to the house," Colin growled.

"I don't think so. How about you tell me what's going on between you and Sammy."

Colin gritted his teeth. "Mind your own business,

Kelly. I'm not one of your bar patrons dying to bear my soul to you."

"How 'bout to Sam? Would you bare your soul to her? Maybe you already did."

"Fuck you. You have no idea what you're talking about."

"Maybe not, but I'm gonna give it a try. I think while our golden boy Braydon has been otherwise occupied you took it upon yourself to entertain Sam, pretty little thing that she is. At first it was all just charity and compassion for a stranger left alone among a pack of wolves, but then you realized there was a lot more to her then you first saw. The more time you spent with her the more you fell for her. And now she's leaving and you're too much of a pussy to admit you may be human after all and actually go after what you want most."

"You don't know what you're talking about," Colin nearly snarled.

"Maybe not, but I do know that in my entire life I never saw you look at anyone the way I caught you looking at her this morning. Do you love her?"

Before he could answer he heard Braydon yelling from the house and marching toward them. "Yo, Colin! I need to have a word with you."

"Great," Colin muttered under his breath.

Braydon marched right up to him and shoved him in the chest. "What the fuck do you think you're doing?"

Stunned that he was being attacked Colin shook his head. "What are you talking about?"

"I'm talking about Sam. I ought to kick your sorry ass!

What the fuck did you think would happen? It would all just go away?"

"What would go away?" Kelly asked.

Before Colin could tell Kelly to take a hike, Braydon turned to him and snapped, "Stay out of it."

"Fuck you, Bray. And fuck you too, Colin."

Braydon turned back to Colin and pushed him. "She's up there about to cry, and it's all your fault."

"Who's crying? Sammy?" Kelly asked and they each ignored him.

"What do you want me to do, Bray? I never made her any promises."

He hated that she was hurting, but they had each known this moment was coming.

Braydon growled at him. "Then you don't do anything! You had no right to play with a girl like her knowing you were never going to change your plans! She fucking loves you, asshole. And you're so goddamn pigheaded you're going to let her go so you can go play monk and take vows of poverty and celibacy and any other sacrifice that makes your pompous ass feel more like a righteous martyr."

His brother's words stunned him and he reacted without thinking, punching Braydon square in the nose.

Utterly shocked by his actions, Colin reared back. It was a knee jerk reaction, one he hadn't had since he was a kid, horsing around with his brothers. But this wasn't horsing around. His brother's accusations stung. Disgust for his barbaric behavior set in before his arm even returned to his side. But Braydon wouldn't know that. No, rather than evaluate their emotions on a sophisticated level, Braydon found it better to throw an uppercut that knocked Colin right on his ass.

All hell broke loose. Punches flew and knuckles collided with flesh. Somehow Kelly got tossed into the melee and Luke was suddenly there ripping them all apart.

"What the bloody fuck is going on?" Luke screamed.

Colin caught his breath and stared hard at Braydon who had blood smeared from his nose to his cheek. Kelly, the scrappy little shit, looked like he just stepped out of a cover shoot. Colin tasted blood and ran his thumb under is lip. Yup, blood. Luke looked from one brother to the next.

"What the fuck?" he asked again.

"Sorry," Colin said to the three of them.

"What the hell happened?" Luke asked.

"Nothing," Braydon said, not making eye contact with him or Luke.

Luke looked at Kelly and Kelly held up his hands, "Don't look at me. I was dragged into this."

Blown away by the stench of bullshit coming from his youngest brother Colin snorted out a disbelieving laugh.

Kelly looked at him. "What? I was."

He was done with all of them. Turning on his heel to return to the house Colin said to no one in particular, "I'm leaving." Thankfully no one tried to stop him.

As Colin passed the guesthouse he spotted Tristan waiting at the door. Odd thing was he didn't have shoes on. "If you're looking for Luke, he's that way."

When he returned to the house he marched straight up

to his room and shut himself in. After locking the door behind him he went through the bathroom and locked the door leading to Sam's room. He sat on his bed and cradled his pounding head. He needed to think for a minute. Think and pray.

CHAPTER 15

*S*am heard the door lock, locking her out of Colin's room and felt as if a part of her broke away from her soul. It was starting. He was pulling away. How would she ever get through these last few hours? She went to the door and softly tapped against the wood.

"Colin?"

She listened, but heard nothing. She flinched when she heard the sound of something crashing against the floor and glass shattering. Her hand instinctively went to the knob. She jiggled it, but it was locked from the inside as she'd suspected.

"Colin, please let me in."

She waited a moment longer and then saw the shadow of his feet peek out below the door. Her hand went to the wood, as if she could somehow touch him, get through to him. He was hurting too.

"Colin, I know you're there. I know you can hear me. Please don't shut me out. Please."

The shadow of his feet retreated followed by the soft click of his door closing once more. Samantha choked as the weight of her tears became too much. He wasn't being fair. They had one more day. It was his fault they couldn't be together and she understood that from the get go, but now he was cutting their time even shorter. Who gave him the right?

She silently cried until she had the sense to know her tears were useless. If he wanted to shut her out, let him. Angry that she couldn't even use the bathroom to clean up her face, she grabbed her debit card and driver's license, a few twenties from her wallet, and headed out the door.

Luckily, the first person she saw was Kelly. She knew he had figured out what was going on to some extent and at this point she really didn't give a shit who knew what.

"Hey, love, you feeling better?"

Sam knew she looked a fright, but there was nothing she could do about it at the moment, not without the use of her damn bathroom.

"Will you take me somewhere, Kelly?"

"Sure. Where do you need to go?"

"Away from here."

He considered her request, his gaze scrutinizing. Something he saw in her expression must have told him she needed to escape. Without asking for further explanation, he reached in his pocket and pulled out his keys.

Dangling them from his fingers he said, "Let's go."

Kelly drove an old beat up truck that smelled of worn

in leather and sex. There was an Irish trinity pendant hanging from his rearview mirror and Samantha watched it twirl and lean from side to side as they drove to God knew where. She didn't care where he was taking her so long as it was away from Colin.

She appreciated that Kelly didn't try to fill the silence with meaningless babble. She wanted to simply stew for a while.

The truck slowed as they pulled up to the ball field. Leaning back, Kelly reached across her lap and opened the glove compartment. He pulled out a flask and she said, "Are you sure that's a good idea if we have to drive back?"

"It's not for me, love. It's for you."

She stared at him as if he were crazy. Whatever Maureen had given her earlier felt like it burned a hole through her esophagus. She really hoped it wasn't Irish whiskey again. Not wanting to offend him, especially when he had helped her run, she said, "It's not even eleven in the morning."

"It's five o'clock somewhere. Come on."

She followed him to the dugout and they sat on the same bench they had occupied that first game.

He handed her the flask. "Wanna tell me what's going on, Sammy? I know it has to do with Colin and I know what you feel for him is more than what friend's should probably feel for their boyfriend's brothers."

She considered confessing everything to Kelly, but in the end chose the whiskey. Taking the flask from his hands, she unscrewed the cap and brought the cool metal nozzle to her lips. Even the fumes smelled like turpentine. She shut her eyes and tipped back a sip.

Sam sputtered and coughed as it made it past her throat and started a fire deep in her belly. "Oh, God, how do you drink that?"

He laughed. "Now what kind of Irish lass are you if you can't drink your Tullamore Dew?"

"A sober one."

"Ah, now that's no fun. Give it another go. The second time's not that bad."

She gave him a skeptical look and held her breath as she took another sip. *Nope, still horrible.*

Kelly got a good chuckle out of her contorting face as she suffered through each swig.

Over the next several minutes he coached and coaxed her into several more sips. The whiskey didn't burn as much anymore. They decided to take a walk around the bases and wound up lying in center field watching clouds roll by.

"Are you feelin' a bit better now, love?" he asked in an Irish lilt.

She giggled and had no idea why. "Yes. Why do you guys all fake Irish accents?"

"Ah, we are not fakin', love. The Gaelic's in our blood. It tis what it means to be a McCullough. We know how it makes the lassies mad with lust so we try to talk normal-like most of the time."

"I think you're all a bunch of drunks."

He laughed and faced her. He really did have the most mesmerizing eyes. His heart shaped face and scrappy elfin hair made her feel like she was in the company of a fictional character of lore.

"Now, look who is talking. I give you one wee flask and yer tongue becomes as sharp as a sward. I believe you'll fit right in just fine with the lot of us. Look at ye, lyin' in the middle of a field, piss drunk, before you've even had lunch. It's like my Morai always said, *A McCullough lying on the floor is the only kind of McCullough who will drink no more.*"

"Well I'm not a bloody McCullough!" she said tipping the flask to her lips and taking another sip. When she found it empty she shook it above her face and frowned.

"A-ha, seems to me you've taken all yer toasts."

"Do you have any more?"

He laughed. "'Friad not, love. I'll have to be getting you home soon anyway. I've work in a few hours."

"I don't want to go back."

He turned to her and watched her for a moment. His blue eyes seeing parts of her she wished she could keep hidden, but such was the sadness of being drunk in a ball field.

"Do you love him, Sammy?" he whispered.

"Yes," she whispered back.

"Then he's a fool."

Enough said.

They lay in the field for a while longer, not talking about anything too serious. Somewhere in the back of her mind, Sam knew she was getting sunburn and probably had a dozen more freckles on her nose to show for it, but she didn't care.

When Kelly finally helped her to her feet she toppled right back to the ground and realized how drunk she actually was. The dugout wavered like a seesaw and home base looked like a tilt-a-whirl.

He helped her to the truck and even buckled her in. As he walked around the car to the driver's side, dread built inside of her at the thought of returning and feeling dejected even more. Kelly climbed in and paused when he saw her expression.

"No, no, we'll have none of that. I didn't give you my good hooch so you could piss it away on tears and sorrows. Where's the smile I saw minutes ago?"

"I lost it," she slurred, slouching against the seat to face him.

"Well, perhaps not all is lost. Your time here is not over yet and farther more Colin is no bloody better than the rest of us. He's no priest as of yet. Who's to say how things may change between now and then?"

"He wants to take his vows, Kelly. He'll do it. I know him."

Kelly smiled sadly at her and lovingly touched her cheek. She would've been uncomfortable had anyone else done so, but that was just Kelly, openly affectionate. "He wants you too, love. That's the crux of it all, that he can't have you both. He loves his church. She's all he's ever opened himself to, but he loves you too, Sammy."

"It doesn't matter. I can't compete with Gob."

"Gob?"

"You know what I mean. God! This is all your fall. You and your damn whiskey. God, I can't compete with *God.*"

"Ah, but the church and God are two different matters entirely. No one said if he has you he can't have his God as well."

"That's not what he wants. I know he loves me, but he loves the church more. I would always be the mistress who ruined what could have been a perfect marriage."

"Well, if that's true then he'd better be damn sure because I have no doubt that someone will wife you up in no time a'tall. And while an Irishman may be able to go twenty years without kissing his wife, he'll kill the man that does."

That made her smile.

"Thanks, Kelly. For everything, but Colin couldn't hurt a fly."

Her eyes grew heavy so she shut them for a bit.

"WHAT HAPPENED?" Braydon asked as Kelly carried Sam through the kitchen door.

"Nothing. I just got our girl here a wee bit drunk. She's fine."

"She doesn't look fine. How much did you give her?"

"Just a flask full, I swear it. She needed a break from reality for a moment."

Braydon gave Kelly an exasperated look. "This coming from a guy who thinks reality is a result of an alcohol deficiency. Nice."

"Where's Colin?"

"I don't fucking care. Here, give her to me and I'll take

her to my room." Braydon lifted Sam out of Kelly's arms and she groaned. "I got you, Sam."

He carried her up the stairs and into his room. The bed was made so he laid her on top of the covers. She began to make little snoring noises and he tried not to laugh.

What the hell was wrong with Colin? He reached out and swept her hair over her shoulder.

"What happened?"

Speak of the holy devil.

Braydon turned and saw Colin standing in the door. He hid his satisfaction at seeing his brother with the shadow of a bruise on his jaw and a split lip.

"You care?"

"Shut up, Bray. Yes, I fucking care!" Colin hissed.

"That'll be two Hail Mary's."

"Knock it off."

"Why should I? You're still the same self-righteous prick you've always been and apparently you have no plans of changing."

When Colin didn't reply he turned to see if he left. The hurt he saw in his brother's eyes made him regret his last jab. Maybe he'd gone too far.

"Is that how you see me?" Colin rasped. "A self-righteous prick?"

"No, that was a little harsh. I'm just not real happy with you right now."

"I'm not real happy with myself," his brother confessed. "What happened to Sammy?"

"Kelly got her drunk."

Braydon laughed when he saw his brother's jaw tick.

"She needed it," he said. "Next time try talking to her instead of running away. If you really plan on letting her go tomorrow, for good, then at least have the decency to be there for her today."

"I never meant to hurt her, Bray. You have to know that. I just…I don't know what to do."

"You certainly have a choice to make, but I can't make it for you and neither can anyone else. If you ask me, the answer is obvious."

"I never meant to fall in love with her."

"You falling in love with her doesn't surprise me in the least. It's the fact that you somehow managed to get her to fall in love with you. Love that isn't given easily is not something you throw away, Colin."

"I'll never stop loving her. It isn't wasted."

Braydon couldn't see things from his brother's perspective no matter how hard he tried. "Then what are you doing, man?"

"I don't know." Dismissing any further conversation Colin asked, "Are you taking her to dinner tonight?"

"I don't see the point. You should be taking her."

"I can't."

"See, that's the thing, Colin. You can."

"Take her to dinner, Bray. Give her a nice last night here."

"And what do you plan to do for her?"

"The most honorable thing I can think of…leave her alone."

CHAPTER 16

hen Braydon left the room, Colin knew he should follow. Samantha lay sleeping on the bed, face squished against the side of her arm, nose red, and hair a mess. He went to the door to leave through the hall, unsure where he'd go, but rather than leave, he shut the door and turned the lock.

Colin went to his room and locked his door as well.

It was nearly three o'clock. In his mind the day was shot. He should've gone to the church to get some painting done, but his heart wasn't in it. Turning the wand hanging from the blinds, Colin shut out the sunlight filtering into the room.

He walked to the other side of the bed and stood watching her as she rested in drowsy tranquility. Damn Kelly for getting her drunk. She'd probably wake up with a headache. Not a great way to spend her last day.

Done with his introspective analysis, Colin forced his

mind to stop thinking and simply did what he needed in his heart, no matter how unwise. He climbed onto the covers and scooted behind Samantha's body until her back was pressed to his front. He held her close, hating that this might be his last chance at holding her in such a way.

Her warm body heated his and her clothing smelled of fresh cut grass. Her hair tickled his chin. He loved her. Onlookers had always made such awed references about giving up the right to marry once he became a priest. Such dignified sacrifice for God our Savior. Colin now saw things differently.

Love was an agony that embedded into the soul and infected the mind so completely there was no escaping its reach once it got its claws in a person. Evading marriage was not a sacrifice he made for God, but a mercy God granted him. To his mind, the stronger man was the one brave enough to risk loving a wife, to chance loving her with all of his being until there was nothing left of him, and knowing there always was the possibility of losing her. Colin was not so brave.

He rested beside Samantha for the better part of an hour. He held her gently in his arms, memorizing her scent and the placement of every freckle upon her cheek. He marveled at how full the crests of her dusty eyelashes were and how soft, yet defined, the line was that shaped her lips.

He couldn't stop remembering the old Irish proverb. *A man is incomplete until he marries. After that he is finished.*

Whoever married this magnificent woman would be doomed.

Sometime later she awoke with a deep sigh followed by a pained moan. Her body stretched within his embrace and he whispered, "Have yourself a wee little nip, did ya?"

She froze.

Turning slowly to face him, she said not a word, but watched him as if testing his presence to see if it was real or the fabrication of some dream.

Finally she whispered, "I'm mad at you."

"I know. I'm mad at me too."

"You locked me out."

Shame knifed through him. How could he explain to her that he was weak, that when he saw her he forgot his place and the commitments he set forth for himself? She took everything important to him away and flipped him inside out until he was barely recognizable as himself. He couldn't.

"I'm sorry. I needed some time alone."

The hurt reflected in her eyes tore through him like a blade that had been resting in the flames of a blazing fire. Would he ever forget the fact that he hurt her? Was there a penance great enough for him to forgive himself for such a crime?

"What are you doing here, Colin?"

"I couldn't stay away."

"And now that you're here, will you go again?"

"You have to go to dinner with Braydon."

She shook her head. "I don't have to do anything. Braydon cares about taking me to dinner about as much as I care about being there with him. I don't want to lose the few hours it'll take. It's my last night."

"I know." Nor did he want her to go. "But Sammy, I can't take you. People would talk."

"Do you think once you become a priest you'll never dine in restaurants, Colin?"

"No, but…my family…they'll want to know why I'm taking you instead of Braydon. It'll stir questions. It's bad enough Kelly and Bray already have an idea about what's going on, but if the women were to find out…"

He shook his head.

The women finding out would definitely not be good.

SAM TRIED NOT to wince at his words. She'd been away for only a matter of minutes and it seemed every time he opened his mouth he crushed her heart a little more. She'd always be second choice to the first man she ever loved. She would never be more than a dirty little secret. She was the Hester Prynne, the mistress to his first love—The Church—while Colin was the noble unwavering one.

She was fighting tears and a nagging headache thanks to Kelly's flask full of whiskey. Sighing, she rolled away from him. At first she didn't think he'd allow her to get up, his hands tightened on her hip, but then he released her, just as he would tomorrow.

"I should probably shower," she said, trying not to look at him. Then, because for some reason she wanted to hurt him she said, "So I can get ready for my *date.*"

"Samantha," he implored, but she ignored him.

"Do you mind going so that I can get changed?"

Silently he watched her and then stood. He walked up to her as if to kiss her or perhaps simply lay a hand on her, but did neither. "It's for the best, Sammy."

"Maybe I don't really feel like being the best right now, Colin. Maybe I'm a little tired of always trying to get everything right."

He looked down, and she knew she was bullying him. Stupid man. He was going to let her just disappear. He couldn't be satisfied with knowing they had no chance at a future. No, he had to squander their last opportunity to spend time together. She walked to the bathroom door, towel in her hand, and waited for him to leave.

Without making eye contact her gaze followed his slow steps to his room and she shut the door. This time she was the one to lock it.

CHAPTER 17

*D*inner was nice. It was good for Sam to get away from the others with Braydon. If not her boyfriend, he was still her friend. They talked about school, her graduating, and his senior year. They referenced many inside jokes that only a Villanova student would understand. It was a very pleasant evening.

When Sam and Braydon returned home, the house was settled. Maureen and Frank were watching Antiques Road Show in the den. Kelly was working. Sheilagh was out with Patrick and friends. And Finn—Maureen was displeased to state—was out on a date with his ex, Erin.

Sam never asked where Colin was. He'd made it clear that even their last night together was not worth the others' suspicions. She was at first angry, then sad, then resigned. This was what she had agreed to, two weeks, nothing more. She'd known all along nothing would change his path. She told herself not to take it personally and was really trying hard not to.

These past two weeks Sam had learned things about herself that she never knew. She learned how to kiss a man properly. She learned what it was to truly be intimate with someone, the incredibly freeing sense of letting go in those lost moments of time. She faced her fear of water.

Once she returned home her fears would likely return. It had been Colin's presence, his gentle coaxing and pride, which had encouraged her to face down her demons. No matter what, he would not let her sink.

Sam sat in the den for a while chatting with Maureen. She was really going to miss the woman. Maureen had packed a basket of homemade bread and a cooler of several loafs that were frozen so Sam would have decent food when she returned to school. She also washed and folded all of her clothes and had Frank purchase her train ticket. Sam was overwhelmed with gratitude for this woman who was perhaps the greatest matriarch of this amazing family she'd come to love.

When the two parents went to bed she sat quietly on the couch a seat away from Braydon. She wanted to trap the scent of this home and keep it with her for all time. Braydon watched her thoughtfully.

"You okay?"

She took a long slow breath. "I'll be fine."

"We have to be at the station by twelve tomorrow. We should probably leave here around eleven-thirty at the latest."

"Okay."

"You know you're welcome to come back anytime, Sam. My family loves you."

She made non-committal sound, because that would never happen.

"He won't always be here, Sam. After summer is over he'll go wherever they tell him. He may not even stay in the U.S. I know he really enjoyed himself when he was in Ireland."

She smiled sorrowfully. "Like the rest of you, his presence is written into the bones of this house, Braydon. His absence won't erase the memory of him, not here or in my mind once I go home. It'll be hard enough never truly knowing where he is or what he's doing. To come here and wonder if he may pass through or if he'd recently held a cup, touched the banister where my fingers land, or sat in a seat now empty...that would just be too hard."

"You could always write him."

She shook her head. "No. There's no point drawing out what can never be more. What your brother and I shared was here, in this moment in time, on this mountain, and will never survive anywhere else. Once he makes his vows there will be no undoing them. I wouldn't want to do that to him, remind him of what can never be again."

It was surprising that Braydon could discuss such things with her. She appreciated his friendship, saying certain things out loud to him made her reality easier to accept, as if with each spoken word she was making her own vows to let Colin go.

Braydon eventually stood and stretched. He kissed her

on the cheek and told her he would see her in the morning.

It wasn't long before Sam was shutting out the downstairs lights and climbing the steps herself. When she reached her door she paused. The yellow glow of light fanned out onto the wood planked floor from below Colin's door. He was so capable in so many matters, yet with love he was just a boy.

A FEW HOURS later Sam awoke to someone touching her shoulder.

"Sammy, wake up."

She grumbled and slowly lifted her lashes. It was still dark. Her eyes squinted as her vision cleared from blurry to merely fuzzy and she saw Colin standing over her.

"Colin? What time is it?"

"Four. Come on," he whispered.

"Where are we going?"

"To the lake."

"It's the middle of the night."

"I know, but I promised you I'd teach you how to swim before you left."

Disappointment flooded her sleep-addled brain. "I don't want to swim."

He pulled her out of bed anyway. "We have to. It's the one thing I can give you. Now come on, put some pants on. Where are your shoes?"

She groggily stood in place and watched him shuffle

around her room searching for her things. He handed her
a pair of pants and she tossed them on the bed.

"What are you doing? Put them on."

"I have to pee," she grumbled and shut the bathroom
door.

The florescent lights of the bathroom helped her wake
up painfully fast. Washing the sleep out of her eyes at the
sink, she proceeded to brush her teeth. She probably
wouldn't get a chance to go back to bed, but she could
sleep on the train.

When she entered the bedroom again Colin sat on the
bed holding her flip-flops. She climbed into her jeans and
buttoned the snap. Colin handed her the sandals and she
slipped them onto her feet. Gazing at him, she sent him a
pointed look that said, at this hour this was as ready as she
was going to get.

It didn't occur to her until they reached the lake that
she'd forgotten to slip into her suit. As Colin pulled off his
shirt she stilled, mesmerized by the way the moon glinted
against his abs and shoulders. He tossed his shirt to the
sand and faced her.

"I forgot my suit."

He looked at her for a moment appearing to consider
their options. Without a word he walked to her and lifted
her tank top over her arms and tossed it to the ground.
She had been sleeping so she was braless. The cool night
air tickled her flesh and her nipples tightened. He stepped
closer and the hard nubs pressed into his chest.

Head lowering, his eyes reflected the light thrown by
the moon. His soft lips grazed hers and she sucked in a

breath. Pulling her flush to his front, a thousand butter-flies released in her belly as he kissed her.

He did not kiss her as a holy man or as a friend saying goodbye, but as a lover kissing his woman before embarking on a journey that he knew left little chance of his return. He tasted her and savored her, drank from her. Her body bent back as he tipped her head farther to take more of her. Her fervor rivaled his as she kissed him back.

They broke away from each other breathless. Fingers unbuttoned her jeans and slid them down her legs leaving her bare and standing before him in only her plain cotton panties. He took her hand and her soul anchored itself to his. Safe.

They walked with slow silent steps to the water and there was no apprehension, no fear of how this part of the earth could swallow her whole. She understood that there were greater things to fear, less physical pains. Drowning emotionally was a demon she now knew that made her old fears look like child's play. She was foolish enough to follow him for the simple joy of it, the same as she had followed Meghan that wintry day they had lusted for an adventure.

There would always be different landmarks in her memory. This lake, this evening, would mark her time with Colin. It would represent her wordless farewell to the first man she ever loved. She pushed all mutinous thoughts away so that she could purely embrace the now.

The slumbering water jostled and rippled as they stepped down the bank. The depthless forests across the lake was only an inky backdrop to the majestic waters.

Stars reflected on the surface winking with little ripples. The moon spilled into a wide silver puddle that danced with each step they took.

The water crested her knees and her body shivered. Colin held her close and never lessened his grip on her hand.

By the time her lower belly was wet she was anxious to move in up to her shoulders to slow the chill of the night air upon her flesh.

Colin moved her in front of him and held her back flush against his heated body as he guided them deeper. She had a moment of panic when her feet lost contact with the ground, the picturesque lake suddenly a deep abyss, but Colin didn't let her thoughts take over.

His hands caressed her under the fluid weight of the water. His touch never moved beyond her stomach or shoulders, but her body awakened nonetheless.

When they reached the point they had gone to previously, Colin turned her to face him. He expected her to try to float on her own.

He widened his arms and held her by the hands as her body coasted away from his. Her legs instinctively kicked and swirled beneath her, working to keep her head above water.

She found it easiest to work in a pattern of swirl-swirl-kick, the swirls using less energy than the kicks. Her fingers gripped his hands tightly. They were her training wheels. Colin smiled and gently instructed her on ways to move her body.

When she noticed that he too was floating and no longer

had his feet on the ground her concentration broke and she lost her pattern. The break in her momentum caused Sam to sink slightly. The moment the water touched her jaw she panicked and sputtered and instinctively reached for Colin's body and tried to climb up his broad shoulders.

He laughed softly. "It's okay. You're doing fine. I got you."

It took him being insistent and heavy-handed, but he somehow managed to pry her off of him.

"That's it. Just keep kicking." His left hand released her right hand. "Now swirl your arm around. Don't panic or move too fast. It's like peddling a bike. Sometimes a long slow stroke's all you need."

Sam was breathing fast, but more from nerves than exertion. She held his right hand tightly in her left and swirled sideways figure eights with her right on the other side of her. Her feet found their pattern again, his larger feet acting as their rudder.

When they faced the little floating dock in the distance she saw they were moving forward. Her legs now hung slightly behind her rather than below and with each kick she propelled herself closer to the dock. Understanding what she was doing she smiled.

"I'm doing it! I'm swimming!"

"Yes you are!" Colin laughed, finding as much joy in her achievement as she. "Come on. Let's see if we can make it to the dock."

She mentally measured the distance and refused to let her mind see it as daunting. It was a goal she needed to accomplish, a right of passage that would say more about her self-preservation and resolve than anything else could. Steeling herself for the crossing, she took a good deep breath and kicked long and hard.

They swam in silence, Samantha's focus never leaving the prize. Colin held her hand and they became one, united, unsinkable. Faster than she thought possible the small dock loomed before her, much bigger than it had appeared from the beach.

Her movements became uncoordinated as her muscles began to quit a moment too soon and her mind tried to figure out what to do now. Needing her right arm to continue swirling to keep her afloat, she did the only thing she could. Her survival instincts took over and she released Colin's hand and slapped her palm onto the cool weathered wood of the floating dock.

His hands caught the wood and they each slowed to catch their breath and give their muscles a moment to revive. He grinned at her, shimmering blue eyes flecked with green glittered like the two deep pools of water. She could drown in those eyes.

He pointed out a ladder she hadn't noticed and instructed her to climb out so they could take a rest. Although her legs shook, her mind was wide-awake, adrenaline pumping through her at her major accomplishment.

She climbed out of the water and stood on the dock. Her eyes took in her new vantage point and saw the beautiful view anew. When she turned full circle, cataloging the spectacular panoramic display, Colin was standing before her.

Rivulets of water slipped over his chest. His damp flesh appeared blue under the moonlit sky.

Her body shivered as a breeze kissed her shoulders. Sam wondered if these mountains could talk or if the wind was God's whisper to them.

Colin's smile faded and he looked at her in a manner she had never seen before. There was such unspoken meaning in his expression. Her smile fell as well. His hand reached for hers, squeezing reassuringly. Sam stepped closer. Slowly, without haste, he leaned down and pressed his lips to hers.

His mouth was warm, a contrast to their cooling skin. She stepped into Colin's arms and he held her as he kissed her. Her hair was wet at the tips and the pieces clumped together over his arm that had wrapped around her back. Her panties had sealed themselves over her flesh like a second skin and her breasts hung heavily as she pressed them into his chest.

Her fingers traveled over his broad sturdy shoulders and down his arms. His tongue tickled hidden corners of her mouth and teased the soft pillows of her lips. Seemingly in accordance, they both lowered to the dock as one, Colin holding her as he guided her to her back.

His mouth nipped at her jaw and sipped from the crevice between her shoulder and neck. She arched and sighed when her nipples abraded against his flesh. His palm reached for her breast and squeezed her. She needed the pressure, needed to know he held her tight, not by chance, but out of want.

His thumb tripped over her nipple and his lips found her other breast. The heat of his mouth enclosing over her hardened tip was heaven. He suckled her breasts deeply until they became red and pointed. His tongue passed his lips and she watched as he licked at each proud peak. When his gaze met hers, she saw the shameless seduction in his eyes and her insides melted.

Colin's hands found the edge of her panties and peeled them away from her hips. The material slurped and clung as he tried to separate it from her skin and they giggled. He tossed the wet material aside and it landed with a soft splat.

Heavy palms slowly pressed her knees wide. If ever there was an expression of reverence, Colin was wearing it. Lowering his head, he brought his mouth to her sex and softly kissed her there.

His tongue pierced her folds and traveled in and out of her channel then up and down her crease. His thumb found her clit and began to run in insistent circles while his other hand pinched at her nipples. Her bottom raised off the dock as the sensation became too much, too fast. She moaned and cried out, uncaring of her passion echoing off the forest walls. The orgasm happened so quickly, it blindsided her.

Her legs trembled as Colin placed a few soft kisses on her thighs and sat back on his knees. Focusing on one bright star that still shined in the pinkening sky, she breathed as her heartbeat slowly return to normal. Colin pushed back between her knees and kissed a trail up her belly and to her breasts.

When he reached her mouth awareness stepped in and she tensed. He was naked. His arousal hung heavily against her belly as he kissed her. Her body tightened as she wondered what his nudity meant. His length dragged between her legs and over her sex. His skin there was hot and smooth, yet hard at the same time. He was large, but Colin was a large man so that made sense.

Her sex wept for him to become a part of her. They kissed slowly and passionately for several minutes and with ever slight change of their position, his erection seemed to settle closer to her opening, as if it had a mind of its own and knew where it needed to go.

Her moisture coated his flesh and the image in her mind only made her wetter. His cock slipped over her folds, nudging ever so slightly past her lips. His hips were broad between her thighs and her legs spread to accommodate him.

There was no thought about the hardness of the dock or the dawn creeping up on them. The only thought she had was of him being with her, filling her, making love to her once and for all. She knew she couldn't keep him, but she wanted this part of him. She wanted his virginity and needed to give him hers.

Instinctively she maneuvered her hips under him and somehow aligned his sex with hers, using skill she didn't know she possessed, and thrust her body up at his. He sunk into her and they both hissed and stilled.

He broke the kiss and turned his face away from her,

resting his forehead on her shoulder as he breathed. She knew he was struggling. He was inside of her, but not yet deep enough to breach her, to break the mark of her virtue. He panted and she waited.

Slowly he raised his head and looked down at her, a sheen of unshed tears in his eyes. "You're the only woman who will ever know this side of me Sammy. This part of me belongs only to you." He slammed his hips forward entering her completely.

There was a momentary shock and pinch, but her elation at having him inside of her overrode those lesser feelings. The fullness and completeness she experienced in that moment was indescribable. He seemed to be analyzing the overwhelming sensation as well. His eyes remained closed, his expression pinched, and she hoped she did not just force him to do something he hadn't wanted to do.

Insecurely, she whispered his name. "Colin?"

He breathed a sigh and slowly opened his eyes. In that moment she saw more than the man. She was seeing his naked soul, bare and vulnerable in a way he'd never showed anyone else.

"Dear God, Samantha, never had I imagined…"

Words seemed to fail him. She raised a hand and brushed her fingertips along the side of his face. He pressed his cheek into her palm.

"I love you, Colin."

"I love you too, Samantha. More than any man should love any woman."

He adjusted his arms and braced his palms on the

wood beside her shoulders. The first thrust was slow. His body pulled from hers and her sex fought to hold him there. When he pushed deep, her slickness accepted him without hindrance. They moaned and found a rhythm as one. He slid over her, gliding in and out, the pressure building with each sure thrust.

The weight of him between her legs was something cherished, knowing she would not feel the weight of a man there again, likely for a long, long time. When he drove into her deeply she felt it all the way to her shoulders as if her spinal cord was tingling out to every nerve of her body. He waited, seated deep inside of her, allowing her to experience the fullness with each stroke. When she rotated her hips beneath him she could cause him to press into soft tissue that was especially sensitive to his presence. She loved the feel of her mound pressing against his pelvis, his hair there abrading her deliciously.

Lifting her hips, they moaned in uncontainable pleasure. While his flesh rubbed coarsely over her clit his length reached a new sweet spot.

They repeated the motion and realized they were onto something incredible. Mimicking the move again and again, coming back to it faster than the time before, they began to grind and thrust their bodies together, Colin picking up power with each pump of his hips.

Sam grasped the back of his neck tightly as he drove into her with forceful, quick strokes. They moaned and murmured to the beat of his thrusts. Sam's back slid against the weathered dock and Colin lifted one arm and held her hip to keep her in place.

He plunged into her with such intensity that her body coiled tighter than a snake ready to spring. There was probably some ironic biblical parody about a serpent and Eve seducing Adam leading to the downfall of man, but Samantha allowed no judgment to tarnish this moment for her. There'd be a day that she would have to answer for her selfish sins, but that day was not today.

Their slick bodies became frantic, as if they were trying to not just be one with each other, but break through one another. Finally, her center twisted too tight and, like a universe being born, she shattered from the inside out. Colin gave a guttural groan and fed himself into her one last time before heat filled her and eventually seeped down her thighs.

He kissed her hard, passionately, and she refused to cry.

As she came back to herself her mind slowly filled with unutterable fears. It was not a vibrant dawn, but a melancholy morning. The crystalline skyline beckoned the blue, but Sam saw the coming clouds. Dawn's magnificence was doomed to fade on such a day and she suddenly felt engulfed by the waters that surrounded her, as if she'd have to swim alone evermore.

"I want this to be our goodbye, Colin," she whispered. "This is how I want to remember you."

He looked at her, such resigned sadness surrounding his eyes, but said nothing, only nodded.

· · ·

WHEN THEY PULLED up to the house a while later everything was quiet. There was only a moment of silence, weighted in unspeakable regret and longing that passed between them before Sam climbed out of the car. She stood facing Colin, as he seemed to search for the right words.

It was better this way. She didn't want to hear his goodbye. Words would only cheapen the memory. Standing stoically before him, she looked him in the eyes.

"I wish you the best of luck, Colin. Thank you for these two weeks. I'll never forget them."

As she was about to shut the door he quickly said, "Sammy..." She paused and gazed at him. The pain in his eyes was too much to bear. "We could write. Maybe see each other one last time before August."

She shook her head. "No, Colin. I will not share you with a monastery. You chose your church and she's the only mistress you can have. Please, just let me have this memory without turning it into some shameful secret we'll always have to hide."

"We could be friends," he pleaded.

"No."

She convulsively swallowed back the lump forming in her throat. "I'll never be able to look at you as only a friend. This is goodbye. We can't..." Why was he making this so hard? She was losing her resolve. "Please don't try to contact me. Goodbye."

She shut the door to the car and walked up the porch steps without looking back. When she heard him pull out of the driveway her shoulders sagged and she pressed a fist to her mouth as she began to cry. Stifling her emotions, knowing there would be endless time to cry later, she quickly wiped away the few tears that had escaped and raised her chin. She would not look back. Opening the door, she quietly slipped inside.

IT WASN'T WATCHING the cabin fading away in the distance or the sight of Braydon waving goodbye from the train station platform that did her in. It wasn't the voicemails waiting for her from her parents saying how lovely their trip was going or the letter from the school she student taught at asking her to come in for a second interview. Nor was it the lonesome hike home from the train station through the labyrinth of walkways and crossroads that made her loss sink in. It wasn't the quiet echo of her keys dropping onto the table in her silent and empty apartment either. No. It was the rain.

Samantha walked past the lightly dusted tables and the forgotten article she had left unread on her sofa. She sidestepped the few weeks of mail, knowing it was without a single letter from a friend. She went to her window and pulled back the drapes and watched as the clouded sky finally broke in two and began to cry. And with the deep blue grayness blanketing the world, she wept.

Surrendering to it all, Samantha wept for the moments she never allowed herself to cry for Meghan. She wept for the family she would never have with the McCulloughs. She wept for Braydon's understanding and Luke's secret. She wept for the tiny part of their home that marked the day Frank had given his heart to Maureen and the moment of truth when she saw Italian Mary help Morai the way only a true friend could.

She wept for her parents' loss and for the blessings they gave her anyway, without ever blaming her for taking their baby. And when she found herself sitting on the floor of her empty apartment, trembling with the weight of emotions she'd spent years fighting, she cried for him.

She let her sobs take her away to a place she had never had the courage to go. She knew she might never come back to herself again after admitting her heart had broken, but she cried anyway. She sobbed past the point of feeling raw and into a state of numb acceptance. She cried because he loved her, because he let her go, because she would never forget those sacred moments they shared at the water, and because she would never have him again. She cried harder than she'd ever allowed herself to cry. And she knew that as the last tear fell, she'd never allow herself to cry so freely for him again.

Hours later, Sam woke on the floor of her apartment as the sun faded behind the Philadelphia skyline. Another webbing of cracks spread over her heart at the reminder she would never again see those purple mountains that had been her view the day before.

After showering and forcing herself to eat a cup of powdered broth and tepid water, she changed into her pajamas and crawled into bed where she remained for the next several days aside from the time she needed to go to campus for class. Moving like a zombie, promising herself that this feeling would soon pass, but with each day she suffered the disappointing reality that her heart was still broken.

She wasn't sure if she was even passing her classes, let alone maintaining her GPA of straight A's. Yet she couldn't muster the concern to even pretend she cared. When her four-week term finished she was surprised to see that she had actually achieved two low B's. It wasn't until Sam faced the fact that she had to be out of her apartment by the end of June that she admitted how far she had gone off the deep end.

She faced the disaster her home had become over the last month and wondered how she had lost such track of herself. It was as if days had come and gone, yet she had no recollection of them passing. Four Saturdays she had no memory of. Thirty evenings of staring at the television set, but no memory of what shows she had watched. When she threw away the twentieth empty pint of Ben and Jerry's littering her end tables and nightstands, she finally admitted she was depressed.

All Sam wanted to do was sleep. She woke up tired and went through her days exhausted. She cared about nothing and found it hard to remember what it was that once moved her to try so hard. Sometimes Samantha would find herself crying and not even realize she'd been doing so. She no longer listened to music, as every song reminded her of him. His name was barred from her mind, knowing he would only ever be a secret she could not betray.

As she packed up her belongings that had marked her

time as a college student, but had no place in her real home, she touched and held memories that now seemed insignificant, and small, memories that told nothing of who she really was.

When every corner of her apartment had been cleaned and all that remained was an empty box with her one cup coffee pot resting beside it, she removed her key from her ring, placed it on the counter, and locked the door.

Driving home was a blur. When Sam arrived, her mother and father greeted her in the driveway with genuine smiles that fell short at the sight of her. Samantha knew she looked terrible. She had lost weight and seemed to have perpetual bags under her eyes.

"Samantha?" her mother said, concern lacing her voice. "What is it, baby?"

Unable to hold it all inside, Samantha fell to pieces and sobbed in her mother's arms. Her parents shuffled her into the house and watched as she cried, but she never breathed a word about why. She only promised them that it would soon pass and she'd return to herself once more.

The concern in her father's eyes was a tough pill to swallow. He looked at her as if he saw through her. The more he gazed across the table at her, the more familiar that eerie stare seemed. When she was lying in bed that night she realized she had seen that pained look in her father's eyes once before.

It was the look of impotence, being completely help-less when his child needed him. He had looked that way the day of Meghan's funeral. It was wrong to burden her parents with her own grief.

Lying there in bed that evening, she vowed her broken heart would be hers to keep and no one else's. There would be no more crying for her. She would move on and, once and for all, accept that Colin would never belong to her.

At the end of July she had her second interview with Suzanne Antonelli, the principal of the school Sam had student taught with. She was offered a position with the English department on the spot and gladly accepted. She should have waited until she finished her other interviews, but she'd been so exhausted lately and the entire job hunting process was draining and she wanted it over. Sam needed to know where she was going so that she could begin setting goals again.

On the last day of July, the eve of August the first, she would be facing her demons once more. At some point that following day Colin would no longer be Colin McCullough, but Father Colin McCullough forevermore, a man married to his Heavenly Father and never to belong to or love another living being more.

CHAPTER 18

*S*heilagh had waited all summer. She'd waited and bided her time for that one week a year when the Clooney's all disappeared to the Outer Banks of North Carolina for a week of relaxation without the rest of the family. Patrick had told her that Tristan declined their offer to join them. Although he'd roomed with Ryan, Patrick's older brother, and was practically a member of the family, he still did not want to intrude on what had always been a longstanding, private, Clooney tradition. And so it was time.

Flipping down the visor, she applied a fresh layer of gloss to her lips and fluffed her red hair over her shoulders. As she climbed out of her car parked at the foot of her cousin's property, twenty feet from Tristan's truck, she adjusted her skirt and brushed the wrinkles out of her fitted tee.

She knew her legs looked fantastic in her four-inch

espadrille wedges and they added to her confidence as she sauntered up the drive. The house was dark with the others gone, but the porch light burned an orange glow around the front door. There was no overhang over the porch so when it started to drizzle Sheilagh tried not to worry too much about what it was doing to her hair.

She rung the bell and waited. Her heart raced as she heard someone coming. She knew exactly what she was going to say and if everything went as planned she would be a very happy woman come morning.

The door opened and she tried not to look too anxious at the sight of Tristan barefoot in jeans with nothing else. The jeans were zippered, but not snapped and they hung low on his tapered hips. His sculpted abdomen was ridged and his chest was smooth and hard. He had a silver hoop running through one flat nipple and a leather necklace with one lone shell around his neck.

His jaw was strong and shadowed as if he hadn't shaved in days, but Sheilagh knew he probably had that morning. His hair was mussed and badly in need of a cut. He looked as if he'd been lying around in bed all day.

"Sheilagh?" The Texan lilt that made him extend the *sh* of her name always made her melt. She loved the sound of her name on his tongue.

"Hey, Tristan."

She gave him that coy gaze that was ridiculously girlie, even for her, and something only he could get her to do.

"What are you doing here? Is everything all right?"

"Everything's fine. I just figured with Pat and the

others gone you were probably lonely and I wanted to stop by to see if you needed some company."

He gave her that look he always did when she flirted with him. It was as though her father were standing behind her with a shotgun aimed at his balls. She knew it was her age that freaked him out, but she was an adult now and he would have to get over it.

"Uh, now isn't really a good time."

She took a deep breath and smiled. It was now or never, right?

"Look Tristan, I know you think I'm just Ryan's little old cousin who doesn't know what's good for her, but I'm here to tell you you're wrong. I have feelings, Tristan, and I know you feel them too."

The drizzle was now soaking her shoulders through. She caught him taking notice of what the weather was doing to her breasts below her thin t-shirt and hid a smile.

"Why don't you invite me in and we can talk like two adults?"

He swallowed slowly and cursed under his breath. Good. She was getting to him. She took a slow step closer to him and he cleared his throat.

"Look Shei, you're an awesome girl. You're fun and beautiful and someday you're gonna give some lucky guy a run for his money, but I'm afraid that guy ain't me."

She didn't let his rejection deter her. She'd heard all his flimsy excuses before. If he really wanted her to believe he wasn't interested he would have to give a damn better reason than the ones he had come up with in the past.

"Can we just talk for a minute? You don't need to

invite me in, but…" She pouted and gave him the most cajoling look she could muster. "I'm getting wet."

"Fuck. Here." He stepped back so she could get out of the rain, but still managed to block her way into the house. She didn't mind. His insistence that she stay out allowed her to creep closer to him in order to avoid the rain. He smelled divine, like cut wood and pine.

"Look," she said, risking a touch to his arm. He looked at her hand resting on his forearm. She loved his muscled skin under her fingertips.

"Don't pretend that the two of us haven't been dancing around this for the past several months. I know you think I'm attractive and I know you're aware of what I think of you."

"Sheilagh—"

She stepped closer until her rain dampened breasts and tummy pressed against his hard, bare chest. She looped her arms loosely around his neck and whispered, "Don't tell me you never thought of just letting it all go, Tristan, and taking what we both know you want."

When she pressed her lips to his she felt him relax for a brief second before he tensed again. He grasped her arms in his hands and removed them from his shoulders, stepping back farther into the house.

"I can't do this, Sheilagh."

"Why?" She didn't want to sound like the petulant child she knew she sounded like, but why? Why couldn't they?

"Because I'm seeing someone."

Her posture faltered. She had to have misunderstood

him. One of his excuses not to date her was that he didn't have any interest in dating anyone.

"Who?" Her voice was suddenly strained and raspy.

Tristan's eyes showed his displeasure in hurting her, but she needed to know.

"It's not important."

"It is to me. You told me it was nothing personal, that you didn't want anyone, so pardon me if I find it imperative to know who was able to persuade you otherwise when I, who was willing to be anything you needed or wanted me to be, could not."

He brushed his knuckles over her cheek and she hated herself for being so weak and having such little self-respect that she allowed the contact.

"Don't do this, Sheilagh. When I told you it wasn't anything personal I meant it. You're sweet and one of my friends, but no matter how much you think you can be what I need, you can't."

Pain, as though a hundred heated blades sliced her wide open, caused her to almost double over at the blow of his words. Her eyes blinked rapidly forcing back the tears that threatened to come.

"I…I don't understand."

He looked down. "Look, I can't explain right now—"

"Oh my God. You're not alone. She's here now, isn't she?"

She was going to be sick. Sheilagh practically stumbled away from him and off the porch. He stepped forward into the rain as if to comfort her, but she was so betrayed in that moment she couldn't bear his touch. And just as she thought her heart had plummeted to the lowest of lows she discovered a whole new level of agony.

Tristan tensed as a familiar voice called out. "Babe? Where'd you go? I thought you were going to join me in the shower."

No. This has to be a bad dream.

She shook her head and Tristan said, "Sheilagh, it isn't what you think."

"Luke?" How could this be? Tristan liked women. He flirted with women. He wasn't gay and neither was her brother. "You and Luke?"

"You're misinterpreting the whole thing, Shei—"

But his false words fell on deaf ears as her brother opened the door, looking for his lover and wearing nothing but a towel. Once he saw her he paled. "Sheilagh."

"Luke." Her lips went numb and she had to force her words to form correctly.

His mouth opened and closed as he thought of something to say. "I...I was doing some renovations at the guest house and I needed to shower so I stopped here to get cleaned up."

She was about to tell him how ridiculous his bullshit lie was, but Tristan spoke first.

"Don't bother, Luke. She heard you."

Luke stiffened as if Tristan were insinuating something he would never consider when it was, in fact, his reality. She wondered if Tristan enjoyed knowing her asshole brother thought he was too good to admit he was fucking a man like him. Did it hurt him to be denied and hidden like a shameful secret? Sheilagh would've never been ashamed of him. She would've been proud to love him, but now she understood why she never would.

There were no words. She saw the hurt in Tristan's eyes at Luke's unspoken denial. She instinctively wanted to comfort him and punch her brother, but Tristan had hurt her too. Everything was suddenly different and Sheilagh didn't want to be there anymore. Turning on her heel, she ran through the rain and back to her truck as her tears won and she began to cry.

She didn't know what had truly upset her. It wasn't the fact that she'd just discovered her brother or Tristan were gay. She held no prejudice about peoples' sexual orientation whatsoever. All she knew was that the man she had set her heart on for almost an entire year had suddenly become completely and undeniably off limits to her forever.

As unfair as it was, Sheilagh knew she would have instantly despised any woman with Tristan, but he hadn't been with another woman. He'd been with her brother. She wondered if the others knew about Luke. Had they all pitied her for being so naive?

Her heart ached. Her eyes burned. And her pride stung. She wanted to kick herself for not being more intuitive. She had been so certain she knew him when really she knew nothing about him. Never in her life had she felt like such a fool.

WHEN SHEILAGH WOKE up the following morning she felt slightly better, but the moment her mind returned to the idea of her brother lovingly caressing and kissing Tristan, the crushing ache filled her heart again. Luckily the day was going to be a busy one that would leave little down time to think on how pathetic she was.

Colin was making his holy orders. His Ordination was to take place at two o'clock at Saint Peter's. The week before they had all gone to the new restaurant in town to toast his journey and while he had begun his path into priesthood when she was just a girl in pigtails, it was today that his course would truly begin.

Everyone had long ago come to terms with the fact that the eldest McCullough son would never marry. There were no more regrets among the naysayers of the family. Everyone had accepted Colin's choice and, over time, developed respect for his devotion. Today would be a proud day for not just Colin, but the entire McCullough family.

They were out the door and on the road before many people had even awakened for the day. The plan was to make it to Philadelphia by noon so they had time to eat lunch and arrive at Saint Peter's early enough to find seats for their large group close to the altar. When everyone split up into the four cars making the trip, Sheilagh was careful to avoid the car holding Luke.

The city was insane. All her life she'd grown up surrounded by enormous mountains, yet being placed in the slots between so many tall skyscrapers made her feel incredibly insignificant and small. Everyone was so fashionably dressed and styled. Even the men made her feel like an unsophisticated hick.

ALMOST PRIEST

People moved at warp speeds and smog and honking horns polluted the air while everything from forgotten shoes to empty coffee cups littered the ground. Pages of newspapers twirled up from the curbs dancing gaily in the air for a moment in homeless winds then fluttered back to earth. No one seemed to bat an eye at such disorder.

When they drove through Center City so that Bray could show them why he loved Philadelphia so much, she was speechless. The architecture was magnificent and although she'd seen pictures, none had done these historic buildings justice.

She suddenly understood why Braydon had wanted to attend school in such a bustling place. Here, even the pavement pulsed with life.

They ate lunch at a corner delicatessen that considered eight pounds of food an appropriate serving size for one person. None of them finished their meals. She felt Luke looking at her throughout lunch, but kept her eyes averted from his gaze. She knew he was worried she would tell the others his secret. She wouldn't, but figured to let him worry, serve him right for being ashamed of having a relationship with Tristan. Tristan was a good man and he deserved better than that.

When they arrived at Saint Peter's, Colin was off somewhere out of sight, likely spending his last moments as an independent man reflecting on the enormity of what he was about to commit to. The others at the monastery welcomed them and allowed them to use their facility to freshen up before the ceremony.

Saint Peter's Cathedral was a beautiful structure. She

275

had been so sure she'd never leave Center County, yet, since arriving to this part of Pennsylvania, she was no longer so certain. The city definitely had its appeals. In the past twenty-four hours, so many things she assumed were absolutes had changed. She dreaded to see what other dependable truths would surprise her as being only illusions.

Many had come to watch her brother become an ordained priest. Bishop Adrian sat with his back to the center of the pulpit, his tall mitre gleaming under the chandeliers. Colin looked impeccably handsome in his white robes and golden sash. It was the first time Sheilagh could recall that her eldest brother looked nervous.

The ceremony began with a prayer and then the bishop questioned other priests about her brother's worthiness. When Bishop Adrian announced his approval of the others' choice everyone clapped. Once the applause quieted the bishop began to question Colin directly.

Colin stood with his back to the pews and faced the bishop who sat comfortably in a throne like chair.

"Colin McCullough," Bishop Adrian began. "Before you enter the order of priesthood you must declare before the people your intentions of such an undertaking. Do you resolve, with the help of The Holy Spirit this charge, without fail, the office of priesthood as a worthy fellow worker with the order of bishops in caring for The Lord's flock?"

Colin's voice echoed through the large church. "I do."

"Do you resolve to exercise the ministry of the word,

worthily and wisely, preaching the Gospel and teaching the Catholic faith?"

"I do," Colin answered and her mother fished a handkerchief out of her purse to dab her lashes.

"Do you resolve to celebrate faithfully and reverently in accord with the churches tradition the mysteries of Christ especially the sacrifice of Eucharist and the sacrament of reconciliation in the glory of God and the sanctification of the Christian people?

"I do."

"Do you resolve to implore with us God's mercy upon the people and entrusted to your care by observing the command to pray without ceasing?"

"I do."

"Do you resolve to be united *more closely* everyday to Christ, the high priest who offered himself for us, to the Father as a pure sacrifice, and with him to consecrate yourself to God for the salvation of all?"

The parishioners waited quietly for Colin's reply. This one was perhaps the biggest vow of all, a promise to never put another before God and hold his relationship with God above all others. When Colin hesitated a moment Sheilagh leaned forward straining to hear. The bishop seemed to be waiting as well. Father Tucker, the priest they had met earlier, shot a sideways glance at another rather large priest, yet no one said a word. Everyone simply waited for Colin to continue with his vows.

When she heard her mother hiss, "Jesus, Mary, and Joseph," she began to worry, but then Colin cleared his throat and began to speak.

CHAPTER 19

he start of the school year was a blessing. Samantha had been so busy readying her classroom and preparing lesson plans she was left with little free time to think of her own personal turmoil, too exhausted to hold much of a thought in whatever free time she had. On the other hand, her business led her to overlook other things that normally would've come to her attention sooner had she not been so preoccupied with her new job. Important things.

Late October, one Sunday evening, Sam was helping her mother change the linens of the B&B section of the house. They had just centered a beautiful Victorian quilt onto the bed in one of the more posh rooms when her mother asked her to sit for a moment at the room's small floral sofa.

"I want to talk to you about something, Samantha, and I don't want you to get upset with me."

Whatever her mother had to talk about, it sounded serious.

"What is it? Is Daddy okay?" She always worried about her father's health since he had gotten sick.

"Daddy's fine. I want to talk about you."

"Me?"

She nodded. "Do you like your new job, honey?"

Sam knew her mother didn't want to talk about her job. They talked about it everyday. There was no need for a formal discussion, but Sam humored her anyway.

"Yes."

"Are there any boy teachers there? Maybe one you had your eye on when you were still a student?"

"No, Mom, the only male teacher there is the music teacher and I'm pretty sure he's gay."

"Oh. Well, how about back at school? Were there any old boyfriends, a young man you may have gone out with a few times? You know you can talk to me about this stuff. You're an adult now. I mean I know you're living with us, and I love having you here, but I also know you aren't here because you can't be out on your own. You've always been very responsible, Samantha."

What was she trying to say? Did she want her to start looking for an apartment?

"I know I can talk to you, Mom. And you know you can say anything to me as well, right? And no, there were no old boyfriends from college. I was too wrapped up in studying to date."

Her mother pursed her lips.

"What is it you want to ask me, Mom?"

Her mother took a deep breath and let it out quickly. "Samantha, honey, I went to the store and stocked up your room in June before you came home. I knew something was wrong, but I also knew you weren't ready to talk to us about it, but honey…how long are you going to keep this to yourself?"

Sam's eyes widened. Did her mother and father somehow know about Colin? No, that was impossible. No one knew about that. She quickly blanked her expression.

"I don't know what you're talking about, Mom."

She sighed and took Sam's hand and patted it lovingly.

"Please don't get mad at me for saying this, honey. When you came home you looked terrible. You'd lost so much weight. I'm glad to see you looking more like yourself again, but darling, you have never been a girl to get fat. You can't expect us, when we watch what you pack in your lunches for work and put in your mouth at dinner, to believe that that's what's happening here. Why won't you just tell us?"

Sam looked down at her body. True, she'd put on quite a few pounds, but she had a lot of stress with starting a new job. And no matter how much she loved her mother and father, moving back in with her parents at age twenty-four was stressful too. Not to mention that ice cream seemed to be the only distraction that worked when she felt like crying, which was a lot. Maybe she should start walking in the mornings.

"I know I put on some weight, but I'm adapting to a new life and I guess I'm a stress eater."

Her mom dropped her head as if she were disappointed with Sam's excuse. Maybe she was worried about her health.

"Don't worry, mom. I'm going to start walking tomorrow. I'll be back to normal in—"

Her mom looked up at her with tears shimmering in her eyes and Sam shut up. Why was she so upset?

"Darn it, Sammy, I don't know why you can't be honest with me. I don't think I'm that judgmental of a person."

Completely confused, Sam said, "Mom, I really have no clue what you're talking about."

"The box of tampons I put under the sink in your bathroom in June's never even been opened," her mother suddenly blurted.

"Wha—" *June, July, August, September, October...shit.* "Oh my God."

"Did you really think we wouldn't have noticed, Sammy? You're showing, for crying out loud."

Sam didn't think the idea of her parents not noticing was too hard to believe. It had somehow slipped her own attention. Sam was going to pass out. She hadn't had a panic attack since June, but one was coming on.

Her mother continued. "I've put it together that whoever the father is you two are no longer an item. I am not so old that I don't get how things like this happen. I don't know if he's someone who wants to be involved in this child's life or not, but no matter what, your father and I are here for you. We support your decision to do the responsible thing."

Sam couldn't breathe. Her mom rubbed her back, knowing the attack would likely pass if she calmed down.

When Samantha was finally able to pull in a full breath of air her mother gave her a sad smile and asked, "Will you tell me about the father, honey?"

"He's a father," Sam said under her breath.

Her mother nodded, totally misinterpreting the type of father Sam had meant. "Does he plan to be a part of the child's life?"

Sam swallowed and shook her head. "No."

Her mother pressed her lips together solemnly. "Well, he'll still have to help you financially."

Vow of poverty, was the first thought to run through Sam's mind.

"I'll never ask him for anything."

Some of the pain she'd been lugging around for the past four months suddenly slipped away. She owned a part of him after all.

Her shaky hand tentatively touched her slightly protruding belly.

"This is my baby. Mine."

ADJUSTING to the idea of motherhood was surprisingly easy for Samantha. She immediately contacted her OB/GYN and—shock of all shocks—she was pregnant. She tried not to over berate herself for being such a moron and not putting two and two together. It helped when her obstetrician explained that lots of pregnant moms complain about feeling like they are walking around in a fog and not being able to remember everyday things.

Once the doctor had verified that she was in fact pregnant, Samantha considered contacting Colin. She looked online for a phone number to the McCullough's home. She could just call Braydon at school and get the number, but she didn't want to have to answer any questions until she spoke to Colin. Then it occurred to her that Colin was likely living at Saint Peter's again, or they at least would have a better knowledge of where he was. So she looked up the church online and that was when she had the idea of flipping through archived church bulletins.

When she reached August's newsletter her heart dropped to the pit of her stomach. On the first page was a calendar and there on the first of August was written, Ordainment of Colin McCullough.

He had done it. He'd gone ahead and become a priest. She knew he would have, but for some reason seeing the proof of the act was like dying a hundred deaths all over again. She tried not to get too upset knowing it wasn't good for the baby. After that day she vowed she would never tell a single soul who her child's father was, including Father Colin McCullough.

The baby was due on March fifteenth. By Christmas she was the size of a house. Her mother had gone baby bonkers once the pregnancy was openly acknowledged. Sam suspected her mother would never want her to move out once the baby was born. Being that Sam was on her way to being a single mom with a child to worry about, the idea of staying with her mother and father close by didn't bother her in the least.

When she told them she would stay they had the guest

cottage converted into living quarters for her and the baby. It had already been remodeled for the guests of the B&B so there really wasn't much to change. Sam simply purchased a few personal touches for herself and the baby and brought in a few extra appliances like a microwave and mini-fridge. For the most part they'd still be eating with her parents for most meals. It was just enough privacy, but still gave her the comfort of knowing her parents were close by.

On New Year's Day her mother surprised her with a baby shower. It was small and nice. All the girls from work had come and Sam felt much loved.

She couldn't help but imagine how different her shower would've been if Maureen McCullough had been involved. She imagined all the aunts and Morai and Italian Mary and smiled fondly at the fantasy. If only the circumstances were different. Then she banished the thought.

Her mother had been wonderful to her since finding out. To wish Maureen was there somehow felt disloyal. Yet, Sam knew her not telling Maureen of her coming grandchild was pure treachery in itself. All in all, thoughts of Maureen and the rest of the McCulloughs made her feel confused and guilty so she tried to think of them as little as possible.

For the most part it was easy not to think of the McCulloughs. They were hundreds of miles away and no one close to Samantha knew of their existence. If ever she did think of them or him, no one knew it but her.

The baby began to move a lot. Sam would lay awake at night watching her stomach flutter and poke. Gestating was a fascinating thing. It made her sad that not only was Colin missing her pregnancy, but that he would never know what it was to experience parenthood with this level of intimacy. If things were different, Sam believed Colin would've adored witnessing his child grow.

By March Samantha had completely given up on style. She was fairly certain she was having a girl because her looks had turned to shit. Her hair remained in a simple ponytail. All of her dress slacks were traded in for comfy yoga pants she hoped were dark enough that co-workers didn't realize they were essentially sweat pants. If they did they didn't say anything. Resigned to empire cut blouses, she accepted pregnancy was not a job for the vain. On top of all that, antacids had become a major food group.

She spent an extra twenty minutes a day trying to get out of chairs and learned that low seating was something she should never chance without a buddy to help her back up. It was easier to simply stand, but then her ankles started swelling to the point she thought she would need new shoes, and her sciatica began to pinch and ache. So sat she did.

She had been sitting at her desk one afternoon working on lesson plans for the sub that would come when she started her maternity leave, enjoying a soft pretzel and ridiculously large banana smoothie, when there was a knock at her classroom door.

"Knock, knock."

Sam looked up and almost choked on her pretzel, the dough turning to lead on her tongue.

"Braydon," she wheezed.

"I thought I'd find you here. I was in the neighborhood and figured I'd ask if you worked here. Low and behold here you are."

She knew she was being rude, but she had so not prepared for this. "It's really not a good time. I have a lot of work to get done before next week."

He stepped farther into her classroom anyway. Sam slumped lower in her chair. She might as well have been trying to hide a beach ball under a tissue.

"You look great. Different."

"Thanks. You look good too."

He came and plopped his keys down and sat right on the edge of her desk, making himself right at home.

"You'll never believe who's applying to Villanova."

"Who?" she asked mechanically.

"Sheilagh. My mom, who still talks about you all the time by the way, says she's really grown up in the past few months. No one knows what happened, but it's like she went to bed one night a bratty child demanding respect and woke up an adult prepared to earn it. She'll probably get in. Shei's always been smart. Kelly's still the same old—"

"Braydon, what are you doing here?" she finally interrupted.

He seemed intent on updating her on every McCullough and there were certain McCulloughs she could do without hearing about, especially this close to her due date and being so emotional. Not to mention that she had to pee again and didn't want Braydon to notice her condition.

"I was worried about you. My mom tells me that Colin—"

"Please don't bring him up. I really can't deal with any thoughts of your brother at the moment. I'm busy and I have to get back to work. I'm sorry."

She knew she gave her feelings away, but she had to if she wanted him to keep Colin out of all conversation. He gave her a sad smile that Sam took as his understanding her dismissal was more a self-preservation thing than anything personal.

"Okay, Sam. Well, I'm glad I saw you. I'll let you get back to work. Congrats on the new job and maybe I'll stop by before school lets out."

"Sure. Closer to June would be best. I won't be…as busy then."

He smiled seeming pleased that she'd like to visit with him at a less hectic time. "Okay then. You still have my number. Call me if you ever want to grab a drink or something. Just as friends, Sam. I hope we're still at least that."

She smiled. "We're still friends, Braydon."

"Good."

When he finally left Sam leaned back in her chair and breathed a huge sigh of relief. She hoisted herself out of her seat and waddled toward the bathroom before her bladder exploded. She was halfway to the door when Braydon suddenly breezed back in.

"I forgot my keys—"

They both froze.

There was no hiding her belly.

His eyes grew to the size of saucers. "Jesus fucking Christ, you're pregnant?"

Sam hung her head. Her life would've been so much easier if she could have avoided this moment. She was about to sit back down and explain herself, but instead said, "Yes. And no doubt a million accusations are running through your head, most of them likely insulting, but I'm not going to listen to a single one until I go pee. You're welcome to sit. I'll be back in five minutes. Just remember, Braydon, knowing what's right doesn't always change what is real."

"But Sam—"

"Not until I pee," she said and wobbled out the door.

It took longer than five minutes for Sam to waddle her way back to her classroom. With every hour that brought her closer to her due date her belly seemed to drop lower. She felt like her baby could fall out of her at any given moment.

When she entered the room she could tell Braydon still hadn't accepted what he had seen. He sat in a student's desk in the front row and reminded her of a kid. His face was pale and his expression was one of complete bewilderment. Waddling to her desk, she sighed as she sat down.

"Braydon, it's okay. Really. I'm okay."

"You're pregnant," he said this as if it was news to her. Then he shook his head as if it were simply impossible. "Colin's?"

She pressed her lips together. She'd never told anyone who the father was. Braydon looked as though this revelation was costing him and she could make that all go away with just one lie. All she had to do was deny Colin's paternity, but for some reason she could not lie to Braydon.

"The baby's father isn't an issue. He or she will have all the love they need. I'll be every bit as much of a father to this child as a mother. My child will want for nothing when it comes to being loved and nurtured."

He scowled at her. "You can't do this, Sam. My family has a right to that child's life. That's my niece or nephew in there."

Overprotectiveness blanketed her like a second skin. If the McCullough's knew Colin was the father he would undoubtedly find out. It would ruin his future and he would resent her for the rest of his life. He had made his choice and he didn't choose her.

Sadness morphed into anger.

"What do you propose I do, Braydon? Walk into Saint Peter's or wherever your brother is and ask for the use of a manger because I am about to bring the child of a holy man into this world? You know I can't do that to him."

"He's not at Saint Peter's."

"Well, wherever he is." She waved away the technicality. "There's nothing he can do."

"You're wrong, Samantha," he snapped. "You should have contacted him the minute you found out. Contacted us. Something! You've gone all this time, keeping it from us, lying—"

"You have no idea what I've had to endure, Braydon." The start of tears choked her. "He chose the church! Not me, but a life of poverty, service, and celibacy in spite of what we shared! He practically promised himself to God from the cradle. He told me all along nothing would change his path and I understood that."

Tears slipped past her lashes and down her cheeks.

"My baby changes nothing. If it did, he would only resent me for putting him in this situation. He would *blame* me."

"You're wrong," he said so certainly. "Colin would never blame you for something he took equal part in. You need to come home with me. You have to tell them."

"No," she resolved. "Tell them if you must, but I'll never return to your home again, Braydon."

"He's in Center County, Sam."

And that was why she would never return. The image of him in flowing robes and white collars made her chest ache so painfully she gasped and choked on a sob.

"It's too late. He made his vows to the Catholic Church, not me. Nothing can ever remove that promise. Colin's word to God would be something unbreakable, not by circumstances, temptation, or even love."

"No, Sam, there's so much you don't understand."

"And I have no interest in comprehending, Braydon. Please try to understand. I have not told a single soul who the father is. I wouldn't do that to Colin. You are the first person I've admitted it to. Colin finding out would be such a burden—"

"Or a blessing," he interrupted.

"No, Braydon, it would be a burden. It would ruin everything. Please, please try to understand that this is not how I wanted things to work out, but it's the best solution I have if I want to protect Colin."

He was quiet for a long while. As he looked past her shoulder as if seeing a vision only meant for him, he said, "The day of his Ordination you should have been there. I know he wanted you there, but knew it would be too hard for you."

"Braydon, please don't do this to me," she begged but he ignored her.

"He looked so right in his robes up on that pulpit beside the bishop. It was how we always imagined him. First the other priests testified that he was worthy of the priesthood. Then the bishop began to question him. Colin promised before us all to always give his service to the Holy Spirit. He vowed to preach the Gospel and teach the Catholic faith."

Her heart felt like it was being crushed. Like her chest was caving in. She silently sobbed as Braydon continued.

"He vowed to always hold faith in the mysteries of the church, to honor and believe in the sacraments. But when the bishop asked if he vowed to always love God above all others he promised nothing."

Sam hung her head, guilt riding her hard, and wiped her eyes with the heel of her palm.

"We waited and eventually he did speak, but he made no such promise. Before my entire family, the priesthood, his mentor Father Tucker, and the Bishop, Colin declared himself unworthy. He asked for more time. Said he had unresolved matters that were plaguing his heart and making it impossible to surrender himself completely to the Lord."

Pieces of his words finally penetrated the pain.

"What?" Dear God, she had caused him this confusion. Guilt, harder than she had ever felt before, lanced through her.

"Everyone was shocked, but Kelly and I, we understood what his dilemma was. It was you, Sam."

"I'm sorry," she said pathetically, her tears falling unchecked. "I never wanted to cause him trouble. That's why I can never tell him. This will only complicate matters further for him. He's meant to be a priest. I can't interfere in that any more than I already have."

"He's meant to serve God, which he is. He's working for the parish teaching theology at the grade school, but Sam, he's completely miserable. He may have given his word to serve the church, but he had promised such loyalty since he was a teenager. To swear it before others was nothing new. But he could not promise to bond himself solely to God when he gave you his heart first. Don't you see? He's lost everything when he had it all. He's lost his way. He lost his church. He lost you. And now you want to keep his child from him too."

"What if he still wants to go back? What if he's only taking some time to reflect?"

Braydon shook his head. "How's he supposed to make any decision without having all the facts?"

What if he rejected her again? Sam didn't think, between the pregnancy and the stress of becoming a new mom in the next week or so, she could handle the heartache of Colin's rejection again.

"Look," Braydon said, standing from the desk he'd occupied. "I was planning on driving home tonight. Why don't I wait until tomorrow morning? If you change your mind meet me here at the school at seven o'clock."

"And if I don't? Will you tell them?"

His lips formed a firm line of displeasure. "I don't know."

CHAPTER 20

*P*erspiration cooled on Colin's skin under his heavy flannel as he swung the ax down hard and split the log on the chopping block with practiced precision. March had certainly come in like a lion. The blustery winds smacked at his face and his breath clouded before him. His boots crunched over the snow as he tossed the split wood to the pile and grabbed another log from the woodpile.

Braydon's little car pulled into the plowed driveway at the edge of the property. Damn selfish of him to leave their mother waiting for him last night only to change his mind last minute and decide to come this morning. He tossed another log onto the pile and the hair on the back of his neck prickled.

His mother's steps onto the front porch came the moment Braydon parked the car. Everyone else in the world might stop for his brother's arrival, but Colin continued to split wood. He usually spent his entire Saturday chopping firewood and shoveling snow until his arms felt as though they would fall off his body and his mind was too exhausted to think, allowing no idle time for self-pity.

The car door opened and Colin grunted as he swung down the axe. The weight of the heavy blade slicing through the wood and splintering it into two was oddly comforting.

"Finally!" his mother crowed. "And just in time for lunch."

"I've brought someone with me, Mum," Braydon said and for some reason his words caused Colin's aim to slip and he nearly sliced the heavy axe right into his leg.

Irritated at the distraction, he kicked the fallen log aside and stacked another log upon the block. This time slamming down the axe with twice as much force and missing nothing.

His mother gasped. "Holy Christ." The oath was enough to cause Colin to wait a split second before swinging down again. "Samantha?"

His breathing ceased and the heavy axe fell from his hand. He pivoted so quickly he almost tripped over the log he'd kicked aside. There she was, bundled in a heavy down jacket, long dark hair blowing in the heavy winter wind, looking as stunning as ever. He couldn't move. His feet were frozen to the ground.

Braydon noticed him first, but next Sammy's gaze found him. His shoulders raised and fell as his breath sawed in and out of his chest. He resented the cloud of moisture his breath created as it blurred his view.

Braydon looked back to their mother and said, "Let's catch up inside. It's freezing out here and Sam really needs to use the restroom."

When Colin saw Braydon take Samantha's elbow and help her up the stairs a possessive animal inside of him roared in objection. Ignoring the mess he'd left at the chopping block he marched up to the porch and inside the house after them. Why was she suddenly here? Did she know he had not made his Holy Orders? He had so many questions, but when he stepped inside she was gone.

He looked at Braydon and his brother said, "Bathroom."

His gaze watched the door to the powder room as he accusingly asked, "What's she doing here, Bray?"

"Don't sound so put out. She hasn't had an easy time of things lately. She needed to be here and she's really emotional so try, for once, not to be a prick."

He frowned at Braydon, wanting more of an explanation as to why Sammy had been having a difficult time. Were her parents okay? Did something happen with her job? Was someone sick or God forbid, her? The door to the small bathroom opened and she stepped out and paused when she saw them all standing there waiting for her.

A moment of unspoken yearning passed between them and then she blanked her expression, but not before Colin caught the look of pure regret and desolation in her eyes.

His mother bustled back to the hall and sternly said,

"Well, what's everyone just standing around for? For the love of Mike, boys, let the poor child use the loo in peace. Come on, I put on a fresh pot of coffee. Bitter outside." She turned and hustled back into the kitchen. As they all followed she barked, "Braydon, take Sammy's coat."

Colin had yet to say a word. He simply watched the two of them, wondering what this was all about. Had they somehow gotten back together? Had Samantha's feelings changed?

A look passed between Sammy and his brother and he scowled. They seemed to be sharing some sort of silent exchange meant to be kept a secret from the rest of them. Sammy gave an uncertain nod then her fingers went to the zipper of her coat. Colin watched her eyes, mentally begging her to look at him, see him. He waited, never taking his gaze off her face, but she kept her eyes averted from his stare.

Their mother grabbed a handful of mugs from the cabinet and set them on the table. "What a pleasant surprise it is having you back in our home, Sammy! I must tell you Braydon has not—"

Colin flinched and quickly turned at the sound of several mugs crashing to the floor and shattering into pieces. His mother's face paled and her fingers fluttered to her mouth. Quieter than he ever heard her speak she said, "Mother of God, is that a McCullough in there?"

Colin quickly turned back to his brother and Sam to see what the hell she was talking about and almost stumbled on his arse. Samantha's stomach was swollen to a size that seemed impossible for her small frame to support. There was no doubt in his mind what he was seeing. She looked at him and the apology he saw in her eyes broke his heart. That was his child. She was carrying his child!

He nearly took her in his arms and swore, but paused as it occurred to him that she was at the end of her pregnancy and had kept this from him for nine bloody months. He gave her a furious look, as her betrayal became a living thing snaking through his veins. She immediately looked away.

"Braydon, tell me you just found out about this and that is why none of us have known," his mother admonished.

Braydon's look of shock at her misunderstanding matched his own.

Samantha cleared her throat. "Um, it's been a really long ride and I'd like to have a moment to speak with Braydon in his room if you don't mind. I promise we won't be long. I know you have a lot of questions and I'm so sorry to spring this on all of you like this, but if you will excuse us for a moment..."

Her confidence and words faltered when she again glanced at Colin's stormy expression.

Braydon chimed in and said, "Just give us a moment to settle ourselves from the ride, Mum. We'll be back down in a little bit and I promise we'll explain everything."

He took Sam's elbow and gave Colin a pointed look before they left. Colin and his mother stood stock-still and watched them go.

As he heard Braydon's bedroom door close he turned

to his mum and said, "I'm going to change. I'll be back down in a bit."

SAM SAT on Braydon's bed and watched him pace as they each waited. The sound of Colin's footsteps followed. The opening and slamming of his bedroom door was the only warning they had before he marched into Braydon's bedroom through the connecting bathroom and crashed the door into the wall. She tried not to cringe at the look of disdain he shot her. She knew he would be upset.

"Somebody better start talking," he growled. She'd never seen him like this. He seemed so different, harder.

"Col—" Braydon began, but Colin cut him off.

"Why are you even here, Braydon? This has nothing to do with you."

Braydon stiffened. "Oh, okay," he snapped sarcastically. "I'll just head back downstairs then and tell Mum you've got everything under control. Don't be a bloody moron! And if it weren't for me, she wouldn't be here. It wasn't easy convincing her to come, you ingrate."

Colin shot her a look that was so severe she had to look away. "You kept this from me on purpose."

"I thought you joined the church. How was I supposed to know you didn't? It wasn't like you left Saint Peter's and came knocking on my door."

"How could you keep this from me?" he roared and Braydon hissed his name in warning.

"What was I supposed to do, Colin? You didn't ask for this."

"What if I had taken my vows like I was supposed to in August? I would have been honor bound to the church and…you would have let me swear my life away without ever knowing I had a child?" he sounded so wounded her eyes glazed with unshed tears.

"You didn't want this. You made it perfectly clear what you wanted and never was it me, let alone a child."

She didn't see the point in explaining that she hadn't discovered her circumstances until October. She deserved every scornful word he could throw at her. How had she ever convinced herself it was okay to keep this from him?

"You have no idea what I want," he whispered. "I never would have thought you capable of keeping such a thing from me."

Tears blurred her vision and the fact that he made no move to comfort her only made her pain multiply.

A few moments of silence passed and then he announced, "I have to get out of here."

"Where are you going?" she cried.

"I don't know, but while you've had months to adjust to this news, it's still brand new to me. I can't be around you right now."

The agony his words caused was worse than anything she'd ever experienced or imagined. He stormed out of the bedroom and a moment later she heard his heavy footsteps tromping down the stairs. She looked up at Braydon with watery eyes and fell completely apart.

All her strength abandoned her as he took her in his arms and held her as she sobbed.

· · ·

KELLY WAS NEARLY RUN over when Colin stormed out of the house. Apparently he was in another stormy mood.

"Whoa, what's up with you?"

"Out of my fuckin' way, Kelly," he growled, and Kelly would have normally let him take his brooding arse elsewhere, but this was not the typical bad mood Colin had adopted since summer. This was something serious. He grabbed Colin's arm and jerked him to a stop.

His brother smacked his grip away and pushed him. *"I said back off!"*

"Whoa, Col, it's me. What's going on?"

Colin's shoulders began to quake as he pulled in a hard breath. When he looked back at Kelly his eyes transformed from angry pits of deceit to broken windows of his soul. His mouth trembled and pressed together, but it was not enough to hold back his tears. For the first time in his life, Kelly saw his older brother fall apart.

"She lied to me," he rasped and Kelly did the only thing he could think of and pulled Colin into his arms.

"Hey, hey, hey. Who lied to you?" He squeezed him fiercely as his brother struggled to stifle and swallow his building sobs.

"Sammy."

Kelly pulled back and looked Colin in the eye. "Sammy's here? Since when?"

Colin, apparently gaining control over his emotions once more, roughly swiped at his red eyes and stepped back, putting distance between them. "She just got here. She came with Braydon."

"Well, that's great!"

It was stupid for Colin to continue playing the martyr. So what if he didn't become a priest? He was still a model Catholic. He didn't understand why his brother insisted on torturing himself for the past months. Kelly knew why he couldn't make his vows. What he didn't know was why Colin had yet to go collect Sammy and make her a McCullough. It was like he'd given himself penance.

"It's not great. She fucking lied. All this time she could have come back here and she didn't."

"Uh, not to sound like a dick, but you could've just as easily gone to her and you didn't. So aren't you guilty of the same thing?"

"I'm not carrying her child!"

"Whoa... What? Sammy's pregnant?"

"Yes! And she looks about ready to pop and figured just now maybe she should share this news with me. And according to Bray, she didn't even want to do that. He had to beg her to come here and do what was right. What I had every damn right to know nine fucking months ago!"

"Okay, settle down," Kelly said, trying to digest all of this. "First of all, she probably didn't find out about the baby until she was a couple of months late. By then she may have already assumed you had taken your vows. She may have been trying to protect you the best she knew how. Second, I sure as hell hope you didn't hit her with a barrage of accusations when she told you. You know Sammy. She doesn't have a deceitful bone in her body. This has probably been more than stressful on her. And thirdly, mazel tov! You get to be a father after all, just not the kind you thought you were gonna be."

Colin didn't quite look like he was ready to bust out the cigars yet. He looked pale and terrified.

"I'm not even sure what I said to her. I was just so shocked, but I know I wasn't nice." He shamefully bowed his head and whispered, "She was crying and I walked away from her."

This time Kelly pushed him. Colin tripped backward, not expecting the blow. "What the fuck is wrong with you, man? She came all the way here to tell you in person and you fucking yelled at her? Jesus, I know you've been in a shitty mood since she left, but that's not her fault. It's yours, you fucking dope!"

Kelly rubbed his cold hands angrily over his face. "Where is she?"

"Braydon's room," he said in a barely audible voice.

Kelly didn't even give him the courtesy of a goodbye. He simply walked into the house and left him there to stew in the misery that was his own making. When he reached Braydon's room he knocked twice then walked in. Sam sat on the edge of the bed crying in his brother's arms.

He walked around and nudged Bray out of the way then crouched down in front of Sam.

"Hey, beautiful."

"Hi, Kelly."

She gave him a teary smile. Yup, she was definitely pregnant.

"I heard you're carrying some precious cargo."

"I'm enormous."

"Aw, well, that's just because even the wee McCullough

lads have big cocks. He's probably regular size everywhere else."

She sniffled and laughed. "What's your excuse if it's a girl?"

"Well, in that case, she must have her mother's brains and therefore have an abnormally large melon."

She laughed and punched him playfully in the arm. "Jerk."

"Don't worry, love, she probably has her mum's looks too and therefore no one will think twice about her big head."

Her chuckle was a half sob. She wiped her nose against the back of her hand and he teased, "On second thought, I don't know. I remember you a lot prettier with a lot less snot on your face."

He reached over and plucked a tissue from the box on the nightstand. He blotted her eyes lovingly and held the tissue to her nose.

"Blow," he instructed, and she did.

"That's better," Kelly said, taking her hands and holding them away from her body. "You look stunning, Sammy, snot and all."

"I've missed you, Kelly."

"You too, love. I can't believe you've got my little niece or nephew in there. It's bloody fantastic!"

"I think you're the first in your family to see it that way."

"Impossible. My mother's probably already knitted it eight sweaters since you arrived."

She looked at Braydon and her expression said she

LYDIA MICHAELS

believed the opposite. Braydon quickly reassured her, "No, Sam, you can't go by her initial reaction. She was just shocked."

Sam let a hysterical laugh bubble past her lips.

"What?" Kelly asked, wanting to know what had suddenly amused her.

"She thinks the baby's Braydon's," she confessed and laughed again.

Bray blushed and Kelly snorted.

"Well, it looks like she has another surprise coming. What do you say we let you get cleaned up and you meet us downstairs so we can clear up Mum's confusion?"

Her smile fell away. "What about Colin?"

He pressed his lips together. He should have punched his brother in the head while he had the chance.

Colin had done nothing but walk around the place in a perpetual bad mood for the last several months and now that he actually had a blessing before him he was too thickheaded to appreciate it.

"Colin will come around, but you don't need his permission to celebrate with the rest of us. You've got McCullough blood in you now. We need to commemorate such news with some fine Irish whiskey."

She gagged. "None for me thanks."

"No, love, none for you."

When Sam joined the others downstairs she looked a lot better than she had, but was still a bit unsure of herself. Like he suspected, his mother was bursting with excitement over the news. This would be her grandbaby and

306

therefore one of the most spoiled children to ever grace their mountains.

Sheilagh and Finn eventually joined them and congratulated both Sam and Braydon on the news. No one corrected everyone's misconception that Sam was carrying Braydon's child. This seemed to make Sammy uncomfortable, but she said nothing when Braydon only shrugged it off.

They spent the entire day in the kitchen, laughing and telling stories of when they were babies. Around five, Luke and their father joined them. He was glad to see a smile split his father's bearded face when he heard the news. He lovingly hugged Sam and placed his big mitt on her stomach welcoming her to the family.

They were finishing dinner when Colin finally returned. Everyone aside from Kelly, Braydon, and Sam greeted him with a smile. All the merriment that had been in Sam's eyes moments ago vanished. Colin stood in the doorway of the kitchen as if he didn't belong.

"Colin," his father greeted happily. "Did you hear the news? Braydon's going to be a father!"

Colin's shoulders visibly tensed as he scowled at Braydon. His jaw ticked and everyone quieted not understanding his reaction.

"Colin," Braydon began apologetically.

"I aught to kick your ass," Colin growled.

"What the hell has gotten into you, Colin Francis McCullough?" their mother asked, appalled at her eldest son's manners.

Braydon stood up and tipped his chin at their older

brother. "Do it. I'd love an excuse to knock some sense into you."

"Everybody sit down!" their father barked. "What the bloody hell is going on here?"

"Oh. My. God," Sheilagh suddenly chimed in. "It's not yours," she said turning to Braydon.

"What's not yours?" their mother asked.

"The baby," Sheilagh informed the rest. "It's Colin's."

As one, everyone slowly turned to face Colin. He at least had the decency to not deny it.

Their mother uttered a long drown out, "Ohhhh." She looked to Sam, and Kelly almost laughed. His mother was clearly embarrassed for the girl. She looked down at her plate and gently said, "Oh, my poor girl, I know all my sons are handsome, but you've gone ahead and had yer fill now. How will we know who the father is? And—"

"Maureen, quiet," his father interrupted. That was a first. He looked to Colin and asked, "Is this true, son?"

Colin nodded and their father looked to Braydon. "And you, Braydon? What is your part in all this?"

Blushing, Bray admitted, "The baby isn't mine. I never thought it was. It would be impossible. I just didn't correct all of you when you made the assumption."

Everyone turned to Sam who kept her gaze glued to her lap. Colin finally stepped beside her and said, "All of you can just clam up and mind your own business for a spell. I need to talk to Sammy alone and she doesn't need the rest of you passing judgment on her. If you want to judge anyone, judge me. I'm the only one who pretended to be something I wasn't. She was never disloyal to me or to Braydon. If you don't believe me, ask Bray, but we're going up to my room and I don't want anyone to interrupt us until we decide to come down."

He took Samantha's hand and helped her from the table. She looked at him a bit insecurely, but followed him nonetheless. As soon as they cleared the threshold everyone began talking at once.

CHAPTER 21

*S*am stepped into Colin's room and went right to the window. She had missed the view. The mountains were beautiful covered in snow. The trees looked like little confections sprinkled with powdered sugar.

The sound of the door shutting and the snick of the lock scattered all of her thoughts away. She turned and faced Colin.

"Colin, I'm so sor—"

He held up his hand. "Stop. I've had time to think, and I don't want your apology."

She swallowed hard and blinked back tears. "Okay," she rasped.

"Do you want to sit?"

She didn't want to feel more vulnerable, but she was starting to get Braxton Hicks, and the last thing she wanted to do was go into early labor before she made it home to her parents. So she nodded and sat down on the bed. He waited patiently as she arranged the pillows against the headboard and tried to get comfortable. There really wasn't any comfort left at this stage of the pregnancy, but she fiddled with the pillows and tried for it anyway.

Colin let out an exasperated sigh and walked over to her.

"Here, let me." He held her forward by the arm as he fluffed and placed the pillows so they wouldn't slip behind the mattress.

"There," he said softly and eased her back.

Sam sighed in pleasure and he watched her for a moment making her feel terribly exposed. When he looked at her like that she never knew how to look back. She had forgotten how quickly he could disarm her with a glance.

"God, you're beautiful, Sammy. I tried to convince myself I was embellishing my memories of you, but really I wasn't giving you enough credit."

That was the first kind thing Colin had said to her since she arrived earlier. It was the first thing that even remotely reminded her of the man she thought he was, the man she fell in love with.

She couldn't stop her tears. Her emotions were out of control, and she was too exhausted to combat them at the moment.

He pulled her into his arms and the sensation of him finally holding her again was too much. She cried long and hard for all the times she told herself he'd never touch her like this again.

"I am so sorry for the way I treated you earlier, Samantha. You didn't deserve my anger or the cruel things I said. I'm sorry for acting like a complete arse."

"I didn't know. I swear I didn't know," she babbled as she cried into his shoulder. "I didn't even realize I was pregnant until October. Like an idiot I thought I was depressed and getting fat. I replaced you with two guys named Ben and Jerry. My mom was the one who brought it to my attention. By then I thought you were already ordained. I did try to look you up, I swear, but I wasn't sure where to call. I found Saint Peter's online and came across their bulletin and on the bottom I saw your ordainment. Why did they put it on the bulletin if you never went through with it?"

"They must have published it beforehand and never removed it. I planned on going through with it, but when the bishop asked me to swear to always love God above all others, I couldn't. I knew it would be a lie. Remember how I told you I realized I wanted to become a priest when I discovered a certain passage in the bible?"

She nodded against his shoulder.

"It's from the Old Testament. It says, *'It becomes like a fire burning in my heart, imprisoned in my bones: I grow weary of holding it in.'* That no longer represents my passion to serve God. It is my love for you that burns in my heart, hotter and stronger than any love I have ever known. You're written into my bones and I realized in the past few months I would never be able to erase your presence inside of me. You have become a part of me and I love you so fiercely sometimes I fear it'll swallow me whole and I'll no longer recognize myself."

He kissed the top of her head and down the side of her face.

"Oh, Sammy, I grow weary holding it all inside. So many times I wanted to say to hell with it all and come find you and demand you come back to me, but I didn't think you would ever forgive me for letting you go. I was such a stupid fool to think I could wash away what we shared. I don't think I will ever stop loving you and I don't ever want to. That day of my ordainment, it was as though God was whispering to me, telling me he had a different plan. That plan was you, Sammy."

His lips found the corner of her mouth and kissed her there. The familiar, almost forgotten touch filled her blood with such wanting she thought she would die if he stopped touching her.

"I'm so sorry," he whispered against her mouth.

"I'm sorry too."

His fingers sifted through her hair and her ponytail loosened. He pulled her to him and kissed her hard as if he could not be gentle in that moment. She kissed him back with equal passion.

Her fingers went to the buttons of his flannel shirt and began quickly undoing them. His hands coasted down her back and held her firmly.

She felt like a whale when she tried to lean farther into him. She wanted to press herself against him, but her belly prevented her from doing so.

When she undid the last button she yanked his shirt off of his shoulders. He was bigger than before, more muscled, harder.

"I want to see you," he breathed as he scattered kisses up the sensitive side of her neck and nibbled the lobe of her ear sending shivers through her body.

"I'm fat," she whispered, as she ran her hands over his bared flesh.

He held her away from him and looked at her sternly, "No, Samantha, you are beautiful and that is my child you're carrying. Do you know how magnificent that is to me, what a miracle it is to be creating life? Let me see you."

Well, if he was going to put it that way... She lifted her shirt over her head then undid her hideously functional maternity bra. Tossing the offensive garment aside, she leaned back on her elbows and let him look his fill. His gaze was fixated on her belly. It was huge. Her belly button had somehow turned inside out and her skin was stretched thin.

He looked up at her in complete awe.

"You are the most stunning beauty I've ever looked upon. I don't think I have ever even seen a painting of the Virgin Mary as breathtaking."

She blushed when his focus moved to her breasts. They resembled nothing of what they were that summer.

"You're nipples are darker," he said and her blush intensified until she actually felt as though her face was on fire.

"The doctor says that's normal."

He looked at her with a mixture of excitement and curiosity. "And what about everything else? Have you had any other issues? Any trouble with anything? Does the doctor say you and the baby are healthy?"

"We're both fine. Aside from a little heartburn I've had a fairly easy pregnancy. It makes me terrified for the delivery. I'm afraid because everything has been easy God will punish me with a thirty pound newborn."

He laughed. "If it's a boy he'll likely be close to ten pounds. We were all big. But if she's a girl, well, Sheilagh was only six-two. No matter what though, I'll be there with you the whole time, Sammy. I'd take the pain for you if I could. I promise I'm not going anywhere."

Her heart elated at his words, but like a knee jerk emotion her mind told her not to believe having Colin would ever be possible.

"What are you thinking? You look sad."

"I'm wondering if this is really happening, that I'm actually here with you. I've dreamed this moment, or moments like this, a thousand times, but my mind always tells me I'm an idiot for entertaining such fantasies."

He cupped his palm to the side of her face. "My love for you is no fantasy, Samantha. It's the most real thing I've ever known."

For once, she shed tears of joy. "I love you too, Colin. Thinking I would never be able to touch you again, kiss you, laugh with you, swim with you, it was the worse hell I've ever known. I don't ever want to be without you again."

"Marry me. Be my wife, Samantha, and make me whole again. I'm miserable without you."

She laughed through her tears. "I've never wanted to belong to a family the way I want to belong to yours. I want to belong to you. Yes, I'll marry you, Colin McCullough."

He kissed her, and she knew that everything would finally be okay.

When they pulled apart they gazed at each other with unrefined lust in their eyes and unconditional love in their hearts.

He carefully unlaced her shoes and placed them beside his bed. Strong fingers plucked her socks from her feet and tossed them aside. She tried not to blush when he pulled her pants and panties away leaving her completely nude before him. She wasn't sexy. She could barely pull off sexy when she wasn't pregnant, but the way he looked at her made her feel more desired than she ever thought possible.

He placed both hands over her belly, forming a heart with his fingers and thumbs around her bellybutton, and pressed a kiss there. She watched, mesmerized, as his thumb traced the sign of the cross over the tight flesh of her abdomen as if he were anointing their child, blessing their baby.

He whispered promises as he spread kisses over her flesh, to their child, to her, and to God, and when the intimate moment had passed into something too large to voice he finally stood.

He never took his gaze from hers as he removed his

pants and the last of his clothing. Her gaze strayed, the intimate moment pressing into parts of her still tender from losing him. The last time they'd made love it had been dawn. She hadn't looked at him. When she finally saw him in all his naked glory she swallowed hard.

Yes, that would definitely get a girl pregnant.

He reached for her. "Come here."

She let him help her to her feet and they stood toe to toe as he kissed her. His hands cupped her full breasts and she moaned into his mouth.

"Are you sensitive there?"

"Extremely," she admitted.

His head dropped lower and he gently pulled one dark nipple into his mouth. His tongue flicked over the nub and her thighs pressed together. It seemed ergonomically impossible for them to actually make love in her condition, but she sure hoped Colin had a plan, because she never wanted him so badly.

"Do you think you can manage on your knees, Sammy?"

Liquid poured from her center, coating her swollen folds. She nodded. He turned her, swept her hair over one shoulder, and kissed the back of her neck. His soft, warm lips traveled down her spine and back again until she was trembling with desire.

"Please, Colin."

He helped her onto the bed and carefully climbed up behind her. The touch of his hard thighs against her much softer ones was enough to make her come apart. Holding her hips supportively he fitted his knees between hers. "You'll tell me if it is too much, Sammy."

"It won't be."

"But you'll tell me if it is."

"Yes," she agreed and his hard arousal nudged against her sex.

He parted her moist folds and began stroking slowly back and forth, making shallow dips into her wetness. His erection became slick with her cream. No barrier lay between them aside from Colin's worry.

"Colin, the doctor assured me there isn't a man alive large enough to do any damage to me or the baby. As long as you're gentle everything will be fine."

Her encouragement and the shared wisdom of her obstetrician seemed to be the only persuasion he needed. He pressed forward and filled her completely. It was incredible. Again she wanted to cry for how amazing it felt to be with him again, the touch of his skin to hers, his amazing warmth blanketing her.

He slowly moved in and out of her and they each moaned with pleasure. His hands held her lovingly and petted over her shoulders and thighs. Soft lips kissed the nape of her neck reverently and, again, he whispered his undying love for her. It wasn't long before they were both coming apart.

They didn't return to the rest of the family that night. Neither did they attend breakfast that following morning. It was the first time they could hold and openly love one another without shame or guilt and they reveled in the freedom of such gifts.

Aside from dozing a few moments between conversations, they had barely slept. By Sunday at noon Samantha's stomach had begun to grumble. Colin insisted she stay in bed to get some sleep while he went downstairs to rustle up some food.

He didn't have to go far. Someone, likely Maureen, had left a covered tray outside their door with muffins, orange juice, a jar of milk in ice, cereal, and even a pickle, which they assumed was intended for Sam in case she had some sort of clichéd craving.

They ate in bed and awoke sometime that evening long after the sun had set. "I need to call out of work tomorrow."

Colin handed her the phone and waited as she left the message. It was wrong, taking off so close to her maternity leave, but there was no way she could make it back in time and be able to function in front of a class of thirty-five sixteen year olds.

After she hung up the phone Colin announced, "I'm driving you back. I want to meet your parents and ask your father's permission to marry you."

"What will you do if he says no?"

"Steal you away and make you my bride anyway, just like my father did with my mother."

"Is this really what you want?"

"I've never wanted anything more, Sammy."

She laughed. "Colin, do you have a name you always wanted if you ever had a son or a daughter?"

"I never thought I would have children, Samantha."

"Oh, right."

"Do you have names thought up?" he asked.

"Well, if it's a boy, I think we should name him Colin. I never imagined naming him after you because I never imagined confessing who his father was, but now that the secret is out, I would really like to name him after you."

"Never in my life had I imagined a son of my own blood bearing my name. I think that's magnificent. Thank you."

"And if it's a girl…"

"If it's a girl," he prompted.

"I want to name her Tallulah Meghan and call her Lula for short."

"Meghan for your sister?"

"Yes."

"And where did you come up with Tallulah?"

"Well, I have this book that tells you the origin of names and their meanings. Tallulah's Gaelic, which is fitting since she'll be a McCullough, but I love it for what it means."

He smiled at her sweetly. "And what does it mean, Sammy?"

"Water."

She saw he too fell in love with the name as soon as he discovered its meaning. He kissed her softly and whispered, "I cannot imagine a more fitting name for my daughter. I love it."

"I love you."

"I love you too, Samantha. And I'll never stop."

EPILOGUE

Tallulah Meghan McCullough was born at three thirty-five that following Wednesday. She had her father's dark hair and piercing blue-green eyes, but her mother's nose and mouth. The entire McCullough clan had come to town to meet the newest McCullough. The fact that the Dougherty's owned a bed and breakfast worked out perfectly, because there was actually a place to put them all.

Although Sam had surprised her parents by returning home with the father of her child, they welcomed Colin with open arms. Sam tried to explain how their situation had come about as tactfully as possible and her parents had gotten quite a chuckle out of the scandalous affair.

The *Thorn Bird* references never ended. For the rest of the night they referred to Sam and Colin as Meggie and Ralph, but they each took the teasing in stride. She wasn't anything like Meggie. She'd found her happily ever after and in the end, Colin had chosen her before all else.

Samuel, Samantha's father, gave Colin his blessing and her mother was only slightly disappointed when they turned down her offer to have the wedding at the B&B. The property was beautiful, but Colin and Sam were already in agreement that there was only one place sacred enough to make their vows.

Labor had been terrifying, but in the end it was not as bad as she had assumed it would be. She was grateful Tallulah was a girl and not a ten-pound McCullough boy. They returned to the Dougherty home that Friday, mom and baby doing wonderfully well. Dad on the other hand was a bit of an old hen the way he clucked over the two of them, but Sam loved him all the more for it.

When they settled Lula into her bassinette and went to find the others, they walked right into a surprise shower, this time including the McCulloughs. The aunts doted over the newest female McCullough and Colin asked Sheilagh to be Lula's Godmother, hoping it would soften the blow of losing her position as the female of the family holding the McCullough name. Braydon proudly accepted when they asked him to be Godfather.

A week later everyone traveled out to Saint Peter's for the Christening. Colin's dear friend Father Tucker performed the Mass and no one seemed to bat an eye that Lula's parents still were not married. Everyone seemed to understand it was a result of the circumstances quite beyond their control.

The morning of the christening Colin did give

Samantha her ring. It was a simple silver Claddagh with a diamond in the center of the crown. She loved it immediately.

Father Tucker accompanied the family back to Center County. Although Colin and Sam were not getting married in a church and therefore could not have a Catholic ceremony, it had been very important to Colin to have Father Tucker there to at least lead them in prayer.

On Tuesday morning Maureen and Karen, Sam's mother, helped Sam dress in a gown that had belonged to Morai. It was stunning and Sam was flattered Colin's grandmother had offered it. Once her hair was done and her last silk covered button was fastened, Sam slipped on a pair of warm white boots and a heavy white wool coat and followed the women out to the cars.

Thankfully it was only in the lower fifties that day and not overly blustery. The lake was calm and beautiful as always, but nothing looked as magnificent as Colin standing at its bank in his grandfather's kilt and a formal tuxedo jacket.

Colin finally made his vows. They were not to an institution that would never love him back, but to a woman he knew would always care for him and hold his heart tighter than any other ever could.

His daughter looked almost as beautiful as his wife that day by the waters that had become so sacred to him and Samantha, those waters that taught them each how to love when, for their own different reasons, they thought they never would.

This was their lake. It held their secrets, their fears,

and their most sacred memories of coming to know one another. It was a place of hope for them both, a place of peace, a place of escape. They were their waters and they were more sacred than any other place on earth.

THE END

If you enjoyed ALMOST PRIEST, you will love BEAUTIFUL DISTRACTION, the next story in the McCullough Mountain Series

Skip ahead for a sneak peek inside

ABOUT THE AUTHOR

Never miss another book release!
Click here to sign up for Lydia Michaels' Newsletter.

Follow Lydia Michaels on Instagram and Facebook!

What to Read Next?
Click here to claim your FREE Book from Lydia Michaels!

Billionaire Romance
Falling In | Sacrifice of the Pawn | Calamity Rayne

Small Town Romance
Wake My Heart | The Best Man | Love Me Nots | Pining
For You | Almost Priest

Emotional Favorites
La Vie en Rose | Simple Man | Wake My Heart | Sacrifice
of the Pawn | Forfeit

Romantic Comedy
Calamity Rayne

Erotic Romance
Breaking Perfect | Protégé | Falling In | Sugar

First Books in Binge Worthy Trilogies and Series
Almost Priest | Falling In | Wake My Heart | Forfeit | Original Sin

Paranormal Vampire Romance
Original Sin | Dark Exodus | Prodigal Son

LGBTQ+ & Menage Romance
Broken Man (MM) | Breaking Perfect (MMF) | Forfeit (MMF) | Hurt (Non-Consensual) | Protege

Sexy Nerds & Second Chances
Blind | Untied

Teacher Student, Workplace, and Age-Gap Love Affairs... Oh my!
British Professor | Pining For You | Breaking Perfect | Falling In | Sacrifice of the Pawn

Single Dads & Single Moms
Simple Man | Pining For You | First Comes Love | Controlled Chaos | Intentional Risk

Dark Psychological Thriller & Tortured Hero Romance (TRIGGER WARNING)
Hurt

About the Author

Lydia Michaels is the award winning and bestselling author of more than forty titles. She is the consecutive winner of the 2018 & 2019 *Author of the Year Award* from *Happenings Media,* as well as the recipient of the 2014 *Best Author Award* from the *Courier Times.* She has been featured in *USA Today, Romantic Times Magazine, Love & Lace,* and more. As the host and founder of the *East Coast Author Convention,* the *Behind the Keys Author Retreat,* and *Read Between the Wines,* she continues to celebrate her growing love for readers and romance novels around the world.

In 2021, Michaels released the groundbreaking, non-fiction series, **Write 10K in a Day**, to commemorate her career in the publishing industry. She looks forward to many more years of exploring both fiction and non-fiction writing, teaching about the craft, and learning from the others in the author community.

Lydia is happily married to her childhood sweetheart. Some of her favorite things include the scent of paperback books, listening to her husband play piano, escaping to her coastal home at the Jersey Shore, cheap wine, *Game of Thrones,* coffee, and kilts. She hopes to meet you soon at one of her many upcoming events.

You can follow Lydia at www.Facebook.com/LydiaMichaels or on Instagram @lydia_michaels_books

Other Titles by Lydia Michaels

Wake My Heart

The Best Man

Love Me Nots

Pining For You

My Funny Valentine

Falling In: Surrender Trilogy 1

Breaking Out: Surrender Trilogy 2

Coming Home: Surrender Trilogy 3

Sacrifice of the Pawn: Billionaire Romance

Queen of the Knight: Billionaire Romance

Original Sin

Dark Exodus

Calamity Rayne: Gets a Life

Calamity Rayne: Back Again

La Vie en Rose

Breaking Perfect

FREE! - Blind

Untied

Almost Priest

Beautiful Distraction

Irish Rogue

British Professor

Broken Man

Controlled Chaos

Hard Fix

SAMPLE BEAUTIFUL
DISTRACTION

"**S**hit."

The uneven flapping of rubber slapped against the dirt road and Finnegan McCullough tugged the battered wheel of his truck, hauling his flatbed to the shoulder. That was the second tire he'd lost in a month. The roads on their family property were eaten up from a long, icy winter.

Climbing out of the truck, his yellow work boots stomped over the dried, packed clay as he took in the damage.

"Bloody hell." There was no patching that.

From the bed of the truck, he grabbed the jack and donut. Heat beat through his flannel as he dropped to his knees and—

What was that sound?

He paused. This far out in the woods there were only bears and no bear he'd ever seen had made noises like

LYDIA MICHAELS

that. His lungs stilled as he tilted his head, focusing on the sound. The slow buzz of insects and then—*there it was*—soft, breathy pants, a steady pulse of soft taps. It sounded like...fucking.

Narrowing his eyes, he squinted at the horizon as the late afternoon sun pierced the green canopy. He turned, but saw no one. Abandoning the jack and spare, he stood and beat the ginger dust off his knees. Whoever was getting their jollies in his family's woods was about to be interrupted. This was private property.

His long, clipped strides rounded the truck and came up short. The noise was coming from a dense part of the woods where a narrow path was rutted into the earth. A twig snapped under his foot as he brushed aside a fern and stepped onto the rough trail. Too late.

Something big slammed into him and white light flashed behind his eyes as he stumbled backward. Pain exploded in his face like when one is blindsided with a basketball. There was a shrill scream.

"Son of a bitch!" His fingers pressed into his eyes as he waited for the sharp smarting to dissipate. The screaming wasn't helping matters.

Cracking his eyelids, he took in the panicked screamer as her body twisted to flee, only to land roughly on the gravel. She twisted again and continued to scream. Her chest moved under a cotton tank top. A trail of sweat worked its way down her flushed cheeks where the threads of earplugs hung.

When she continued to shriek and scrambled to her

feet, he yanked out an ear bud and snapped, *"What the hell are you doing?"*

She hurdled back, her breasts heaving as she threw up her arms. "Don't touch me!"

He scowled. "Don't touch you? You nearly broke my nose and you're on *my* property. I could shoot you if I wanted."

Her rosy cheeks paled and her blue eyes went as wide as saucers. Full, pink lips opened and closed like a trout. Scrambling to her feet, she glanced over her shoulder. Her flaxen ponytail, dark with perspiration, swished and smacked him in the face. Her panicked eyes glanced back at him and she bolted past him.

"Hey!"

Her round, little form burst through the trees and he cursed. Where the hell was she going now? Cursing, he took off after her. Nothing like chasing some broad after nine hours of sweating his balls off in the lumberyard.

His truck cut off her escape and his fingers latched onto her arm. Slamming her back into the rusted door, she screamed again and he winced.

Her panicked cries only cut off when he shook her. "Stop screaming!"

"Please don't hurt me!" she babbled.

He frowned. "Who are you?"

"Mmm—Mallory. Mallory Fenton."

"What are you doing on my property, Mallory Fenton?"

"I didn't realize it was private property. I was jogging in the community park and must've gotten confused."

"Jogging? The parks three miles from here."

Her brow rose. "It is? I didn't realize I went that far."

He released her arm and stepped back. "Well...this is private land."

"I'm sorry. I didn't know."

They had to watch for poachers this far out, but she didn't strike him as the type. "No harm."

Her gaze traced over his face and her brow knit. "You're bleeding."

Running a finger under his nose, he drew back his hand and found a dab of red. He'd live. "Yeah, I was nearly bulldozed by a rogue runner."

She winced and lowered her eyes. "I'm really sorry. I didn't expect to run into anyone out here. Literally."

"Well, maybe next time you might want to try running on the high school track."

Her lips trembled and she looked away. In a quiet voice, she mumbled, "Sorry." Her expression shuttered.

Did he say something wrong? Now that the panic was over, she seemed to withdraw. They awkwardly stood there for a moment and she shifted. "Um, I guess I'll just head back the way I came."

He stepped aside. Her fist pressed into her ribs as if she had a cramp. She didn't look like a track star. Her skin was flushed to her chest, which was notable. Her hips filled out her shorts and her thighs jiggled as she stepped back onto the rough path. He frowned. She wasn't jogging. Her steps appeared tired and lagging.

"Are you planning on walking all the way back to the park? It'll be dark before you make it out of the woods."

She sighed and glanced up at the sky. She was still breathing heavy from exertion. "This is what I get..." she muttered under her breath. Then, in a stronger voice, she said, "I'll be fine. Sorry I trespassed on your property."

Center County was a pretty tight knit community. Finn had never seen her before. She must be new. That was probably why she didn't realize this entire mountain was pretty much McCullough land. He sighed. "If you can wait a few minutes I can give you a lift."

Her beaten-in Nikes crunched over the gravel as she turned, her expression weighing his words—as well as his serial killer qualities, he imagined.

Holding out his arms, he said, "I'm not a psychopath. It's easy to get lost in these woods if you don't know where you're going. I'd hate to see that happen. I got a flat. If you can wait a minute while I fix it, I'll drop you wherever you need to go."

Her lips tightened. "Are there really bears and stuff in these woods?"

He chuckled. "You could say that. I definitely wouldn't want to be walking unarmed at night."

Ground scraped under her rubber shoes as she stepped closer. "My car's at the bottom of the trail." She was sweaty. Her skin glistened under the remaining sun.

He nodded, a bit distracted by her soft form. The fabric of her cotton top was darker where perspiration had run between her breasts. Golden beams of sunlight threw shadows over them and the temperature began to drop, the same way it did every night in these parts. Her nipples pressed through her clothing. She was packed into that sports bra under her clothes.

She cleared her throat and his gaze jerked back to her face. "Sorry," he muttered and quickly turned to grab the jack.

She didn't say much as he fixed the tire. The rim fell like a ton of bricks into his flatbed and he stood, wiping the grease off his fingers onto an old rag. His gaze inspected her. She was average height for a girl, sort of plump and curvy, and she definitely didn't look like a runner. "You're not from around here, are you?"

"I just moved here. I'm from Philly." She kept staring at him.

"My brother goes to school there. Villanova. You know it?"

She smiled and nodded. Her teeth were a straight line of pearls. "Yeah—"

His hand went to his hip as his phone started chirping. He held up a finger telling her to hold that thought and brought it to his ear.

"Hey."

"Fin, where are you? I've been sitting here for an hour."

He glanced at his watch. "Sorry, babe. I had to work over and then I got a flat."

"Another flat?" Erin asked, and he grit his teeth at the suspicious tone in her voice.

"Yeah."

His girlfriend sighed. "Well, when are you coming to pick me up?"

He glanced at the girl. What was her name? Melissa?

Maloney? Mallory? Yeah, Mallory. "I gotta take care of some shit and then I'll be there. Give me an hour."

She huffed into the phone. "Why don't I just meet you there?" She said this in a tone that spoke nothing of favors and understanding. He wasn't being baited.

"That'd be great. I'll see you when I get there." His thumb rolled over the end call button and he stuffed it back in his pocket. He turned to Mallory and noticed her expression changed as she looked at the ground.

It was getting dark. "You ready?" he asked.

She nodded and silently went around to the passenger side of the truck. The door whined as she pried it open. *Gonna have to get some WD40 on that.*

MALLORY SANK INTO THE BROKEN-IN, leather, bench seat. She was such an idiot. Her doctor had given her a world of crap at her last physical because of her weight. He basically freaked her out, warning that if she didn't get her act together she was going to run into a shit storm of health issues because her family's medical history was a hodge-podge of diabetes and autoimmune diseases. He successfully freaked her out and she'd—like everything else she did—barreled head first into a plan. Like always, she'd wound up embarrassing herself. Now she was lost, getting a ride home from some mountain man who was like a wet dream in flannel.

She sighed. Of course the first time she ran into—literally—a hot guy in Center County, she'd nearly plowed him down like a bull in a china shop. And, of course, she was a fat, sweaty, panting mess when he saw her. And, *of course*, he had a girlfriend, so why the hell did she care? Yeah, that all sounded about right.

She clicked her seatbelt, stretching it as far as it could go. She was all too aware of how the strap hugged and accentuated her ugly parts.

The truck roared to life. Closed in the roomy cab with him she could smell his skin. What was that? It wasn't like the cologne guys wore at home. This was a piney smell, sweet like sap with some briny, manly edge to it.

"We'll have to take it slow so I don't lose the donut too."

His voice was gravelly and distracting. Almost as distracting as the mention of donut. *Mmm...Boston cream— stop! You don't eat that crap anymore. Think of carrots. Delicious, raw, slices of—*oh, fuck it. She wanted a donut.

As they drove over the bumpy pass of road, she eyed him slyly. He was tall. His long, muscled arms handled the steering wheel with evident strength. He was owning that flannel shirt too. Guys didn't dress like that at home. This wasn't the Kurt Cobain type flannel. No, this flannel was his bitch. It was soft and faded, and stretched over his broad shoulders like a second skin. She frowned as she realized she was jealous of a shirt.

Averting her gaze, she stared out the window. Behind the soft reflection of trees going by in the dark she caught her reflection. Dear God, she looked hideous.

Her hand smoothed her ponytail and she winced as her fingers touched the damp, sweaty mop. Yeah, this is why she went to the park and not the gym or the high school. Nothing like working out next to Redneck Barbie to make her feel more like a slob.

Was his girlfriend the Barbie type? She glanced at him again out of her peripheral vision. Yeah, probably.

Her shoulders slumped into the seat. She just wanted to get back to her car and get home. Mallory sighed as she considered the steamed broccoli that waited for her there. God, she wanted a Philly cheesesteak.

"Do you run a lot?"

His question caught her off guard. "Um, I'm trying to. I need to lose some weight." She winced. *Smooth, Mallory. Draw his attention to your flaws. Like he didn't already notice.* She recalled his comment about being nearly 'bulldozed' by her. Nothing like having a hot guy compare her to twenty-ton truck.

"Girls worry too much about their weight."

"According to my doctor, I don't worry enough." Why was she telling him this? *Shut up!*

He glanced at her then back at the road. Thankfully, he made no further comment on the issue. He probably agreed. "What made you move to Center County?"

A chance at a new beginning. "Work."

"What do you do?"

"I'm a secretary. I'll be working at the high school in the fall."

"Oh, yeah? My sister-in-law teaches there. My brother, Colin, is really involved with the afterschool programs too."

"Colin McCullough?" He'd been on the panel of people to interview her.

"Yeah, that's him. You know him?"

"He interviewed me."

"No shit. Small world. You should like it there. They just redid the gym. If you wanted, I could talk to Colin about letting you use it."

Not this again. "That's okay. I'd rather stick to the park."

He nodded like he understood her reasoning when she knew he didn't. "Just make sure you mind the markers. Sometimes people sneak on our land to hunt. You don't want to get inadvertently shot."

No, that certainly wasn't on the agenda. She nodded.

"How often do you run?"

Not enough. "Every day."

His brows lifted. He was probably calculating her weight and calling her a liar. Well, she was trying. She'd only just started this new 'lifestyle'. Like calling it that instead of a diet made it better.

"I don't run unless something's chasing me," he said, and she laughed.

"I hate it." The confession slipped out before she could pull it back.

"Then why do it?"

"Because I don't want to be fat or die from some illness that stems from obesity."

He scowled at her then turned back to the wheel. "You *are not* obese."

"Uh, yeah, I am. Morbidly, actually."

"How much do you weigh?"

She balked. "You did not just ask me that!"

"Sure I did. How much? I bet you can't be more than one-seventy."

Well wasn't he sweet. She hadn't seen numbers that low in years. "You're way off."

"Girls overdramatize things. How much? One-eighty?"

"Stop asking."

"Why won't you tell me? It's just a number."

"You're not supposed to ask girls how much they weigh."

"Why? I'd tell someone if they asked me."

"Yeah, look at you. If I were built like you, I'd probably run around naked." Holy shit, did she really just say that?

He laughed. "That's always an option."

She stared at her lap. What was wrong with her? *So many things...*

"Come on, give me a number."

"No."

"Please."

"No!"

"Pretty please..."

"Why do you care so much?"

He shrugged. "You piqued my interests. I'm of the inquisitive sort."

She sighed and rested her elbow on the door, ignoring him.

"I weigh one ninety."

It was all muscle. She shot him a look telling him to drop it. Finally, when they pulled into the park, he relented. "Is that your car?"

"That's me."

The truck slid beside her tiny Chevy and he put it in park. She busied herself by wrapping the strings of her ear buds around her iPod.

"Well, thanks for the lift."

He turned and nodded. God, he was sexy. His eyes were incredibly blue against his tanned skin. His jaw was strong and dusted with brown shadow from his stubble. He should be doing Bounty commercials.

When she realized she was just sitting there staring and he had better things to do, she grabbed the door handle and yanked it open. It made a loud cranking sound. She jumped out of the truck and her knees nearly gave out. She overdid it today. "Well...thanks again."

"Nice meeting you, Mallory Fenton."

"You too." She shut the door and went to her car. He waited until the engine purred to life before pulling out.

Her head fell to the steering wheel. "You're such an idiot," she mumbled. She glanced back and saw the tail lights of his truck disappear. It was dark and scary in the park at night. Throwing her car in reverse, she quickly made her way home. It wasn't until she got to bed that night that she realized she hadn't even asked his name.

DON'T STOP THERE! Download Beautiful Distraction now!

Printed in Great Britain
by Amazon